"I loved having for KING & COUNTRY ████████████████
birthday party on *The View*. As the mothe███████████████
I believe this film and novel is a powerful story that needs to be
shared with the world."

**—Candace Cameron Bure**
Actress, Talk Show Host, Producer, and *New York Times* Best-Selling Author

"This is a beautiful story about the value we have, the extent love
will go to find us, and how God see's us for who we're becoming
rather than who we were."

**—Bob Goff**
Author of the *New York Times* Bestseller *Love Does*

"Throughout the *Priceless* story, Joel and Luke courageously stand
on the front lines of a real culture war, vividly illustrating what it
means to protect, cherish, and honor women and family."

**—Elisabeth Hasselbeck**
TV Personality, Best-Selling Author, and Mom

"We've seen Joel and Luke come and preform at many of our
Celebrate Recovery Summits, and we've witnessed firsthand how
for KING & COUNTRY's lyrics have moved hearts. Now we're
excited to see how their book *Priceless* challenges and affects lives."

**—John Baker**
Founder of Celebrate Recovery

"Words cannot adequately express the deepest respect and admiration I have for my brothers Joel and Luke and for their first written
work with the fabulous Nancy Rue . . . *priceless!* The message of
this movie-based novel—that every person has infinite value and is
worthy of love and respect—is an answer to the cries of this generation. This story is captivating, and I encourage you to read, and be
changed!"

**—Rebecca St. James**
GRAMMY Award Winning Artist, Best-Selling Author, and Actress

"If you've ever experienced a for KING & COUNTRY concert, then you know it is exciting, riveting, and unlike any other. As Joel and Luke Smallbone temporarily set aside their instruments to pick up a pen and write this novel—you can expect more of the same. This captivating story will have you immersed in the reality of what's happening in our dark world today. Unlike other books (but like their live shows), *Priceless* will point you to where hope can be found, in spite of past mistakes."

**—Kyle Idleman**

Author of *Not A Fan*, Teaching Pastor at Southeast Christian Church

"Seeing these boys grow up and watching them venture into making music and now writing books has been a joy. But the thing that I am most proud of is the message of *Priceless*. We need more books like this that challenge today's culture."

**—Darren Whitehead**

Senior Pastor, Church of the City, Nashville

"I've really enjoyed becoming friends with Joel and Luke. I love the way they spread the *Priceless* message in how they live their lives, both on and off the stage, and this novel comes at the perfect time! Our generation is longing to hear that they have meaning, and I am so proud of these guys for reminding women that they are priceless."

**—Sadie Robertson**

Motivational Speaker

"I've had the privilege of following the journey of Joel and Luke Smallbone of for KING & COUNTRY from the beginning. Their humility, talent, and servant's hearts have allowed these brothers a platform to remind every woman of their worth and every man to respect and honor women. The novel *Priceless* explores the depths of our mistakes and the true beauty of God's forgiveness."

**—Dave Stone**

Senior Pastor, Southeast Christian Church

A NOVEL

# PRICELESS

## SHE'S WORTH FIGHTING FOR

**JOEL AND LUKE SMALLBONE OF**
for KING & COUNTRY
WITH NANCY RUE

WORTHY®
PUBLISHING

Library of Congress Control Number: 2016944212

ISBN: 978-1-61795-730-7

Publisher's Note: The issue of human trafficking is at the heart of this story, so it may be unsuitable for some readers under the age of thirteen. Parents, please use your discretion when considering sharing this book with your child.

*Printed in the United States of America*
16 17 18 19 20 BVG 8 7 6 5 4 3 2 1

# 1

"How GUILTY do you feel?"

"Guilty?"

"Yes. On a scale of one to ten, how guilty do you feel?"

James took his gaze from the stoplight long enough to glance at Michelle. Her hazel eyes were wide, her lips pressed tightly together. She was offering him no clue as to what he was supposed to do with that question.

"How guilty do *you* feel?" he said.

"I asked you first."

She shifted sideways in her seat. He could now feel those eyes trying to suck an answer out of his brain.

"I need more information," he said.

"One means you've already forgotten. Ten means you want to hang a U-turn and go back."

"I got that part. What is it I'm supposed to feel guilty about—or not?"

She shook her head and gave him a mock *tsk-tsk*. "Epic fail," she said.

Another glance as the light turned green. Her dimples were deepening.

"Emerson?" she said. "Our daughter? The kid we just left for an entire weekend?"

James drove the pickup across the intersection. "Is this one of those 'there's no way I can answer this right' things?"

"What are you even talking about?"

"You know. If I say I feel like a jerk because we didn't bring our four-year-old on our second honeymoon, you'll say I don't want to be alone with you. But if I say, 'Emerson who?' I'm a lousy father."

Michelle lightly smacked his arm. "That is so not true. I only want to know if you feel as bad as I do."

"How bad do you feel?"

"Not even a little bit bad."

James pulled a straight face. "What kind of mother are you?"

"The kind who doesn't want her only child to remain one."

"Did I know this weekend was a babymoon?"

She swatted at his arm again. "You know you want another baby."

"I know I like how we're going to *get* another baby."

"You lucked out, then. I looked it up, and they do have places in the Hill Country where you can buy more kids."

James reached across the console and tugged on a honey-colored curl that had escaped from his wife's messy bun. If he could have gotten hold of the tie that held the whole thing together he'd have given it a yank and brought it all tumbling over her shoulders. Just where he liked it.

Yeah. This was going to be an awesome weekend.

"I'm sort of serious, though," Michelle said. She pulled her feet up onto the seat and hugged her knees. "Should I call your mom and see if Emmy's okay?"

"You're kidding, right? Did you *see* the tea party Mom had

going? Looked like they were expecting the first lady. Rotten kid didn't even kiss me good-bye."

"You poor thing. Let me make that up to you."

She slipped the strap of her seat belt over her head and put it behind her as she leaned toward him. James felt a grin melt across his face.

"Look out now," he said. "I'm not sure it's legal to make out on the on-ramp."

Fortunately, she ignored him and brushed her lips against his beard as he accelerated onto the Crosby Freeway. When she rested her warm hand on the top of his thigh, he wasn't sure which was going faster, his pulse or his Dodge Dakota.

"Thanks for getting your mom to come stay with her," Michelle said.

"Thanks for coming with me."

"Thanks for not worrying about the money we're spending."

"Who said I wasn't worrying?"

"James Stevens!"

"Kidding. Kidding."

She squeezed his leg.

"Continuing to kid."

He smothered her fingers with his and wondered, as always, how such a strong, feisty woman could have bones that felt like they would turn to chalk dust if he squeezed them too tightly.

"There's no other way I'd rather spend that bonus," he said.

"We do need a new toilet in the hall bathroom."

"We need *this.*"

"Yes," she said. "We do."

She raised the armrest between them and unbuckled her lap

belt so she could slide closer to him for just a moment. Her cheek rested against his shoulder, the weight of her head pressing into him. He kissed the top of the nest of curls and flipped on the windshield wipers to clear the drizzle that was quickly turning into full-out rain. Houston weather could change faster than he could change channels on the radio. Which he now did, switching from Garth Brooks to classic rock. Nothing like the Eagles to set the mood. "Take It Easy" matched the beat of the wipers and the rhythm that settled in between them.

"I hope it doesn't rain like this the whole time," he said.

"Does it matter?" she said.

Married for five years. Married *young* for five years. And it still didn't make any difference whether the sky rained or snowed or stirred up an F-12 tornado as long as they could hold each other. Life couldn't get any better than this.

"I think we should have some guidelines for this weekend," she said, wriggling closer.

"You mean like rules?" James gave a snort. "Not happening."

"No. I mean like *guidelines*. For getting the maximum pleasure out of our time."

"I love it when you talk like that."

"Not what I mean, Romeo."

"Oh. Bummer."

"I'm talking, like, no calling each other 'Mommy' and 'Daddy' like we do around Emmy."

"I'll give you that one."

"No more than one hour spent shopping for something to take back to her."

"Good luck with that, but okay."

Michelle sat up and pressed her palms together. The freeway

lights freckled raindrop silhouettes on her hands and across the front of her pink T-shirt. James didn't have to see her face to know her expression was only a slightly older version of Emmy's when she was about to give them a long rendition of some discovery she'd just made—like how to make steam on a window with her breath or do bunny shadows on the wall. The two of them couldn't be any more different from his brown-eyed, dark-haired, hulking self.

He nudged Michelle with his elbow. "Two guidelines oughta be enough, right?"

"I'm just getting started."

She held up her index finger. In the gathering dark he could tell she'd given herself a manicure. She hadn't done that since before Emmy was born.

"No talking about bills," she said. "We should pretend we don't have a mortgage and two car payments."

"Okay, I see how this works." James grinned at her. "No getting up before nine."

"I was thinking ten."

"I like it."

"Number five . . ." She uncurled her ring finger. The three tiny diamonds winked in the flash of oncoming headlights. "No—"

*Wait. Oncoming headlights. On a divided highway.*

James smashed the brake and yanked the steering wheel away from the vehicle that bore down on them. Michelle grabbed at his sleeve, her nails digging into the skin on his forearm before her fingers were wrenched away. If she screamed, he didn't hear her—not over the panicked squeal of the tires.

The back end of the Dakota fishtailed, and James tried to jerk the wheel back. But the truck was locked into a spin that kept them in the path of the metal monster hurling toward him.

A sickening crash jarred James into a twist. The air was shocked into silence as the highway tilted and his own lights pointed the way to the shoulder of the road. His side of the roof of the cab hit the pavement and then they slid lopsided and downward into the drainage ditch.

A second crash spewed glass like a shower of jagged spit. The pickup rocked itself still and another stunned silence fell. James felt the blood pounding in his head.

He was hanging upside down.

Upside down and suffocating in the airbag. He groped his way out from behind the airbag and fumbled for the seat belt buckle. Broken teeth of glass bit into his fingers and he drew them back, knocking his elbow into the driver's side window, which shattered and spilled its mosaic onto the road.

He was surrounded by slivers and shards. The buckle he wrestled with was jammed. And the hand he held up to his face was oozing blood.

But all he could think of was Michelle.

"Baby! Michelle—are you okay?"

No spunky voice answered him. Probably muffled by her own airbag.

Except there wasn't one—at least not a deployed balloon like the one he'd just fought back. Still upside down, blood trickled from his face as he tried to move around the crumpled cab.

"I'll get you out, baby!" he said. "I'll get you out. Just hang on."

But as his hand broke through to dead air where the windshield should have been, his reassuring litany to Michelle died on his lips. The thought that slammed into his mind was more image than words—of an unbelted Michelle flying into glass and hurling into the rain.

Terror surged through the muscles in his arms as he knocked at the seat belt buckle until it broke free and torqued himself so he could crawl through the driver's side window.

The frame of jagged glass points tore at his skin. Voices shouted down from the road. Ignoring both, James stumbled through the slanting rain to the front of the overturned truck, still calling out Michelle's name, still promising her he'd save her.

But he couldn't.

Far away, a siren screamed.

And so did he.

# 2

It had to be the single most annoying sound he'd heard in the last ten minutes. But then, what didn't rub under his skin like fifty-grit sandpaper anymore? James followed the horn's blare to the door, already working from a mutter to a bellow just to make it stop.

"It's the mail lady, Daddy!" Emmy announced. She was sitting on the front steps with the ubiquitous grimy teddy bear. "I'll go see what she wants."

He pushed at the bulging screen and let the door slap behind him. "You stay, Em."

He let his fingers touch the top of her head. Her hair felt sticky. Last night it smelled sour when he kissed her good-night. He needed to do something about that.

The Jeep horn continued to blast in impatient spurts at the curb. A series of expletives flipped through his head as he made his way down the driveway. Between that woman in the mail truck and the Houston heat on the concrete cooking the bottoms of his feet, it was all he could do not to spew all of them. Emmy was the only thing stopping him—from that and a list of other things.

The mail carrier leaned the heel of her hand on the horn twice even after James reached her. She peered at him through sunken eyes. Colorless hair was plastered to her round head, and perspiration dotted her almost nonexistent upper lip. It had to be a lousy job. He pulled his sweat-soaked T-shirt away from his chest with two fingers and extended her as much grace as he could.

"What?" he said.

"Got a registered letter for you," she said, every word a grunt.

"From who?"

"None of my business." She pushed a green card and a pen toward him. "Sign by the X."

James read the return address on the form. Bank of America. Fantastic. Signing it would show he'd gotten it. He wouldn't be able to abandon it on the stack of bills that teetered on the dining room table.

"If you don't sign I have to—"

"I'm signing, okay? I'm signing."

James scrawled his name in the blank and stuck the card in her direction. She took it with damp fingers and handed him a bulky bundle of envelopes secured in a rubber band. "This was all still in your box. You might not end up with a last-chance notice if you got your mail on a regular basis."

"I thought it was none of your business," James said.

He took the hunk of letters from her and jumped back just in time to keep from having his toes run over. Gravel sprayed over his bare feet.

Emmy was still too close for him to swear.

Eyes squinted against the remorseless sun, James watched her run, teddy under her arm, across the bare spots in the lawn he'd forgotten to water. All summer. She was barefoot, too, and her soft soles matched the dirt that left dusty puffs in her wake as she played. She was trying so hard to be happy. Would anybody driving by know she didn't have a mother? And not much of a father?

The mail carrier maybe. And his mom. She knew.

James snapped the rubber band off the mail and rifled through it.

Medical bills. Why there were bills when she'd been pronounced dead at the scene he hadn't been able to figure out.

Electric bill. Probably still more than he could afford even though he'd stopped using the air conditioner.

Final notice for the cable they'd disconnected.

Water bill. He'd better bathe Emmy before that got shut off too.

The option his friend Chad had given him was sounding better by the minute.

He looked over at Emmy. She was squatting next to the steps, examining something with just-turned-five-year-old focus. Sunlight tried to play on the top of her curls, Michelle's curls, but they were dark with neglect.

James turned back to the mail. Ads for things he'd never buy again. A postcard from the pediatrician notifying him it was time for Emerson's pre-kindergarten checkup. The kindergarten he still had to register her for.

And one lone sympathy card. From Caroline Meacham. His great-aunt who had probably just heard about the tragedy.

They all called it a tragedy. Or a tragic loss. Or a death difficult to fathom. None of the cards that had packed the mailbox those first few weeks had ever called it what it was: a knife that stabbed him in the heart over and over and would for the rest of his life.

If it weren't for Emmy, he would have cut that short six weeks ago.

Six, five, four weeks ago the cards were still coming. Back then the refrigerator was stuffed with hams and casseroles and fried chicken. The screen door squeaked with the constant coming and going of buddies who sat with him and let him say nothing. And with Michelle's friends who slipped in to do laundry and mop the floors and take Emmy away for playdates.

All that had stopped, except for Chad, who stuck so close it bordered on suffocating at times. Everything else had ground to a halt, including his construction job. The same boss who'd given him a bonus in the spring took a dim view of him not showing up for work past his two-week bereavement leave. Getting out of bed was more than he could handle. Swinging a hammer, wielding a drill, loading a nail gun—forget about it. Even after the foreman came by with the news, James couldn't regret it. Chances were good that he would have turned his tools on himself.

Or someone else. Because even though Michelle had stopped living, people acted like he should keep on. And he hated them for it.

Emmy squealed and stood to face him from across the yard, her chubby knees smudged with dirt. "Look what I found, Daddy!" She held up a yellow blossom that drooped at the end of a long stem. "It's a flower!"

"Sure is, Em," James said. "Where did you get it?"

"Right here!"

Her voice lifted with the exclamation point she put at the end of every sentence. She jabbed a brown finger at the triangular flower bed next to the steps, the bed Michelle had planted impossibly small plants in the week before the accident. He thought they'd all died with her. He sure hadn't done anything to make it turn out otherwise. If he couldn't save her, why would he try to salvage them?

"Okay, Daddy?"

James stared at her. Her dimples dented her face as she pressed her lips together, clearly waiting for an answer.

"What, baby?"

"Can I put it in water so it won't die?"

He nodded. When the screen door closed behind her, he grabbed at his chest, but the stab was insistent. Insistent and cruel.

Only the purr of a well-tuned engine behind him kept him from collapsing to his knees in the yard. One look at the black Lincoln easing up to the curb and his brain went on high alert. He shot a sharp glance at the front of the house, but Emerson was still inside.

Dragging his forearm across his forehead before the sweat could drip into his eyes, James headed for the idling Lincoln. Two thoughts tangled in his head: *Chad never said they'd come to the house . . .* and *This couldn't be any more cliché, right down to the tinted windows.*

The passenger-side window was already lowering when James got there. A face too fresh to be in a Texas summer peered out at him with steel-gray eyes.

"You Paulie?" James asked the driver.

"We don't use first names."

"Mr. Va—"

"Last names either."

James nodded as if he understood. The cliché continued. Next thing he knew the guy would—

"Lift up your shirt. I need to check for a wire."

There it was.

James revealed his bare chest and waited for the command to drop his shorts, but the man seemed satisfied and unlocked the passenger door. Glancing again at the vacant front yard, James slipped into the leather seat.

"You mind if I crack the window?" he said. "I need to listen for my daughter."

"This won't take long."

James took that as a no. He tried not to let his nervousness show, so he discreetly rubbed his palms on his shorts. Cold air whispered from a vent, but he could still feel a trickle of sweat down the middle of his back. He was sure to leave a mark on the leather.

"What were you told?"

James called up his last conversation with Chad. *Don't mention drugs or deals or money. Just say,* "I was told you have a job for me."

"You know what's involved?"

"Simple delivery."

A faint gleam of approval passed through the otherwise expressionless eyes. James let out the breath he hadn't realized he'd been holding.

"Anything else?"

He groped his way back to his conversation with Chad. *Say as little as possible . . . Let him do the talking . . . No—*

Just as the guy's hands fisted on the steering wheel, James blurted, "No questions asked."

"Wrong."

James blinked at the sting of sweat in his eyes. He didn't quite realize until now how much he was counting on this. His own hands gripped the sides of the seat. "That's what I was told."

"Your man obviously doesn't know you. But you seem cooperative, so you get one question."

Yeah. He had a question: *Could I look more clueless?*

"There has to be something you want to know." The iron eyes looked into his. "Your first job. Must be a question in there somewhere."

Now it would be a mistake not to come up with something. James forced himself to let go of the seat and look directly into the man's eyes.

"You'll tell me where to deliver. You going to tell me where to collect?"

What might pass for a smile in this world he was stepping into twitched at the guy's mouth. "Of course. You'll get complete instructions." He said it as calmly as if he were setting James up with a new washer and dryer. James let out another captive breath, only to snatch it back when the eyes narrowed to a laser point. "One thing concerns me."

*What?* James tried to remain calm and build up a false sense of self-confidence.

"Desperation."

James felt his eyes widen. "I'm not—"

"It's all over you, pal. What have you got riding on this?"

"I think that's my business."

"Not so. Everything about you is now our business."

James shifted in the seat. The backs of his thighs stuck to the upholstery, but he no longer cared. The now-familiar anger burned in his muscles.

"I need the job," he said, keeping his voice flat. "That's all that concerns you."

"You don't make the rules—"

A faint knock on James's window startled them.

"Daddy, you in there?"

Emmy, without the exclamation point. Not waiting for permission, James went for the door handle, but the window slid down. Emmy's face came into view, her hazel eyes round and troubled.

"Are you going away?" she said.

"No, baby!" James grabbed the dirty little hand that now gripped the opening while the other one held the teddy bear against her chest. "I'm just talking grown-up stuff. I'll be right out, okay?"

"Can I get in?"

Clearly reassured, she stood on tiptoes and peeked into the car. She was the picture of awe, until her gaze fell on the driver. Her shoulders went into a shy scrunch.

"I bet you can say your ABCs, can't you, sweetie?" he said.

James whipped his head around. The previously immovable face was now a dead ringer for a doting uncle.

"'Course. I'm five years old."

"Okay, then you go say the alphabet, and when you get to Z, your daddy will come out."

Emmy nodded solemnly. James bit down hard on the inside of his mouth.

"Count loud," the guy said and raised the window.

James heard the chirpy, "A . . . B . . . C . . ." and jutted his head toward the face that had returned to steel.

"Talking to her," James said between his teeth. "Not part of our de—arrangement."

"No need to. You won't screw this up." He tilted his chin toward the yard where Emmy was up to M. "You can't afford to."

"Q . . . R . . . S!"

"Don't disappoint her," he said. "You'll hear from us."

The door locks clicked. James kept his gaze leveled at the driver as he felt for the handle. The triumphant "Y and Z!" kept him from flattening the man's nose. Even so, when he got out he slammed the door hard enough to shimmy the chassis. Above the purr of the Lincoln's engine he heard laughter behind the darkened windows.

What was he thinking, getting mixed up in this thing?

Warm arms wrapped around his leg. James looked down into an upturned face poked with dimples, creased with a pressed-together smile. The stab in his chest tore the breath out of him.

This was what he was thinking. This, the only piece of the life he used to have. One job and he could get them back on their feet. He could start over. For her. Only for her.

"Are you sad?" she said.

"Wha-a-a-t?" he said. "How could I be sad when . . ."

Her round eyes blinked. "When what?"

"When I'm about to do this."

He scooped her, tossed her over his shoulder, and jogged toward the front door with a trail of squeals and giggles behind them.

# 3

JAMES DID DO IT for Emmy. He just wasn't very good at it.

Contrary to what he was promised, Paulie Vaca's instructions left out a few essential items. Maybe he overestimated his first impression of James—or his desperation.

In any case, he neglected to mention what to do if James changed his mind in the middle of the delivery. The minute he saw the buyer nervously pacing in the Kmart parking lot, he started to backpedal. The poison he carried inside his denim jacket was the same stuff that had turned this guy into a twitching anorexic who plucked at the hair on his arms and repeatedly sniffed loudly enough to be heard a hundred feet away.

These drugs were going to kill him. Maybe not tonight or tomorrow, but sooner rather than later. And that would make James a murderer.

James looked around for someplace to dump the package before the guy saw him. But with an especially hearty sniff, the guy seemed to smell what James had on him. With a pathetic yelp he broke every rule Paulie said the guy would follow and ran toward James with more speed than his drug-spindled legs should have allowed.

James took off running from him, but any desperation to get out of there was no match for this man's addictive desire. As the distance between them shortened, James fumbled for his car keys. If he could get to his Toyota parked at the other end of the lot, he could escape with the package and look for a place to dump it.

And it may have worked had two cruisers with blinding blue lights not sandwiched him in before he was able to turn the key in his ignition. Panic seized his brain and screamed at him to fling open his own door and take off. To ignore the command to "Stop! Police!" To try to wrench himself away from the body that slammed him from behind and flattened him facedown into the concrete slab.

He only gave up after his hands were pinned behind his back, cold metal cuffs were clamped to his wrists, and an officer pulled the package of heroin from James's jacket.

---

He had tried to do something for Emmy. Now he'd done it *to* her. The judge agreed. So did his mother. Her sentence was more devastating than His Honor's.

Despite the halfhearted effort of the pimply young public defender, Sander Pardue, to portray James as the bereaved widower who had temporarily lost his mind, the Honorable Wilson Benton had no sympathy for, in his words, "people who use grief as an excuse to break the law."

James heard his mother muffle a cry behind him, which surprised him. Just three days earlier, sitting on the other side of the wavy Plexiglas window in the city jail, she'd said, "How could you do this! If you were in that much financial trouble you could have asked me for help."

The words had come out tight. Melody Stevens would never make a scene in public, even there, which for the moment made

James grateful she hadn't bailed him out. She had been furious with her son, but as she scolded James, there had also been tears in her eyes and a tenderness behind her words.

"You can't give up and throw your life away," she had said. "You have your daughter to consider."

James had been unable to answer, his shame balled up in his throat.

"Whatever that judge says, just know this: Emerson can stay with me for as long as it takes for you to put your life back together."

She had held his eyes with hers, the ones that could take down bullies and heal broken hearts and ferret out the truth before the lie was even told.

"I know you can, James," she had said. "It's what Michelle would want."

He knew he had let Michelle and Emmy down, but he'd let her down just as hard.

So although James tensed as the judge prepared to hand down his sentence, he knew one thing: his life was in shambles, in prison or out.

Judge Benton gave him six months for possession with intent to distribute. He dropped the resisting arrest charges because James had thrown Paulie Vaca under the bus. Chad he'd protected. Because, again, what difference did it make?

James didn't resist this time when the guard approached him with handcuffs.

Sander Pardue said something about appealing but looked relieved when James shook his head. He turned to his mother, who was also shaking hers. Dismay and tears reddened her eyes.

"Tell her I love her," he said.

She put her hand to her mouth. The guard folded his around James's arm.

"Please. Tell her."

"Let's go."

"Mom."

She pulled her fingers from her lips and nodded. "Of course I will," she whispered. "Every day."

---

James wasn't very good at prison either. Pimples Pardue assured him he'd get out early for good behavior, but nobody was having that. Paulie Vaca didn't take kindly to being busted by a first-time offender who ran like a little girl. James didn't see him at Joe Kegans State Jail, but Vaca had minions from the showers to the exercise yard. James was punched, kicked, and cut every time the wardens looked the other way, and often when they didn't. He fought back and was saddled with the blame.

James was told more than once he was lucky he didn't get additional time. But *lucky* wasn't a word he'd ever apply to himself. Even on the day he was released and slid into the front seat of Chad's truck, he wasn't free. He would be locked up for the rest of his life.

---

The social worker who visited James in prison the week before he got out had told him the first thirty days would be the hardest and the most crucial. Actually, he'd read that to James without any emotion from a coffee-stained folder. Prison inmates weren't the only ones to have the life sucked out of them when they walked through those clanging doors.

If it hadn't been for Chad, the social worker might have been right. But James's only remaining friend had him set up with a studio apartment, a fridge full of groceries, and a job before he spent his last day in prison. Chad drove him to the apartment complex straight from lockup.

James sank down onto the futon that smelled faintly of wet dog and stared at his hands.

"Why'd you do all this?" he said.

"Are you serious?" Chad handed him a bottled water and dropped into the black corduroy beanbag chair that had clearly been slept in by the same dog. "You saved my hide, dude."

"You don't owe me anything."

"The heck I don't." Chad drained half a root beer and set the can on the floor beside him. "You could have outed me like you did Paulie but you didn't, and I'm not gonna forget that."

"Yeah, but all this . . ."

"You can pay me back when . . . or if . . . It's no big deal."

That wasn't actually the point. James didn't want to be expected to do any more "jobs." He couldn't go near that life. Not if he was going to get Emmy back.

James could see in Chad's eyes that he was already thinking about the next idea, the next thing, the next move that was going to make him rich. He fingered his short ruddy beard, professionally trimmed in contrast to James's prison stubble.

"I gotta keep clean, Chad. For Emerson."

"I know what you're thinkin'," he said, "but it's not like that. I gave up all that crap—and the booze. Heck, I even gave up swearing." He grinned, which involved only one side of his mouth. If James remembered right, women loved that about Chad, but for some reason that thought made him want to throw up.

"So, this job you got me . . . ," James said.

"Where I'm working. It's construction. You won't be making what you did before, but it's a start."

"Boss know I've done time?"

"Yeah."

"How'd you pull that off?"

"I told him your sob story."

James jerked up his chin.

"Sorry," Chad said, eyes darting. "I shouldn't have said it that way. Besides, it was more about how freakin' good you are at what you do."

James took a visual survey of the apartment. The kitchen and the space where they sat was one room. A pocket door separated it from a phone booth–size bathroom. A row of hooks appeared to be the closet. Except for the poster of a black Harley that Chad had stuck on the wall above the futon, the walls were bare and unfriendly. It was no place for Emmy.

"How much is the rent on this?" he said.

"Don't worry about it—"

"I said how much?"

Chad made an attempt to cover his startled look.

"Sorry," James said. "It's gonna take me awhile to stop talking like I'm inside."

"Forget it. It's four hundred dollars a month plus utilities. If things work out with the job, you'll start making enough for something bigger."

"I have to save for a vehicle."

"Taken care of." Chad put up a hand before James could protest. "I know a guy who wanted to get rid of his old 2000 Nissan Frontier. I picked it up for you."

"How much?"

"Nothing. He owed me. And it's not worth much anyway. Doesn't even have air."

James was suddenly too exhausted to care about anything Chad was doing for him. All he said was, "The cops aren't going to come looking for it, are they?"

Chad slapped his hand against his own chest. "Man, you gotta trust me. I could be in Joe Kegans myself if it wasn't for you." He leaned forward in the beanbag, rustling its contents under his thin frame. "You and me—we're starting fresh. You get back on your feet and we're even. You get that?"

"Yeah," James said. "I get that."

It was another two months before his life even remotely resembled being "on his feet." He was still driving that beater, still living in the studio apartment, still listening to people fight and crank up their music all hours of the night. He made next to nothing, but he sent his mother whatever he could spare from every paycheck. In return, she sent him a drawing Emmy did of herself and her teddy bear having a tea party. Above an empty chair she had colored an arrow pointing down to it and had scribbled *DADY*. James pulled down the Harley poster and taped the drawing to the wall. It got him through most nights.

On the ninth week after his release, he was finally able to get away to see Emmy in Dallas. But since it was his first visit since jail, he had to first meet with the social worker who had been assigned to their case.

"What case?" he said to his mom on the phone.

She paused for so long he wondered if she'd hung up. "I had to get a judge to give me guardianship of Emmy so she didn't have to go into foster care," she said finally—and carefully. "That makes it a case. Number five-one-two-six-four-five."

James ran his hand down the back of his head. It was the only way he could keep from crushing the cell phone. "I need *permission* to see my own kid?"

"As they see it, you have to earn back your parental rights," she said, carefully choosing her words. "That starts with establishing your visitation privileges."

James pressed the phone against his chest until he could breathe. When he put it back to his ear, his mother was still there, waiting.

"Her name is Heather Powell," she said, "and she's compassionate—for a county employee."

"Has she ever worked in a prison?"

"What?"

"Never mind. Where am I supposed to meet with her?"

His mother gave him the particulars. He wrote them down silently.

When she was done and he said nothing, he could hear her draw in a ragged breath. "Look, son . . . nobody besides you wants you and Emerson back together more than I do. I mean that. But we have to be sure you're ready. We can't send her back to the way things were—"

"Stop! Just stop."

She did.

"I will jump through whatever hoops I have to," James said. "Y'all want me to open a vein, I'm on it."

"That's not funny, James."

"It wasn't meant to be." He shifted the phone to his other hand. "Whatever it takes. Tell this Heather person I'll be there."

# 4

HEATHER POWELL HAD BEEN all wide-eyed and tearful with sympathetic nods and soft, knowing words of encouragement. James had started to let his hopes get too high before she finally had given her professional assessment. Without a hint of emotion, she had stated, "You've made a lot of progress. I think you'll get your daughter back eventually, but right now . . ."

She had stopped to watch him. James remembered thinking, *What do you think I'm going to do? Come across the table at you? Sure, it's crossing my mind . . .*

"Go on," he had said, showing calmness instead.

"You can't provide for her properly. Not yet. I think you'll get there."

"When?"

She had inhaled through her nose, probably as part of the whole speech she had practiced saying. "When you make enough money to rent an apartment with two bedrooms and pay for adequate childcare while you're working, as well as—"

"What kind of money are we talking?" James knew, but it was the only thing he could think of to keep himself from screaming, *How many parents can't give their kids all that? They make it work!*

"After you've paid a deposit and first and last on an apartment?" Heather had said. "Two thousand a month at the very least."

His heart had shriveled inside his chest, but he couldn't let her see weakness or discouragement, so he had forced himself to bob his head as if he were completely on board. As if that amount of money would be within reach in a week or two. As if he had a prayer of ever making a home for Emmy and him. The way Michelle would want it.

"I can see her, though, right?" he had said. "I can see Emmy."

With her fingers steepled under her chin, she had said, "You can see her tomorrow like we planned. If your mother feels comfortable with things, we'll leave your visitation schedule up to her. Though I advise you to keep that to a minimum." The compassion he no longer trusted had quickly returned to her eyes as she said, "You coming and going might make this so much harder on Emerson. And she's the one we're most concerned for, yes?"

*We?* James had wanted to rip that word out of her throat. He screamed inside, *The only "we" is Emmy and me! And I will find a way to make that happen!*

---

He and Emmy—his "we"—sat on his mother's front steps in the broiling Dallas heat. It had been almost a year since he'd last seen his little girl. She looked more like Michelle than ever as she gazed up at him, eyes brimming, throat so obviously choking back the tears. In that year her vocabulary had gone from kindergarten chatter to a collection of words like *accomplish* and *options* and phrases like "And last but not least." Her former chubbiness was stretching out into little-girl lank, and she could skip and reach the toothpaste and make her own peanut butter and jelly sandwich. His mother was right. He was missing her childhood.

But she was still his. That was clear from the minute he'd parked at the curb and she broke loose from her grandmother and took flight from the house and into his arms. In the five hours he'd been there, she had only let go of him twice, both times so she could go to the bathroom. Even then she insisted he wait just outside the door.

It had been, to quote Emmy, "the best day ever," but she stiffened when she saw Heather Powell pulling up in front of the house in her nondescript beige import.

Clicking her way up the driveway in ridiculous heels, Heather's demeanor lacked any of the compassion she had exhibited the day before. Emmy tightened her hold on the teddy bear, whose fur was matted and gray from love and sticky hands. James was pretty sure it had started out being pink.

"Is she taking me away?" Emmy said. She linked her bear-free arm through his.

"No, baby," James said. "You're staying here with Gramma."

"But I want to go home with you. Back to our house."

He couldn't tell her "our house" had long since been taken by the bank. He basically couldn't tell her anything that was actually true.

"I have to work, Em," he said. "And as soon as I've worked hard enough I'll come and get you."

She eyed the figure who had stopped six feet short of the porch. At least the woman was giving him that much.

"How long will that be?" Emmy said.

"I don't know, but I'll be back to see you."

"Tomorrow?"

"Probably not tomorrow, but soon."

He expected her to ask how soon. He'd learned that day that a six-year-old could ask more questions than a *Jeopardy!* contestant. But instead her face collapsed and she buried it in his sleeve. The teddy bear fell to the ground as she squeezed his arm with both of hers.

Behind him the screen door opened, and Heather inched forward. It was so obvious they thought he was going to pick up Emmy and make a run for it, he almost laughed. Like he would blow it now.

"Hey, now," he said into the curls that smelled like strawberries. "Look at me. Look at Daddy, Emmy."

She tilted a streaked face up to him.

"I promise you I will be back. Soon. And I promise you that before you know it, you and I will be together and you'll be with me until you're a grown-up girl."

"That's a long time," she said.

"Yes, it is."

Heather cleared her throat. His mother put her hand on Emmy's shoulder.

"It's time," she said.

At least Mom's voice was kind. Heather Powell, on the other hand, was practically tapping her toe.

"I love you, baby," James said.

Emmy threw her arms around his neck and clung to him. His mother reached out to peel her away, but James stood up and held his daughter and whispered, "I have to go. You be brave."

Emmy pulled her face from his neck and looked so deeply into his eyes he thought she might fall in.

"Will you be lonely, Daddy?" she said.

"I'll miss *you*," he said.

"Then here." She scrambled from his arms and retrieved the once-pink teddy bear from the bottom step, right at Heather Powell's feet. "Take Teddy with you."

"Oh, baby—"

"She wants to go with you."

Emmy pressed it into his hand and dodged her grandmother to get into the house, which meant he didn't have to look back as he passed Heather and headed for his truck. He almost believed his baby girl set it up that way.

Heather followed him, but he didn't stop until he reached the Nissan. He only paused then to unlock the door.

"You're very fortunate, James," she said.

"Yeah? How's that?"

"She's with your mother and not in the system."

James held back the words *Bite me* by sheer willpower. He dropped into his truck and drove away. It was the only good thing he'd done since Michelle died. But it wasn't going to be the last.

---

That optimism tanked by the time he got back to Houston. His face burned from both the hot wind that battered him for 240 miles and the memory of what he'd promised his daughter.

What was he thinking? How was he ever going to get her back? He had about as much chance of getting a raise out of South Houston Construction as he did of winning the lottery. The only thing he knew for sure right now was that he couldn't go back to his hole of an apartment with all of that beating him down. Although he wasn't hungry, he thought it best to eat something, so he pulled into the Neighborhood Bar and Grille. It wouldn't be too crowded on a Thursday night, and maybe Jen was working the bar. She knew when to leave him alone.

She was. For once he'd caught a break. He took a spot two stools over from a guy about his age with a Donald Trump 'do who had either been there awhile or came in loaded. He smelled like he'd showered in gin. The even-younger redhead on the other side of him didn't appear to mind. She seemed content with whoever was vertical.

Jen put her hands on hips that were as barely there as her microscopic shorts. "Did you get the number of that semi?"

"What semi?" James said.

"The one that ran over you."

James felt his fists double until she laughed and tossed her shoulder-length hair that was three different shades of blonde. "You look terrible. You could use a beer."

He nodded. She didn't know. He didn't talk about it to people he hadn't met before the accident. She was always decent to him and she never would have said that if she knew.

But he felt like the stool was spinning.

She planted a sweating bottle of Corona on the counter and held out her palm. "That's six dollars, James."

They didn't do tabs here. It was strictly pay as you go. James pulled his debit card out of his wallet and handed it to her. He cupped his hands around the cold bottle and let the sounds of the place blot out his thoughts. Pool balls knocking together. Some female singer wailing through the speakers about the guy who did her wrong. Laughter erupting from a corner booth. A faint buzz from the neon Coors sign above the bar. It was low life and white trash and redneck, but it was better than lying on his futon with a knife in his heart.

His debit card appeared on the counter. Jen leaned toward him.

"This one was denied," she said. "You got another one?"

"Can you run it again?"

"Ran it twice. Look, it's not a big deal. You got any cash?"

She was speaking in a low, throaty voice, but apparently not low enough. The drunk all but fell off his stool and positioned himself on the one next to James.

"I got a lawn you can mow," he said. His drawl was dense as quicksand.

"Shut up and mind your own business, Travis," Jen said.

Travis waved her off sloppily, glazed eyes on James. "It's depressing, isn't it, James? Can I call you James?"

"Look," James said. "Why don't you take your little girl home? It's probably past her bedtime."

"Seriously." A small drop of spit landed on James's cheek. "Wife gone. Kid gone. Can't even afford a beer."

James seethed, but he stared at the Coors sign and said nothing.

"We don't know each other," Travis said. "But I watch the news. First your wife gets thrown through a windshield. Then you get busted for possession—"

"Hey." Jen slapped both hands on the bar. "You're drunk and stupid, and only one of those things is gonna wear off by morning. Why don't you get a head start and go find out which?"

"You gonna make me?"

"It would be the highlight of my night."

"Look at you!"

"I'd rather you didn't." She turned to James and lowered her voice again. Her eyes had been startled into sympathy. "I'll cover you and you can pay me next time you come in."

"I can't," James said.

"Sure you can." She reached for the tip jar, which was only half full of change and crumpled dollar bills.

"Look at the tough guy over here!" Travis panned the room and then tried to settle his inebriated eyes back on James. "Good thing your wife isn't here to see this—a girl fightin' your battles and payin' your tab."

"Knock it off," Jen said.

"See what I'm sayin'? He's nothin' without a woman to—"

James rose from his stool and grabbed the bottle. Jen reached for it, but not in time to keep him from smashing it over Travis's head. Beer and glass reached the group at the pool table and even the corner booth. The country singer kept bemoaning her fate over the screams of Travis's date. Travis himself teetered for a slo-mo moment before falling backward into her.

"Not in here, James!" Jen shouted at him.

"Ya hear that, Ja-a-ames?" Travis said. "Listen to your mommy."

It was the prison yard all over again. Rage kicked in and James shoved his hand onto the back of Travis's head and slammed his face into the bar.

"Get out, James—or I'm calling the cops!" Jen said.

James froze.

"No cops," he said.

"Then get out. Go cool down someplace, but not here."

James stumbled toward the door and into a barrel-chested cowboy with a cell phone held up to James's face. He snatched it from the guy's hand, but once again Jen shouted a threat to call

911. James let the cell phone drop onto the pool table and went for the door.

"I'm pressing charges!" Travis howled from the bar.

"Keep going, James," Jen said. "He'll never remember this."

James rammed through the door and out into the steamy night. He pushed against the wall of humidity to the Nissan, repeating Emmy's name with every heaving breath until he hoisted himself into the cab. He knew he had to get out of there. Once Jen started wiping the blood off the bar, she'd probably change her mind about that phone call. He stabbed the key into the ignition and turned it.

Nothing. Not even a feeble attempt by the engine to turn over.

James pounded the gas with his foot and tried the starter again, but he was met with a *click* and the sound of his own voice shouting, "Come *on*!"

Both hands strangled the steering wheel as he shook it until the truck rocked. The picture taped to the dashboard came loose and dropped to the floor. James knocked his work boots and several empty soda cans out of the way and retrieved it. Michelle and Emmy looked at him, faces now spattered with wet Coke but smiling. Even the pink teddy bear was smiling.

His pulse raced as he turned the picture over and shook away the droplets that threatened to run the ink. It was still there—the message from Michelle—written in her round, smooth handwriting the day they left for their babymoon and propped on his dresser to find when they got home. When he got home. Alone.

*Let all that we do be done in love. I love you, honey!*

How was he supposed to do that when he ran into hate at

every turn? How long would it be before Emmy would stop gazing up at him because he'd let her down too many times?

He wiped the front of the picture on his jeans and slipped it
into his pocket. His hand was bleeding and shaking and sweating
as he grabbed the teddy bear and got out and slammed the door
shut with his foot. With Emmy and Michelle burning against
his chest and the bear dangling from his fingers, he strode to the
middle of the street and headed for home.

Whatever that was.

# 5

CHAD PICKED HIM UP for work the next morning and handed James a venti black coffee when he climbed into the Silverado. James didn't ask how it was that they worked for the same company, doing virtually the same thing, yet Chad could afford a forty-thousand-dollar truck and daily trips to Starbucks. He was afraid to.

"Thanks for doing this," he said. He burned his lip on the first sip and then carefully took another. At least he could feel physical pain. Everything else had gone numb.

"No problem," Chad said. "I got a wrecker picking up your truck. They're taking it to—"

"You gotta stop doing this stuff," James said. "I'm gonna end up owing you more than I owed on my house. And you know how that ended up."

"We already went through this." Chad pulled up to a stop sign and gave him more than a glance. "You look terrible. You know that, don't you?"

James managed a grunt.

Chad honked at a Cherokee that moved through the four-way out of turn and drove forward. "I'm serious, man. When's the last time you slept? Or ate? Grab that bag from the back seat. There's another breakfast sandwich in there."

"I'm good."

"Your hand's not." Chad nodded at the three Band-Aids James had used to suture the split in his palm. "What did you get into?"

"Broken glass," James said.

He could feel Chad looking at him, but he turned his head and stared out the passenger window until they pulled into the yard at South Houston Construction.

"Want a piece of advice?" Chad said.

"Do I have a choice?"

"Don't go on the job looking like that."

"Like what?"

"Like you just robbed a liquor store and you're on the run." Chad narrowed his eyes. "You didn't, did you?"

"No!"

"Then at least look like you give a rip about being here. Come on—nothing'll brighten your mood like some underpaid manual labor."

"Where do you get this stuff, dude?" James said. But he could feel the creases smooth out of his forehead. He had a job. And they couldn't keep paying him minimum wage forever. Not with his skills.

"The only thing that'll brighten my mood is to work *your* sorry butt into the ground," he said.

Chad gave him a full grin. "Now you're talkin'. I have to hit the john. I'll meet you out there."

James left the Silverado and strapped on his tool belt and bags as he walked past the foreman's trailer. They were five minutes late but he'd make it up—

"Stevens!"

Brent Weisman barked out his name almost before he was out the door of the trailer. Built like a brick barbecue with hamish arms and no neck to speak of, he still managed to carry an oversize Styrofoam cup in one thick hand and balance two glazed Krispy Kreme donuts on a clipboard with the other as he stomped down the aluminum steps. The trailer rattled behind him as the door slammed, but he didn't spill a drop of the coffee.

James stifled a groan.

"Do you actually own a clock, Stevens?" he said.

The sarcasm nettled his skin, but James said, "Sorry. There was a thing with my truck—"

"There's always a 'thing.' And what was it yesterday?"

"You gave me the time off—"

"And what did you use it for? You look like you went on a bender."

James swallowed everything he wanted to say, along with his pride.

"I had personal business to take care of. And here's the deal."

He waited for Weisman to bark again, but when he didn't James ventured on.

"I need more hours."

Weisman feigned choking on his coffee. "More hours? You are not what I would call a model employee, Stevens. How long you been working here?"

"Little over two months."

The foreman squinted through the steam curling from his cup. "And before that?"

Seriously? The jerk knew the answer. James had to draw blood from the inside of his mouth with his teeth to keep from shoving one of those donuts in his face.

"I did six months at Kegans."

"Right. Which I overlooked because your buddy Chad suck-
ered me in with a story about his pal who lost his wife and needed
a job to get back on his feet."

At least Chad hadn't told him about Emmy. If his little girl's
name had come out of this man's mouth . . . He couldn't go there.

"I appreciate the job," James said. "I'm—"

"You're a walking soap opera is what you are. Freakin' *Days
of Our Lives* on a forklift. Look . . ." He took another drag from
the cup and tossed the rest of the contents on the ground near
James's boot. "You don't make good with the hours you have.
Matter of fact, if you don't *start* getting here on time and *stop*
taking time off to do God knows what, you won't have those.
We clear?"

James gave a nod. "Clear."

"Get to work—and I'm docking you fifteen minutes."

James turned away to hide the smear of anger he could feel
on his face.

---

He decided to work through lunch. Because he wanted to make
up the hour, and he didn't have anything to eat anyway. The only
thing in his refrigerator that morning was a container of macaroni
and cheese he'd picked up at the mini-mart. He was saving that
for dinner.

But Chad came by at noon and told him to take off his bags
and follow him. It sounded slightly biblical, which didn't improve James's state of mind. He and God had stopped speaking.
Indefinitely.

Chad led him to the Silverado and let down the tailgate. He

patted a place for James to sit and produced a large brown paper bag from inside the cab.

"You gotta eat something," he said as he hiked himself up.

"I'm not eating your lunch."

"No, you're not. I brought enough for both of us. Cold pizza from Pizza Fino and a Caesar salad. My doggie bag from last night."

Again, James didn't ask how Chad could afford to eat like that or, for that matter, wear the pricey-looking watch he wore—and on the job, no less. He wanted to turn down the slice of Italian sausage and pepperoni Chad handed him, but his stomach refused to let him. He actually hadn't eaten anything since lunch at his mother's the day before.

They ate in silence for several minutes—not typical for Chad—before he tossed a thick remnant of crust into the box and said, "How hard up are ya, bud?"

"I'm okay."

"You're lyin'. I told you if you needed anything, all you had to do was ask me."

"I'm not borrowing any money from you."

"Not offering a loan. How 'bout earning it?"

The pizza turned to cardboard in James's mouth. Here it comes. Like the other shoe dropping.

"Off the books," Chad said. "But it's not what you think."

"It better not be because I'm not doing that stuff anymore." James tried to laugh. "Besides, I'm terrible at it."

"I won't argue with you there. But there's nothing illegal about driving."

"Driving what?"

"A truck. From here to Reno."

"Truck full of what?"

"I usually do it myself, but if you need the dough I can give you this run."

"Truck full of *what*?"

Chad wiped his hands on a rag and tossed it aside. "It's not drugs, if that's what you're thinking. It's just a transport gig, alright? The back's locked. You drive to the destination. Guys on the other end unload it. You bring back the empty truck."

"Then how do you know it isn't drugs?"

"Because these people have never messed with me. And there's no evidence they're into that. It's not like Paulie Vaca."

James abandoned the pizza and shook his head. "I don't think so."

"C'mon, man. Do you really think I'd get you mixed up in that stuff again? After all you've been through?" He jabbed his thumb into his chest. "After what you did for me?"

"These gigs. That how you can afford this truck? Wear the clothes you do? Eat like you do?"

"It helps. And it can help *you*. Let's face it, James: workin' here barely pays your bills. It's not gonna get your little girl back for you."

James jerked. Chad put up both palms. "I'm not trying to yank your chain. I'm just sayin'—make one run and you can get into a nice place. Another run—I can put you in a better truck. I didn't do right by you with that piece-of-trash Nissan." He did the half grin.

James sat with the picture Chad had just painted. Emmy's face was in the middle of it saying, *I want to go home with you.* Which was never going to happen if he ended up in prison again.

Custody would be the least of his worries. He'd never see her again. He knew his mother that well.

"I don't know," he said. "It sounds too easy."

"Right." Chad huffed. "You ever drive twenty-eight and a half hours without stopping? That's why it pays so good. It's an endurance thing. If you can do six months at Kegans, you can do this."

James stayed mute.

"Just think about it," Chad said. "The money's real. If you want it, I can make a call and you leave in the morning."

"*Tomorrow* morning?"

"We don't work on Monday because the job site is closed for inspections. So you take off in the wee hours of Saturday, get there Sunday morning, sleep some during the day, then get back on the road so you can get a little sleep before work Tuesday. Besides," Chad said with a shrug, "you don't sleep anyway, so what the heck?"

He had a point there. But anything that sounded too good to be true usually was.

"Thanks for the offer," James said. "But you take the gig. I'll figure something else out."

"What's that gonna be, man?" Chad said. "What?"

James had no idea.

---

He peeled the top off the mac and cheese container and stared into it. That color orange didn't exist in nature. But Emmy claimed to love it. Every time he put it in front of her. Which had been on all the days he didn't give her a hot dog or a frozen waffle or a peanut butter sandwich. His mother was horrified. Michelle would have been too.

James stuck a fork in it and took a mouthful. It was cold, but he didn't have a microwave. Add that to the list of a hundred and fifty other things guys his age owned and he didn't. There might have been one in the storage unit Mom put everything into when the bank took the house. Who knew where all his things were now.

Man, this stuff was gross.

He was on his way to pitch it in the trash bag that hung on a kitchen drawer knob when his cell phone rang. That was always the first bill he paid. It was his only link to Emmy.

"Hey, Mom," he said. "How's my baby?"

"Doing better," she said.

He didn't ask better than what.

"Can I talk to her?"

"She's watching *Scooby Doo*. I need to talk to you."

James dropped the macaroni container into the trash can with more force than he needed to.

"Heather brought the final paperwork by today."

"Heather who? Oh. Heather." Social worker without a heart.

"I was reading through it to make sure there were no surprises—"

"And there was one," James blurted out. He dropped onto the futon and raked his free hand through his hair. "What do they want now—a urine sample?"

"You were never charged with using, James," she said, her voice tightening. "There would be no reason for drug testing."

"That's not what I meant. Never mind. Go on."

He heard paper rustling. "It says here that even though I have custody of Emerson until you can provide—"

"I know, Mom . . ."

"Well, hon, did you read the fine print?"

"You obviously did." He was fighting to keep sarcasm out of his voice, but he felt himself losing that battle. And at least she was trying. She hadn't called him "hon" in two years. "Just tell me," he said.

"The judge is going to revisit the case in six months."

His muscles went taut. "What do you mean, 'revisit'?"

"Go over your situation with Heather and determine how much progress you're making toward proving that you can support Emerson."

"I *am* making progress."

"I'm not sure our idea of progress and theirs is the same." The paper rustled again and she cleared her throat. "It states, 'A home deemed adequate by the court. An income of three thousand dollars a month.'"

"Yeah, Heather told me all that."

"And the equivalent of six months' salary in the bank for emergencies."

"What?!"

"That's what it says."

"I don't know *anybody* who has that in this economy!"

A significant silence fell before his mom said, "I know, son. It's just the situation—"

"Okay. I get it."

"I just didn't want this to blindside you when the time came. If I could help you financially, I would. But that wouldn't fly with them."

"I don't need you to." James stood up and paced to the sink

and back. His mouth went dry. It was hard to get the next words off his tongue. "I can do this. Don't worry about it, Mom. I can do this."

"I know that. I keep telling you that you can."

James waited for the "but."

"But I have to say that you can't do it the way you tried to before."

"Y'know what, Mom?" James dragged in a breath. "You didn't have to say that. I'm not an idiot."

But as he hung up and punched in Chad's number, he wasn't sure he was right.

# 6

THE AIR WAS ALREADY hot and heavy at 3:30 a.m. when James climbed out of Chad's Silverado and walked in the thin path of light formed by a single fixture at the corner of the warehouse roof. Chad had apologized that Starbucks wasn't open yet, but he'd supplied a Big Gulp–size cup of coffee strong enough to walk across the lot with him.

Two box trucks were parked just out of the light. Impatient exhaust blew out of one and its backup lights glared as it moved away from the building and disappeared into the dark. Chad pointed to the remaining vehicle.

"That's yours, bro. And these are your directions to Reno."

James scowled at the stapled sheets of paper Chad pulled out of his sleeveless denim vest. "I know how to get to Reno. I double-checked last night. Take I-10 to—"

"You have to stop thinking so much," Chad said.

His crooked smile was stiff. Either he wasn't totally awake or he was stressing. James didn't like it. The only time he ever saw Chad uptight was the day he came to visit him in jail, before the trial, and even then all signs of anxiety had faded when James said simply, "You got nothing to worry about."

"They like us to take the back roads," Chad said. "You can

actually make better time because there aren't as many cops. Feel free to exceed the speed limit. Put the pedal to the metal—"

"I don't need any tickets."

"Which is why you follow the directions." Chad pressed the paper into James's hand and nodded him toward the truck. "Two more things. One, you have to drive without stopping except for gas and food and bathroom. There's a deadline that you have to meet."

James nodded. "Two?"

"You don't look at the cargo. Not that you could." He reached down and flipped the overkill padlock that secured the door.

"That's the part I don't like," James said.

Chad draped his arm around his shoulder. "See, I didn't like that at first either, and then I figured it out." He looked around, though at what, James wasn't sure. The place was completely deserted. "They don't want anybody tempted to steal their goods. The way I see it, it's for our protection. As long as that lock stays locked, they can't accuse us of ripping them off."

"So what's in there is valuable?" James said.

"They wouldn't be paying this kind of money if it wasn't."

Chad reached into the other side of his vest and pulled out a thick envelope. "Normally you'd get half up front and half when you return the truck, but I talked them into giving all of it to you now. I convinced them you're good for it."

"Who are these people, anyway?"

"Group of investors trying to save money on transport," Chad said. "Like I said, it's nothing illegal. They're just cutting corners."

James nodded, but his pulse was racing.

Chad held out a key on a plain ring. "Somebody will meet you when you get there. They'll give you a payment to bring back for our people—sealed. Grab some sleep after you get there and then head home. Is your cell phone charged?"

"Yeah."

"Got the charger with you? I'll want to keep in touch—keep you awake. You call me if you get tired."

Chad half grinned. James tried. He couldn't imagine falling asleep. Maybe ever again.

---

By three that afternoon it was clear his imagination hadn't stretched far enough. As he drove into the southwest corner of New Mexico, the sun baked the window and tried to fry his eyelids shut. His cheap Walmart sunglasses completely wimped out and his head ached from squinting.

He'd found a four-pack of energy drinks on the front seat, but those were gone. He'd also discovered a gift credit card in the envelope with the cash Chad had given him. Hoping there was enough on there for a fill-up and some food, he scanned the horizon for a gas station. The heat on the road wiggled like a mirage.

Over the next hill a two-pump station appeared beneath a wind-battered sign that read Gas-Beer-Sandwiches-Bait. He hoped the bait wasn't on the sandwiches. Who needed bait out here anyway? There wasn't a fish for five hundred miles.

Okay, the fatigue was getting to him.

The truck bounced in and out of a pothole as he pulled into the station. When he climbed out of the truck the dust was still settling and he breathed in a lungful of it. Coughing, he planted his hands on the side of the truck and stretched. He could almost hear the kinks popping out of his muscles.

The sign said he had to pay inside, which he hoped was

air-conditioned. The truck was—but barely. Chad wasn't kidding. These investors, whoever they were, gave new meaning to the term *cutting corners*.

No such luck. A large dented box fan blew humid air into his face when he pushed open the door. The greasy dude with the comb-over behind the counter knew how to cut corners too.

"Gas?" the man said. His teeth retained the remnants of his last tobacco chew.

"I'll need some," James said. But first things first. "Bathroom?"

The guy pointed a smudged finger to a liter-size cup hanging by a chain from a nail. A key dangled from it.

"In case you get thirsty while you're in there."

James pulled the thing from the nail and looked around for the restroom sign.

"That was a joke. Don't drink out of it."

James cut the bathroom visit as short as possible to avoid asphyxiation from holding his breath in the stink. The guy watched him return the cup and key, grinning for no apparent reason that James could see. James was afraid to get anything to eat—who knew how long those sandwiches had been sitting there—but he figured a six-pack of energy drinks and a handful of candy bars might be safe. If he ever did this again he was packing a lunch.

As he was headed back toward the counter, he noticed a display of stuffed animals piled on top of a fake barrel with a monkey painted on it. Emmy would go nuts. James stopped and ran a finger down the fur of a teddy bear. Pink. Like hers used to be.

He set it on the counter with the other stuff and handed the guy the credit card. "I'm going to need to fill up too."

The combed-over head shook.

"What?" James said. "You're out of gas?"

"No. I don't take credit cards. Cash only."

"Seriously?"

The man put his hand over the items on the counter and narrowed his already half-closed eyes at James. "You don't have cash?"

"Yeah, I've got cash. I'm just surprised, that's all."

"How much gas you want?"

"Fifty dollars' worth," James said.

This place was giving him the creeps, but he had no clue how far it was to the next filling station. He turned away from the counter and pulled the envelope of cash from his jeans pocket just far enough to draw out a hundred-dollar bill. He stuffed the envelope back in and turned to hand the money to the guy. His suddenly awakened eyes went from the hundred to the bulge in James's pocket.

He grabbed the bill as if he expected James to change his mind. "Watcha haulin' there, son?" he said.

*I have no idea* probably wasn't the best answer to give. This wasn't any of the dude's business anyway. He shrugged and said, "Nothing."

A laugh that clearly hadn't been used in a while wheezed from his throat. "Yeah? Guess I gotta find me a way to start haulin' some of that *nothin'.*"

Yeah. Time to get the heck out of Dodge.

"Change?" James said.

Eyes now shifting warily, the attendant dumped bills and coins into James's palm. He was obviously as glad to see James go as James was to clear out.

Although the sun was making its way down the west side of the sky toward the dinosaur-shaped rock formations, it still braised the back of James's neck as he filled up the truck. If he could have pumped faster, he would have. The attendant was staring at him through the smeared station window, working his mouth like he was literally chewing on his suspicions.

Annoyed as he was, James couldn't blame him. Unmarked truck. Padlock on steroids on its door. Driver with a bank roll that would have put Al Capone to shame. And a hand still wrapped from his recent assault on the drunk at the bar.

He would have taken him for a career criminal too.

James climbed back into the cab. Old Gray Bear sat on the seat next to New Pink Bear. As long as he could keep his mind focused on his ultimate goal, he wouldn't lose Emmy. Or himself.

# 7

WHY DIDN'T HE ever feel this sleepy at home? James had spent hours staring up at Emmy's drawing on the wall in the middle of countless nights, but now, when he had to stay awake, he was struggling to keep his eyes open. And the truck on the road.

He was about to reach for the last energy drink—his fourth in 120 miles—when a blue flash in the side mirror caught his eye. A siren blasted and brought him to full consciousness.

Several expletives threatened to burst from his lips as the police car ate the distance between them and lit up the mirror. Its accusing wail took him straight back to the Kmart and the handcuffs and you-have-a-right-to-remain-silent.

Apparently he also had the right to remain stupid. Whatever he was hauling had to be some kind of contraband. He was headed back to prison for sure. He would have cussed Chad if he didn't know it was all his own fault.

The siren whooped right at his tail. The only thing to do was pull over and put on his law-abiding face. Maybe he *had* dozed off and swerved a little, but he'd pass a breathalyzer test.

He shook, though, as he got the truck off the road. No doubt he'd be asked what he was carrying, and *Nothing* wasn't going to cut it with the cops. Neither was *I don't know.*

As he reached for his license, the cruiser whipped past him, still screaming at whatever it was after. It took James a full thirty seconds to register that it wasn't him. He devoted another thirty to trying to stop trembling.

He was just about ready to pull back onto the road when his cell dinged with a text. His hand was so slippery with terror-sweat he almost dropped the phone.

The message was from Chad. *How's it going?*

James had to wipe his fingers on his T-shirt before he could tap out his lie: *Couldn't be better.*

At least he didn't have to worry about staying awake now. That shot of adrenaline was enough to keep him conscious all the way to Reno. It had to be. He couldn't mess this up. He couldn't get pulled over. He couldn't have an accident . . .

---

And then he was having one. Oncoming headlights bearing down on him. Michelle clawing at his arm with her newly manicured fingernails. His body twisting with the crash . . .

An alarmed horn blast ripped through his gut. James wrenched the steering wheel and got the truck out of the path of an even bigger one barreling toward him.

He could almost see the veins in the driver's eyes as they passed within inches of each other. James jerked the wheel again and knew immediately that he'd overcorrected. His foot jammed involuntarily on the brake and the truck skidded sideways. The rock-and-sand embankment came up to meet him, sending dust and sagebrush flying.

Yeah. He and God were *definitely* not on speaking terms.

James pressed his hands to the seat on either side of him and again forced himself to stop shivering like a neurotic Chihuahua.

His right palm knocked into something soft. New Pink Teddy was lying on its side. Old Gray had taken a dive to the floorboards. James fought off another flashback.

The truck was still running, but he needed to check for outside damages. And fast, because he was losing time. Hardly daring to hope for anything resembling a break, he climbed out and crossed in front of the vehicle, shielding his eyes from the headlight beams and murmuring, "Please-please-please."

The front bumper on the passenger side wasn't even dented. They must build these things like armored tanks. The side mirror was askew and he couldn't bend it back—but at least the truck itself was on a slight incline and wasn't upside down. No drainage pipe had impaled the front end. So why were his insides caving?

Because it was never going to go away.

James put his hands on the side of the truck and pushed back the pain surging into his chest. Crying? *Come on, man! Get a hold of yourself. Truckers don't cry!*

It took a crazy minute for him to realize he wasn't the one doing the crying. The frightened whimpering was coming from somewhere else. He tilted his head. *Dude.* He was hearing it inside the truck.

*What the—*

He took the length of the vehicle in three long strides and pressed his ear to the padlocked door. Cries. Female cries. Hushed by a murmuring voice, but sobbing again.

James stared at the lock—like that was going to give him a clue—and then at something liquid that dripped through the crack under the door. He touched it with the tip of his finger and gave it a sniff. And almost gagged. It smelled like the inside of that nasty gas station.

Chad had been clear that he wasn't supposed to look at the cargo, but forget that. He went to the cab and grabbed a tire iron from behind the seat. He could hear Chad telling him through tightened teeth to get back in and drive on, but the full-out sobs coming from the back of the truck trumped that. *Human cargo? Seriously?*

Shoving aside the mental picture of how this was going to go down in the end, James swung at the lock until his arms ached and the thing snapped. He yanked it from the metal hank and dropped it on the pavement with the tire iron. It still took some prying to get the heavy door open, and when he did, something round and metallic sailed past his head. He let the door slam shut.

He did *not* just see what he thought he saw. Sleep deprivation. That's what it was. Because there was no *way* there were two female bodies huddled together in the back of the otherwise empty cargo hold. Throwing tuna cans at him.

No. Freakin'. Way.

The cries he'd heard before were gone as if they'd been snuffed out. Moving more slowly this time, James pulled open the door and flicked on the dome light to reveal two young Hispanic women staring back at him—one of them rattling off a string of something in angry Spanish that he probably didn't want to comprehend. He'd never bothered to learn the language beyond *por favor* and *gracias* and *el baño*, but he didn't have to be a Rosetta Stone graduate to know she was chewing him out. He had, after all, just thrown them around in the back of the truck like a pair of rag dolls.

He put up both hands and took a step back and shook his head. He even threw in, "It's cool." But the woman obviously wasn't having it. Her eyes blazed at him and a petite finger jabbed in his direction. James guessed, from what he could see, that she was in her early twenties, but she could have passed for thirty.

The other one was younger, a teenager, he'd say. Even crouched in the truck she was taller, but her face hadn't found its adult contours yet. From the looks of her swollen, red-rimmed eyes, she was the one who'd been doing all the crying.

He'd be crying too if he'd ridden for sixteen hours in that mess. The disgusting odor wasn't just in the air. It soaked the two sleeping bags, the pillows, and the backpacks. And their clothes. The accident must have popped the lid off their pee can and tossed it and most of its contents over everything they had with them.

"Do you speak any English?" he said.

He was met with a glare.

"I'll take that as a no." He breathed into his hands. "Okay— are you hurt? You okay?"

No response.

James scanned the filthy truck even as the older one returned to the barking of what were obviously orders for him to back off. Tone of voice crossed all language barriers. Ironically, the one thing that had escaped the splash was a roll of toilet paper. He had to do something, even if it was wrong, and this seemed like the logical next step.

He tore a piece off the roll and mimed wiping at his arms and face.

"You need to clean yourselves off. I'm serious. You reek."

When he motioned toward them with the roll, the younger one shrank back, but the older one nodded and gestured for him to toss it to her. Certain it was going to end up in a puddle, James did it anyway and she caught it with the hand that wasn't still holding on to the teenager.

She chattered something to the teen in Spanish, and to his relief they set to cleaning themselves up. Nothing short of a shower—or maybe sheep dip—was going to really do the job, but at least it was something.

"C'mon," he said, wafting a hand from the truck to the ground. "We still have a long way to go, *sí*?"

They had an entire conversation with their eyes and then both of them stepped down from the truck and continued the cleanup. James found a trash bag that had also dumped itself all over the place and offered it to them to put the used paper inside.

Now what?

James ran a hand down the back of his head and kicked at the can. He couldn't let them ride the rest of the way to Reno back there. He wouldn't do that to a herd of pigs, much less these two. There was something close to classy about them. Something kind of refined around the older one's eyes.

"You should ride up front with me," he said, pointing toward the cab.

The face of the younger one brightened. The older one narrowed her dark eyes at him.

James feigned surrender again. As they stared he talked with his hands, shaping the words they obviously weren't understanding. "No strings. You'll just be safer up there. And more comfortable. Come on—I'm not gonna hurt you."

When he pointed to the cab again, Younger Girl scrambled toward him before Older Girl could grab her. She lifted her chin and gave James one long glowering look that read, *Lay one hand on either one of us and you're taking it right in the groin.*

That, too, was universal.

# 8

"He's nice," Maria whispered in Spanish as they followed the guy to the front of the truck.

"So far," Antonia whispered back. "We're only doing this because we don't have much choice."

Her sister wrinkled her nose and nodded. "You still stink."

"So do you."

The guy was now standing with the passenger door open. The truck was tilted, which would actually make it easier to get in. Antonia just hoped his driving improved.

Maria started to climb in ahead of her, but Antonia pushed her aside and slid onto the seat closest to the driver. At seventeen, Maria was still too naïve to get that a guy was about to make a move on her. He could be halfway down her shirt before she figured it out.

Although . . . the two stuffed bears said otherwise. But then, those could be his tools for luring children—

"Go!" Maria whispered to her.

It was better than riding back there and being tossed around in their own body fluids. She would just have to be on alert.

The guy picked up the bears and put them carefully behind the seat. It didn't look weird, but it could be. Antonia slid across the seat.

When they were buckled in—after some big-faced gyrations from the guy (did he think they were mentally challenged?)—he bounced the truck back onto the road and took off into the inky night.

They'd been over the border for a whole day, but this was the first view she'd had of the United States. Even in the dark it still looked as brown and dry as Mexico, but it was definitely superior to the four gray vibrating walls they'd been staring at. This wasn't going down the way they were told it would. Still, arriving in California smelling like her grandmother's chicken yard wasn't an option.

She shivered. The other thing they hadn't been informed of was that summer seemed to disappear when the sun went down. She was nervous, yes, but she was also chilled in her strapped sundress, and so apparently was her sister, who pressed into her side, arms hugged around herself.

Their driver glanced at her—the first time since they'd started off again—and turned a knob on the dashboard. Hot air blasted from the vents, and Maria immediately stuck out her hands. The guy reached across them to re-aim the vent closest to Antonia, and she eased slightly into the seat.

Until he proceeded to remove his flannel shirt. *That* didn't take long. Maria plastered herself against Antonia.

"No, no, no!" Antonia said to him. Her voice was shrill but she couldn't help it. Everything her mother had warned them about American men was screaming in her head.

The guy continued to peel off his shirt as if she hadn't uttered a syllable and held it out to her. A tattoo of a tree branched down his right arm below the sleeve of his T-shirt . . .

"*Fuego*," he said.

Maria smothered a giggle with her hand.

What in the world was he trying to say? *Fuego* was "fire." And "passion." Not happening.

But Maria took the shirt and spread it over the two of them. It was big enough to cover, and it still held his body heat. Antonia wasn't crazy about the idea, but she said, "*Gracias*."

"No problemo," he said.

Maria laughed right out loud, in spite of the side-jab Antonia delivered with her elbow. The child was so comfortable by then she stuck her hand out from under the shirt and switched on the radio.

"What are you doing?" Antonia hissed at her in Spanish.

"It's okay," the guy said. "Here."

The guy reached over and eased up the volume. She could now see the two tattoos on his left arm, a cross peeking from his armpit and some words cascading down toward his wrist. An old Antonio Orosco song filled the cab.

"Hope you like that," he said, "because it's all you're going to get in the land of illegal immigrants."

He caught his breath. Maria clapped her hand over her mouth and Antonia stared her down until she dropped it. She could almost hear the pieces falling into place in his mind. Maybe they should have stayed in the back. With the pee.

He slowed the truck and pointed to a peeling sign. "Gas and *el baño*," he said. He swiped at his arm with his hand. "Clean up some more, *sí?*"

Antonia gave Maria another elbow jab, and this time she kept her giggles to herself.

"*Sí. El baño*," she said.

By her calculations they had twelve more hours to go. But it might as well have been fifty.

James pulled up to a pump, shut off the engine, and turned to look at his two passengers. In spite of the fumes coming off of them and the tangled hair and the tight faces, man, they were pretty. Especially the older one. Her skin was perfect and she moved as if she were made of air. He could only imagine what she looked like when she smiled. If she ever did.

"I don't know how much of this you can understand," he said, "but we have to make this quick. I could get in a lot of trouble for even letting you out of the truck, much less turning you loose to run around outside."

That sounded so self-centered he was glad they probably weren't catching most of it. Their expressionless faces confirmed that. He'd better go back to miming.

He drew his finger across his lips like he was zipping them closed. They nodded. He made his fingers run across the dash-board and shook his head. The younger one giggled. She was like a teenage version of Emmy.

*Don't go there.*

His back complained when he got out of the truck, but he ignored it and tried not to walk like he was eighty as he led them to the station. When he opened the sign-plastered door for them to pass in front of him, Antonia gave him an appreciative glance—before she slid the mask on again—and for once he was glad Mom had drummed be-a-gentleman-manners into him.

But, yeah, those dresses they were wearing had to go. No amount of washing up in *el baño* was going to make them smell any less like soaked diapers.

He looked around inside the truck stop store, which was crammed from ceiling to dirty linoleum floor. These places had everything from imitation Indian blankets to beef jerky. He spot-ted a rack of cheap women's clothes and headed for it, the "cargo" trailing him. The dresses didn't look like anything he'd ever seen Michelle wear, but time was crunching behind him at this point.

He pulled out a bright blue one with flowers embroidered across the front and inched it toward the older girl.

"Go ahead," he said. "It's on me."

She might have shuddered, or maybe he imagined that, but she took it. The younger one helped herself to a pink one and raised her eyebrows at him.

"Sure. You get one too," James said. "Get washed up and changed and I'll meet you back here. Wait, give me the price tags so I can pay for these."

All he needed was to get picked up for shoplifting. The African-American woman at the register was already looking at him like she expected him to hijack the whole collection. Although that might be the least of his offenses. So far he'd racked up causing a vehicular accident, driving under the influence of stupidity, and transporting illegal aliens.

That *was* what he was doing, right? They hadn't tried to bolt. In fact, the older one had obviously been ticked when he discov-ered them in the back of the truck. They clearly wanted to go to Reno, no duress involved.

He took the price tags and watched the girls head for the restroom. Okay, so he'd get them there, sans smell and in one piece.

And then he was going to find another way to make Emmy-money.

# 9

Maria came out of the stall and grinned at herself in the mirror. "A real toilet? Running water? I never thought a bathroom could look this good."

Antonia glanced at Maria's reflection and went back to washing her neck with neon pink hand soap from the dispenser. "I'd trade this dress for a shower, though."

"I'd trade that dress for anything. It may be the ugliest one I've ever seen." Maria grinned again. "He's nice, but he has no taste in clothes."

Antonia gave her one of those looks, the pointed kind that only a mother should be allowed to give. "He's our transportation. Nothing else."

Maria pulled her reeking dress off with two fingers and dropped it into the trash can. She felt more human already. "I like that he wears earrings—"

Another look from the mirror. "Why are you looking at his earlobes? We don't even know if we can trust him."

Maria went after her skin with a rough paper towel. "You have to admit he's nice, though. Letting us ride up front. Making sure we're warm. And did you see his cross tattoo?"

"Maybe too nice. We have to be careful. Don't get friendly with him."

"And the tattoo?"

"Don't read too much into that."

That deserved an eye roll. "You sound like Mama."

"No. I do not."

Maria didn't push it. No point getting into another conversation about everything her sister had against their mother. That could take the rest of the night, although it wouldn't bother their "transportation." He knew as much Spanish as she knew Swahili. Which was none.

Antonia dumped a wad of wet paper towels into the trash can and turned back to the mirror to straighten the gold cross that had hung there as long as Maria could remember. She ran her hands through the mane that gave Maria hair envy every time she looked at her. Her sister got Papa's thick wavy mop. She was stuck with the thin straight stuff like Mama's. Unlike her mother, though, she refused to keep it in a knot on top of her head.

"Wish I had a brush," Antonia said.

"Just ask our 'transportation.' I'm sure he'll buy you one. Is it just me or does he act like he didn't even know we were back there?"

"Don't know and don't care. And neither should you. And no, I'm not asking him to buy me beauty supplies."

"I will!"

"No. You won't."

Antonia took the new dress from Maria and lowered it over her head. Maria stood still. Everything looked better on her if Antonia had a hand in it. She was convinced her sister was born with style—while *she* got all the talent. Otherwise they wouldn't be here.

"Look," Antonia said, tugging at the hemline. "I don't agree with much that Mama says, but she does know more about American men than we do."

"She only lived up here for six months—about a hundred years ago."

"Which is still more experience than we have. Even if you factor in the drama she adds to everything, we have to use caution. I mean it." She frowned in the direction of Maria's knees. "Could you have picked a shorter one?"

"You really think this guy is going to try to . . . do whatever it is Mama says American men do to Mexican women?"

"I didn't say that."

Antonia pulled her fingers through Maria's tangles. Maria winced, but she didn't move. Antonia could do more with her hand than Maria could with a blow dryer, a curling iron, and three kinds of hair products. Besides, moments like this gave Maria images of her sister getting her ready to go on stage—

"We just can't let down our guard," Antonia said. "Just because we're riding up front doesn't mean we're home free, so stay quiet. Don't make eye contact."

"For the whole rest of the trip?"

"I think we only have twelve hours to go. I've been keeping track."

"'Only' twelve?" Maria groaned. "Do you think we'll eat soon?"

"No idea. And we're not eating anything we brought with us now. It's disgusting."

"You *think*?" She turned from the mirror to look at Antonia straight on. "I bet he'll feed us."

"Do *not* ask."

"But if he offers?"

Maria could see Antonia trying to keep her eyes stern, but the longer Maria stared into them, the more they softened, until her sister almost smiled.

"Fine," she said. "But just stay focused on why we're doing this, okay? Good jobs. Not just for us but for Papa."

Maria felt the smile fade from her own face. Antonia could be all motherly and strict and serious as a heart attack, but the sadness was still in the tiny crease in her forehead and the droop at the corners of her mouth. That was the thing that made Maria resist the eye rolling and the hair tossing and the exasperated sighs. If Antonia went back into that dark mourning place, they might as well go home and take whatever happened. It was up to Maria to keep her in the light.

She put the smile back on and nodded at Antonia's dress. "I have to say, you make even that hideous thing look good."

"Liar," Antonia said. She kissed Maria's forehead. "But I love you for it. Come on. He's going to think we climbed out the window and made a run for it."

"Right? Why does he think we'd do that? I'm not going to run away from a chance to be the next Taylor Swift."

Antonia gave her that other look. The practical one that turned dreams into to-do lists. "One thing at a time. First we have to *get* to Hollywood. So remember what I said."

Maria let Antonia go ahead of her out of the bathroom so she could deliver just one eye roll at the mirror. She let herself linger for a nanosecond and nodded. Yeah. She liked what she saw.

She hurried out the door and nearly ran up Antonia's calves. Her sister was planted in the middle of the short hallway, her way blocked by a man with a beer belly and a beard that looked like squirrels could nest in it. He was doing everything but licking his chops, as if he wanted to take a bite out of Antonia's cheek.

"Hey, *señorita bonita*," the guy said.

Maria stifled a groan. If people couldn't speak Spanish, why did they even try? Did this person not realize he sounded like a moron?

"Excuse me," Antonia said. In English. The words came out so cold Maria was surprised the guy's scraggly facial hair didn't freeze.

Antonia reached back and grabbed Maria's hand with her already clammy one. Gaze to the floor, Antonia turned sideways to pass him with Maria in tow.

"You two *chiquitas* traveling alone?" he said.

Maria was sure he was going to drool on her as she moved past him. She might have thrown up if she'd had anything in her stomach.

"I'm thinking yes," he said. "You want some company?"

Antonia didn't say anything, although he'd barred her path again. Maria could feel her sister's back go stiff as a stick. Maybe she *would* puke after all. Maria looked around frantically and almost sagged with relief. Their driver was coming toward them, eyes honed in on this guy.

As he stitched his way through people to get to them, he gestured for them both to get out of there. Antonia tightened her grip on Maria's hand and yanked her forward. But the man's grip was stronger. On Maria's arm.

Her hand slipped from Antonia's as he pulled Maria against him. His breath stank of tobacco and coffee and the length of time since he'd last picked up a toothbrush, and she turned her face away, heart hammering.

"¿*Qué pasa, señorita?*" he said.

"Let her go."

Their driver's voice was hard, nothing like the way he'd talked to them in the truck. She waited for the guy to drop her arm, but he only gave her a sickening smile.

"I'm not done talking to the pretty girl," he said.

His nose was almost touching hers, and she squeezed her eyes shut until they hurt. Which meant she didn't see what happened next. She only felt herself being pushed sideways and heard the man squeak as if his air supply was being cut off.

Because, she discovered when her eyes flew open, their driver had the guy pinned against the wall by the throat. His face was already the color of a chili pepper and his eye sockets were stretched almost to his ears. There were going to be eyeballs on the floor any minute.

"Let. Her. Go," their driver said.

The fingers around Maria's arm released and she felt the blood rush back into it. She still couldn't move. Terror held her to the spot as the man against the wall struggled to breathe. Their driver gave him a shake.

"You're done here! You get that? You're done!"

The guy answered with a gasp as he was let go. Antonia clamped her hand around Maria's wrist and pulled her out into the store with their driver close behind them.

Maria looked back at him, not sure whether to be horrified or impressed. One thing was for sure: he was now her hero.

# 10

WITHIN THIRTY MINUTES they were both asleep and had now been out for six hours. That wasn't surprising to James, seeing how they'd ridden for a whole day in the back of a box truck and had been sprayed with their own pee, stuffed into a four-foot cab with a guy who butchered their language, and accosted by some trucker who took them for an easy romp in the sack.

What a tool. The guy had to be half-blind not to see that wasn't what these two were about.

James glanced at them as a passing bus shone its headlights into the cab. The younger one, now spooned against what had to be her sister, had something uninhibited about her. Not like the teenage girls he'd known who might have acted like they had it all together but were quaking in their pumps two layers down. She carried herself like she had a crowd of fans waiting for her around the next corner. Wouldn't shock him. Although she was lanky and had feet the size of johnboats, the Jolie lips promised what she'd be when she grew into herself. Too bad she'd probably lose some of that innocence eventually. That kind of openness was sweet.

The older one, on the other hand, had something about her that said, *I haven't been out much but don't mess with me.* Maybe it was the dark eyes—sharp and quick. Or the sort of compact

look of her body. Yeah, she was small but not puny. She had the
curves of a—

James smeared his hand across his mouth. What was he even
doing? They were his responsibility for the next six hours, but
they could just as well be bushels of produce. Right?

Who was he kidding? They were clearly intelligent middle-
class young women trying to make a go of it in America. Too bad
they couldn't have just gotten on a Greyhound to Springfield,
Missouri, or some other white-bread place. That was obviously
more the lifestyle they were used to.

Not this.

He didn't have any reason to feel as guilty as he did, but there
it was. He glanced over again. The older one moved her arm to
hold her sister closer, sighing softly in her sleep. His flannel shirt,
which they were once again using for a blanket, slipped from her
shoulder, leaving it bare and brown and shiny.

James used only the tips of his fingers to pull it back over her.
She nestled into it, like Emmy did when he tucked her back in in
the middle of the night. The kid could kick off a zipped-up sleeping bag when she was dreaming.

He clenched the wheel and swallowed the lump that rose in
his throat every time he let himself think about her. Sometimes
when he saw her pressed-in dimples in his mind it pushed him
forward, made him get up for work and bypass the beer and eat
mac and cheese so he could send money to Melody. And keep
driving toward Reno with gravel in his eyes.

Other memories paralyzed him, though . . . like the way she
looked the day she made him take her teddy bear and ran into
the house so she wouldn't have to watch him leave her. If he let
her down this time he was done, and that pain would be in her

Michelle-eyes forever. At those moments, it seemed like anything he did was going to be wrong, so he couldn't move at all.

"Don't go all inert on me," Michelle used to say when he'd stare at a busted faucet with the tools all around him and say, "Where do I even start?"

"Do the next right thing" was always her answer.

Somehow that was easier with plumbing or barbecuing or teaching Emmy not to run out into the street. Or maybe everything was just easier with Michelle there.

Would she say this—what he was doing right now—was "the next right thing"? Transporting illegal aliens, one of them a minor? Taking cash from people with questionable motives? Trying a shortcut that seemed more like a trail back to jail by the minute?

Her face tried to come into view, but he shook it away with a snap of his head. He knew what would be in her eyes. Horror that he would try to choke some guy in a gas station, no matter who he was trying to protect. Disappointment that he would even put himself in this position. Despair for Emmy—

A loud ring jolted the vision away. James jerked and clutched the wheel, until he realized his cell phone was going off. Not a good time to talk to Chad, but he couldn't ignore him.

When he looked at the screen, though, it wasn't Chad's name that came up but Melody's. He was in no better shape to get into it with his mom, but he answered with a brusque hello.

"Daddy?"

James's back came away from the seat. "Emmy? Baby?"

"Hi, Daddy!"

He looked at the time. Four a.m., which meant it was five in Houston. He sucked in air and let it soften his voice.

"You're up early," he said. "Where's Gramma?"

"Still asleep," she whispered. "I called you."

"I can see that." James switched the phone to his other hand. "How did you learn to do that?"

"Dad-dy. I'm in first grade."

"You're so smart."

"Yeah."

"Is everything okay?" he said.

"Yes. Are you taking care of Teddy?"

His chest squeezed. "You bet, baby. She's right here with me."

"I wish *I* was right there with you."

Dear Lord, how was he supposed to do this?

"Me too," he said. "I have to work, but just as soon as I can—"

"I need you *now!*" she said.

The exclamation point he always waited for stabbed him in the gut this time. Made him see the trouble in those hazel eyes. Made him say, "How about in three more days? Four more sleeps? Can you wait that long?"

A squeal burst from the phone that could only be translated as *Yes!*

"Okay," he said. "I'll finish my job and you count the sleeps and we'll be together, okay?"

"And we'll have a tea party!"

"You bet. I'll bring Teddy. And another surprise."

"And then I'll go home with you! You're my favorite out of everyone."

His mouth, already shaped for an *okay*, froze in an O.

"I have to go potty now!" she said. "I love you, Daddy!"

He was glad she hung up before she found out he couldn't speak.

He couldn't even breathe.

*What* had he just done? Made another promise he couldn't keep? *How the—*

James put a hand up and stopped his own thoughts. He'd said it. Now he had to do it. No matter what it took.

It wasn't until he dropped the phone in his lap and took yet another swipe at his face that he realized tears were coursing down his cheeks.

And that the girl beside him was watching them fall, with a sheen in her own eyes.

# 11

MARIA PAWED HER MENTAL WAY to the surface and wiped a trail of drool from the corner of her mouth. That must be attractive.

She wriggled away from Antonia and sat up and used the side window for a mirror to fluff out her hair. When she looked over her shoulder at their driver, she realized he and Antonia were looking at each other like they'd just finished some kind of intimate conversation and the last unspoken words were still lingering in the air.

So much for *Don't make eye contact*.

"*Buen día!*" Antonia said—a little too cheerfully if you asked Maria.

Maria glared out the windshield. She didn't think it looked like morning. It was still dark as tar out there, and she could use about eight more hours of sleep. In an actual bed. She stretched out her arms and let her shoulders pop. This must be what it felt like to get old.

The truck slowed and their driver pointed to a blue neon Route 66 sign. He stuck his finger toward his mouth and then rubbed his stomach. "Hombre?" he said.

Maria had to suffocate a guffaw. *Hombre* was *so* not the word for "hungry." Not even close.

"*Hambriento, sí*," Antonia said and leveled her eyes at Maria.

Okay, something had definitely gone down while she was asleep. Before she'd closed her eyes, this guy was still under suspicion. Now her sister was trying not to let him look like a goofball. As he pulled the truck into the diner parking lot, Maria made a vow to get Antonia into the bathroom immediately and find out what on earth was going on. Antonia had that mushy look on her face like she'd just picked up a motherless kitten.

Maria pretty much forgot about that the minute they walked into the diner. The lights were bright and the music soft, and the smells of eggs and chorizo and potatoes with onions wiped everything from her mind except the fact that she was starving. It was all she could do not to grab a piece of toast from a chubby man's plate at the counter and stuff it into her mouth.

Though that probably wasn't okay to do in a place like this. The windows were made of glass blocks, and a ribbon of orange neon light ran around the top of the wall, stopping at intervals to spell out words like MALTS and BURGERS. One of the job possibilities that had come up when they were planning this trip was waiting tables, and right now that didn't seem so bad. Or it wouldn't if she didn't already have another opportunity waiting for her when they got to Hollywood. Still— the uniform on the waitress approaching them with laminated menus was made up of a tight red T-shirt with the words *Route 66 Diner* on the front and cute skinny jeans that would look even better with a wide belt and a pair of ballet flats. She had no trouble imagining "Maria" replacing "Naomi" on the plastic name tag.

Naomi smiled, smoothing out the lipstick feathering around her mouth, and said, "You folks here for breakfast?"

"No! I want a cheeseburger and French fries," Maria said.

In English.

She got an instant poke in the back from Antonia as they followed Naomi to a booth. When Maria slid into it, she could feel their driver staring at her from across the table.

Oops.

"So . . . ," he said, brown eyes bugging. "You speak English."

She nodded.

"You too?" he said to Antonia.

Antonia looked at Naomi and said, "The same for me, please. Cheeseburger and fries."

Their driver acted like the waitress wasn't standing there, pen poised over pad. "Any particular reason you've been letting me make an idiot out of myself this whole time?" he asked.

"I am sorry," Antonia said. "We want to be careful."

Maria thought "we" was stretching it. She would have been chatting him up in English all along if it had been left up to her. She sure wasn't sorry now. The whole pretending she didn't understand a word he was saying thing had gotten way old.

"You eating?" Naomi said to him. His jaw was still hanging like it had come off its hinges.

"I guess I'll take the same thing."

Naomi looked at the menus under her arm. "No need for these then. Drinks?"

Antonia narrowed her eyes at Maria. "Well, go ahead," she said in Spanish. "You've already outed us so why stop now?"

"Coca-Cola, please," Maria said.

Antonia put two fingers up to Naomi. Their driver made it three. Naomi walked away calling out their orders, and a silence fell over the table.

*Awk*-ward.

"I can explain," Antonia said.

"Yeah, please do," he said.

"We have heard stories of bad men in America . . . when women cross the border. Spanish . . . it seemed safer."

As long as she was insulting him to his face, why didn't she just slap the guy? He *was* an American man. And he did save them from *Señor* Bad Breath back at the truck stop. Seriously?

He seemed to think about it for a minute before he nodded. "I get that. Too many guys like that trucker last night."

"Yes."

How about thanking him for saving their *lives*? Maria was actually about to do that when Naomi returned with three plates on her arm, which she deposited on the table without even letting a French fry fall. Waiting tables was probably harder than it looked, although Maria was sure Antonia could do it. There wasn't much she wasn't good at.

Except being tactful.

The burger bun was open with the cheese-covered meat patty soaking grease into one side and a pile of lettuce and a sort of anemic-looking tomato slice filling up the other. But it looked a whole lot better than anything else they'd had to eat in the past two days. If she never saw another granola bar in her life that would be okay with her.

She reached for the ketchup, but Antonia put her hand on her arm.

"Maria," she whispered. "Give thanks."

Oh. Right. But did people pray in restaurants up here?

She bowed her head and closed her eyes and listened to Antonia murmur a prayer that took way too long as far as her stomach was concerned. She did add her own snippet of gratitude, though, because this whole thing could have gone totally wrong. Especially after the pee-spilling incident.

Maria crossed herself and stuck a French fry in her mouth. So awesome.

"We were blessing our food," Antonia said to the guy.

"Yeah, yeah. I got that."

"And we want to thank you for helping us. For feeding us."

His cheeks flushed, which was kind of adorable in Maria's opinion.

"And for these beautiful dresses."

Maria spit potato, barely missing his tattooed arm. Antonia smacked at her, but she was almost smiling. She put out a hand to him.

"Antonia Hernandez," she said.

He took it and said, "James. James Stevens."

Maria just gave him a wave. "I am Maria. Hernandez."

James waggled a finger back and forth between them. "Sisters."

"No," Antonia said, face straight. "Mother and daughter."

"Wha-a-a-t?" he said.

"I am joking."

Maria didn't think that was even a little bit funny, although there were times when it felt like it was true.

"Good," James said. "Because you two don't have to be afraid of me."

"I am not!" Maria said. And, wow, did this burger taste amazing. She chewed happily.

James waited until Naomi put three Cokes on the table and hurried off—waitresses here seemed to do everything fast—before he said, "You're here on purpose, right? You want to be here?"

It was a logical question. They *were*, after all, locked in the back of a truck. Maria hadn't exactly understood that herself, but Antonia had kept assuring her it was so they could travel without anybody seeing them. That didn't exactly work out.

Antonia hadn't answered him yet. She poured ketchup on her burger as if it might be the last bottle on earth. She didn't even like ketchup.

"Yes," she said. "We are from Tenancingo. In Mexico. Our father owed some local men some money. These were not good men."

Maria heard her sister's voice thicken.

"They . . . he died, our father . . ."

James set his burger on his plate and looked from one of them to the other. She didn't see pity in his eyes. She hated when people acted like they were victims and needed to be handfed or something. He looked like he got it. Like he'd felt it himself.

"I'm sorry," he said.

"My mother could not pay these men back," Antonia said. "So we must go to work for them to pay the debt."

James had thick eyebrows, and they arched up now almost to his hairline. "Work?" he said.

"Waitresses or maids at first. Until . . ."

"Big dreams, huh?" James took a bite of his burger, like for some reason it was okay to eat now.

"I am going to be a singer," Maria said. Antonia nudged her with her knee but she went on anyway. Perfect chance to steer Antonia away from the darkness of Papa. "Like Taylor Swift. Do you like Taylor Swift?"

"No," he said. "But I think my daughter does."

Antonia stared at him over the top of her Coke. Maria could

see the bubbles trying to reach up for her nose. "You have a family, James?"

Maria was kind of surprised herself. He didn't look like the fatherly type, except for maybe those eyes. That would explain the stuffed animals. He also didn't look like he wanted to answer the question. She was about to launch into one of Taylor's hits, just to lighten things up, when he finally said, "Just a daughter. My wife died."

Yeah, good thing she hadn't started singing. No wonder he could feel their pain. She saw it now, not just in his sad eyes, but in the lines that fanned out from them. And the way he swallowed so she could see his Adam's apple go up and down, like it hurt. Because it probably did.

"I am sorry," Antonia said.

He shrugged the wide shoulders. "My kid's with my mom right now."

"Ah." Antonia said it as if something now made sense.

None of it was making sense to Maria. Especially the softness that had suddenly taken over her sister's face.

---

Maria went back to sleep almost before the truck left the diner parking lot. Antonia tucked James's plaid shirt around her curled-up body and kissed the top of her silky hair. She was so exasperating sometimes, which was one of the many reasons Antonia hadn't wanted to bring her along at first. But right now, snuggled up next to Antonia with that sweet sleep-innocence sighing out of her, she was a comfort.

And as much as Antonia hated to admit it, she needed that. Maria could always pull her from the pit she so easily fell into since their father died. Her little sister didn't understand how dark it got for her. Maria had a naturally sunnier nature. But it was that light way she had about her that forced Antonia to look up and at least see shadows.

There were plenty of those now as she gazed out at the rosy tinge touching the tops of a long row of brown hills and creating shaded pictures on their barren sides. This didn't look the way she had imagined Southern California to be, this endless straight road across unbroken desert. But at least she was seeing something, thanks to the man next to her.

James. James the widower, with a daughter he'd promised to go and see in just four more sleeps. He wasn't the hard, grim man he pretended to be.

She nodded now at the tattoo on his forearm. "'Let all that we do be done in love,'" she read. "That is very nice."

She heard him draw in a sharp breath through his nose before he said, "A reminder."

Antonia touched the cross hanging from its gold chain around her neck. Through all of this she was amazed it was still there. "I have a reminder too. Similar message, yes?"

The breath was even sharper this time. "I don't know about that."

"No? You do not believe?" She let her gaze whisper across the cross inked into his skin.

For a moment she wasn't sure she should have asked. His hands whitened on the steering wheel, and even in the faint light of dawn she could see the muscles in his jaw tighten.

"I am sor—"

"I went knocking a couple of times," he said. "Turned out nobody's home. So I leave him alone, he leaves me alone."

Antonia let that dwell in the air and waited for him to change the subject. He said nothing, but it didn't feel as if a door had been slammed. Maybe a tiny nudge to keep it open, yes?

"Makes me sad," she said.

"What makes you sad?"

"That you think you are alone."

He glanced at her, forehead wrinkled.

"We are never alone," she said.

"Alone's fine with me."

She rearranged herself on the seat so she could face him. "But what about your daughter?"

The glance he gave her was sharp. "What *about* her?"

"She is not alone because she has you, even when she can't see you, yes?"

It took a moment for him to nod. "I hope so."

Antonia touched her cross again. "It is the same."

His look down at her was more than a glance this time. She didn't see agreement, but she didn't see anger either. Or that slight slitting that often came into people's eyes that fairly shouted, *You are so naïve. You'll get reality someday.* He simply turned his face back to the road. The twitching in his jaw stopped.

"I will pray for you," she said.

"Thanks," he said. "I guess."

She let it drop. At least between them. Inside, she continued the conversation, with God.

# 12

JAMES HAD ONLY BEEN to Reno, Nevada, once, when he was about fifteen, right before his parents separated. The three of them came up for a vacation; as he looked back on it now it had clearly been a last-ditch effort to rekindle some lost flame. If James had realized that at the time he could have told them it wouldn't work.

In the first place, even as a kid he could see that flicker had been snuffed out long ago by constant bickering and resentment and what had grown into a deep dislike between two people who might not have liked each other that much in the first place. Before James would marry Michelle he'd made her promise they would never turn out like that. They wouldn't have. He knew that.

And in the second place, if you wanted to reconnect with your partner you didn't bring your sullen teenage son along and take turns gambling in the casinos while the other one sat in twenty-four-hour restaurants eating bad French toast and running down the opposite parent to take turns with the kid. His mother filed for divorce the day they got back to Texas.

But there was one good memory of that time for James. They were going to drive to Lake Tahoe one morning, a day trip that was aborted at Verdi because his parents were arguing until their veins bulged about why his father tipped the waitress so much at break-fast. Dad got off I-80 to turn back and Melody made him stop so, she claimed, she could throw up before she had to get back in the car with him. It was that bad.

The minute the car crunched to a stop on the gravel, James got out so he didn't have to listen to the straight-up screaming that was about to start. He stomped away, hands shoved into the pockets of his too-big jeans, muttering to the ground that things would be a whole lot easier if they both took a dive over the side, down into the steep ravine.

Something made him look up. To this day he wasn't sure what it was, but when he did, he had to drop his teen angst and pretty much gasp. The crammed-in, neon-lit, slot-machine-clanging town he'd just spent three days in spread out below him. The casinos were there, yeah, standing tall as madams with their glitzy signs beckoning even from here. But from this distance, they weren't the whole city, or even the real city.

Thick trees lined the streets that fingered out from the flashy center, pointing to the trickle of a river and the proud sprawl of a college and the church spires that reached ironically to a sky so blue and cloudless it hurt his eyes.

All of it was cupped in the hands of the brown mountains with their shadow faces. To his left, a huge white *N* had been created on the side of one of them. To James it was saying, *This is Nevada. There is more here than sin.*

James looked now at the directions he had propped on the steering wheel. They wanted him to continue on Route 395, which became Virginia Street, and turn on Fourth, but if he took the backstreets on the other side of Virginia, he could get to Interstate 80. He hadn't thought about that view much in the last ten years, but it pulled at him now. If these two hopeful girls were going to find a decent life here, they had to know what he knew about Reno. Otherwise, they might be seduced by its so-obvious dark side.

He'd been on the road for twenty-eight hours. Whoever was waiting for him would expect him in about forty minutes. James blew that off as he took a left and headed for I-80 West.

Maria was awake by then, and she and Antonia were peering out the windows with puzzled expressions on their faces. They chattered in Spanish, their voices going up as if every sentence was a question.

"What is wrong?" Antonia said.

"Nothing. I just want you to see the whole town before we drive in." James tilted his head toward Maria. "She'll love this."

Antonia gave him a polite nod, but the two of them couldn't have looked more confused if he'd been ushering them onto the moon. Apparently nobody had told them what to prepare for, and if they did, it wasn't this.

A lot had changed in a decade. Housing developments had encroached on what he remembered as evergreen-dotted hills that had rolled from the north side of the interstate. He almost missed the exit at Mogul because there was now a Jack in the Box there. James was having misgivings about what the rest of the town was going to look like from the vista.

But he crossed the freeway and pulled over anyway, in the same clearing designated for stopping and taking pictures where his parents had ended their marriage. One glance told him the city had crowded in on itself and out into the valleys, but the effect was the same. The mountains still held it like protective uncles.

"Let's get out and take a look around," James said to Antonia.

Maria was already out the door, squealing at the majestic Sierras behind them.

"Everything is so beautiful in America!" she called out over her shoulder.

Antonia was, of course, more reserved, but when he met her in front of the truck, the wrinkle between her eyebrows smoothed and she almost smiled.

"Beautiful," she said.

"It can be," James said. "Listen . . . I just . . . if you want my advice—"

He hesitated. She was looking at him—into him—the same way she had earlier. Like she saw something even he didn't see. Not that there was much left there, in his view.

"Yes," she said. "Please."

James pointed to Harrah's and the Silver Legacy and the El Dorado downtown, and beyond them to the east, the overpowering Grand Sierra. "Stay out of the casinos. There's gambling everywhere—slot machines in the grocery stores, drug stores, gas stations—so you can't avoid it totally, but the high rollin' stuff happens in the big places. That can be dangerous for a—" He stopped short of any of the adjectives that came into his mind and settled for, "—a young woman like yourself. I think the rest of the town is pretty sa—"

"James?"

He looked over Antonia's head, which was not hard to do at her tiny height. Maria's entire face was a question mark and her shoulders were hunched up to her ears.

"Where is the Hollywood sign?" she said.

"The what? The Hollywood sign?"

"Always you see it in pictures," she said.

James looked at Antonia, who seemed to hold the same question in her eyes.

"Uh, it's about five hundred miles that way," James said, vaguely gesturing south.

Their expressions were identical: a stew of confusion and disappointment, lightly spiced with anxiety. His stomach started to grab.

"Only sign here is the *N*." He pointed to the large white-rock letter that was still at the base of the mountain he'd learned was called Peavine.

"What is the *N* for?" Antonia said.

"Nevada," he said and watched the anxiety take over everything else in their faces.

"Are we going to California next?" Maria said.

Two thoughts slammed into James's head. One, *kill Chad*. Two, *kill Chad again*.

"I don't know," James said. "My orders were to bring you here. Maybe you get to rest and then whoever you're meeting will take you the rest of the way."

That would make no sense, but he tried to keep that thought off of his face.

Maria broke into a smile and ran to the outcropping of rocks that bordered the vista area. Antonia waited until she was out of earshot before she turned to James.

"What is this town called?" she said.

"Where I'm taking you? Reno. Reno, Nevada."

She stared down into the city. She should definitely not do any gambling. Everything she was thinking was plastered all over her.

James tried to keep his own what-the-heck-is-going-on thoughts to himself. Something was definitely screwy.

But this wasn't his problem. *His* problem was getting this

truck back to Houston and then driving to Dallas to see Emmy and start making a home for her with the money that bulged in his pocket. He'd done all he could for these two. Right?

*Right?*

Maria had climbed up onto one of the rocks and was belting out something about a last kiss, hand rolled in front of her mouth like a microphone. Antonia was staring from her to the city and back again, and if she wasn't thinking about grabbing her sister and bolting, he was hallucinating. Time to lighten the mood.

James dug his cell out of his pocket and set it to camera.

"Will you take my picture?" he said to Antonia. "For my daughter?"

She pulled her gaze away from Maria and reached for his phone. Her barely-there smile was clearly forced but she said, "Of course. Stand here so she will see the beauty behind. Yes."

Ever since his nightmare mug shots were taken, James hated being photographed, but this was all he could think of. Antonia actually got a gleam in her eye and poked at the screen with a dainty finger. Holding the phone up to look into it, she shook her hair back and smiled.

He had been right. He couldn't have imagined what she looked like when she smiled. It changed her whole being. He didn't want it to fade.

"Did you just take a selfie?" he said.

She tried to look innocent and then smiled again. "Yes. Now you."

Before he had a chance to stiffen into a pose, she took the picture and gave it a nod. "Good," she said.

She handed him the camera and waited while he looked at it. The shot of him was better than most. Antonia had caught him with a halfway pleasant expression on his face. The sleepless bags under his eyes didn't show up that much.

James swiped the screen and Antonia's smiled dazzled at him. He looked up to see her giving him the same one now.

"You can . . . um . . . erase?" she said.

"You mean delete?" James shrugged. "Nah. I'll keep it."

"And yours?"

"I'm sending this one to my little one."

"What is her name?"

James swallowed. Hard. "Emerson," he said.

When she whispered it after him, he had to fight not to lose it. He blinked his way through texting the photo to Emerson and slipped the phone back in his T-shirt pocket. Antonia was still gazing . . . into him.

"I am a daughter missing her father," she said, her voice barely loud enough to be heard over the swishing traffic. "And I see a father who misses his daughter. She must be a very lucky girl."

He didn't answer. She didn't seem to expect it.

Maria finished her performance and bounced toward them. Somehow that went right through him. She was an older Emmy, headed for something that might steal it all away.

He hated himself right now.

"Look, I don't want to ask this," he said as he opened the back of the truck. "But I have my orders. I'm gonna have to put you in here again. It smells better since I washed it out at the last gas stop, but—I'm sorry. I really am."

"No sorry," Antonia said.

She also said something in Spanish to Maria, whose face clouded before she hiked herself inside.

"We don't have much farther to go. Maybe ten minutes."

Antonia nodded and turned to the truck.

"Need help?" James said.

She didn't look at him. He barely heard her say yes. He extended his hand, and she took it and stepped lightly in. When she turned to him, her eyes were bright.

"You are a good man, James," she said.

He felt like far less than one as he pushed the door shut and left them in darkness.

---

"It still stinks in here," Maria said to her in Spanish.

"Breathe through your mouth," Antonia said. "We only have to stand it for ten more minutes."

"I hope we don't have to go to California in the back of another truck." Maria pulled her fingers through her hair. "We should have asked James to buy us a brush. You *know* he would have."

Antonia didn't answer, but she actually agreed. He was kind—that was the word for him. And if he was representative of the men in America, her mother was as wrong as she was about most things.

That gave her a reason to think their ending up in Nevada instead of California was probably a matter of a language mix-up with the English-speaking people who had arranged the trip. It didn't mean they weren't safe.

Although she found herself breathing easily, she decided not to pass on her conclusion to Maria. Give the girl an inch of a reason to trust—especially a male—and she was ready to share her life story with him. She let out a sigh.

"You have a thing for him, don't you?" Maria said.

She was leaning against the side, knees pulled into her chest, eyes laughing in the dark.

"No. I do not," Antonia said.

"I see you looking at him. You li-i-i-ke him."

"You're crazy."

"Am not."

Antonia pulled her brows together. "Really? A man with a child and whatever other baggage he's covering up?"

Antonia dug into her still slightly odorous backpack to see if she'd tucked any lip gloss in there in her hurry to leave home. She'd brought mostly food, the remains of which she'd dumped at the last truck stop.

Maria closed her eyes and went back to humming that endless Taylor Swift song about young love gone wrong. The child knew nothing about it, and Antonia hoped she wouldn't for a long time. Even at twenty-one, losing at love had been enough to make her swear off men until she was thirty. Or beyond.

Actually, Trini Garcia never was the love of her life. He was just attentive to the point of being almost smothering—and full of promises. To him, she was his ideal woman. That was what he'd said, until she told him she had to go to America to pay off her father's debt.

She hadn't anticipated him sneering, telling her she'd never make it in the United States. No way she could do it. Not strong enough. Too naïve. Too ignorant about the world.

Antonia straightened her back now just as she'd done that evening, pressed against the outside wall of her mother's house, the day's heat still warm through her dress. As Trini looked down at her with those words on his curled lip, she realized she was never that into him in the first place. And her will turned to steel.

There was one thing you did not say to Antonia Hernandez, no matter who you were. You didn't tell her she couldn't do something, anything she fastened her mind to. Anything at all.

Being jostled around in the back of a hard, stinking truck, heading for the unknown, still nursing doubts about being in a different place than she'd been told—Antonia could handle that. Because she had never slept with Trini. Her first time was going to be on her wedding night, in a moon-drenched room by the ocean with a man who respected her as much as loved her. So, yes, at least she was starting off clean.

Wherever she was going.

# 13

Downtown Reno was still sleepy when James found his way to Fourth and Lake Streets. It was like a town that hadn't had its coffee yet. The few Sunday-morning commuters at the city bus terminal across the road all seemed to be in a unanimous coma, and there was no life around the bowling stadium that dominated the intersection.

Not much life anywhere. Including at the Lake Street Inn. At least, he assumed it said Lake. The *L* on the faded plastic sign at the corner was broken out, leaving a jagged hole and the word *ake*. Probably a statement on the condition of your back after you slept there.

The rest of the place wasn't in any better shape. Planters around the sign and lobby were full of dry dirt and curled leaves. Even the weeds couldn't make it. The doors to the rooms on both levels may once have been light blue but had deteriorated to a dismal gray, as had the linings of the drapes that hung at smudged windows, each barely meeting in the middle, like a jacket on a fat man's belly.

A few nondescript cars, mostly rentals from what James could tell, were parked intermittently, so somebody was staying here. To tell the truth, as beat up as he felt at the moment, he hoped they had a room available.

But the more pressing issue was the girls. Where was the person he was supposed to meet? Chad hadn't given him details, just that somebody would be waiting for him. Right now, his only possibility was a woman across the parking lot wearing what looked like her entire wardrobe and pushing a battered shopping cart loaded with random items. Two cents said she wasn't coming from the grocery store.

James pulled out his phone and texted Chad: *Here but nobody else is. What do I do?*

He watched the screen for a reply and stirred in the seat and drummed the steering wheel. He really didn't want Antonia and Maria to have to sit in the back of this rancid truck any longer than necessary. Still no answer from Chad. What happened to "keep in touch"?

James climbed out of the front seat and crossed the pocked lot to the door marked Lobby. The morning chill that happened here even in the middle of a sweltering summer was already burning off. Antonia and her sister were going to start cooking back there in about an hour.

An unconvincing bell rattled on the door as James let himself in and took a quick inventory. A couple of fake leather chairs, both with rips in them that looked suspiciously like knife cuts. A display of limp, sun-bleached brochures. A plastic plant with a Santa Claus still stuck in it. And not a person in sight. Unless you counted the miniature cutout of Jennifer Aniston next to a box for contributions to St. Jude Children's Hospital. It was empty.

The counter was separated from the rest of the lobby by a Plexiglas window with a hole in the center of it that reminded him of jail. James heard a television droning from behind it through a doorway hung with strings of orange beads. He banged the counter bell with his palm, which brought a grunt from the same direction.

The beads parted listlessly and a guy with a partially bald, partially shaved head emerged wearing a wife beater the color of weak tea and carrying a soda bottle. He spit into it as he approached the window. The contents of his mouth drained down the inside and joined the rest of the brown gunk at the bottom.

Nice.

He looked at James through the greasy glass with eyes whose whites had turned to road maps. James couldn't say much about that. Last time he looked in the truck's side mirror he himself looked like he'd been on a two-day binge. He kind of had.

"Can I help you?" the guy said through the hole.

By now James hoped he couldn't—that he knew absolutely nothing about anything related to Antonia and Maria. But he couldn't just stand there like a clown either.

"I'm . . . uh . . . here with a truck," James said.

The guy blinked—and even that seemed to take effort. "Okay," he said.

"Right?"

This was going well.

The guy spit into the bottle again and let his lower lip sag. "So, you want a room or what?"

"Listen, never mind," James said. "Sorry to bother you."

"Not any sorrier than I am." Another spit and he disappeared through the curtain of beads.

Now what?

James exited the lobby and gave the place one more long survey. A female hand tried to tug the drapes closed in one of the lower-level rooms. A maid's cart was parked in the stairwell.

Cigarette smoke wafted out from behind a soda machine.

And then a long black passenger van turned into the lot and pulled up next to the truck, two guys in the front. This had to be it.

James crossed to meet the man who slid from the driver's seat, and his hope built as he got closer. The dude looked about five social classes up from the motel manager, and when he saw James he broke into an open smile.

In pressed slacks and a pin-striped vest, the guy was beyond just neat. The silk short-sleeved shirt looked even pricier than what Chad wore. And it wasn't just the clothes. He was polished, rather than merely clean-cut. Barbered hair and beard. Recently buffed nails. Ray-Ban shades. In his midthirties, he'd apparently done well for himself.

He looked from the truck to James, and James nodded. The grin broadened.

"*¿Que pasa?*" he said. "How *are* you?" His voice was confident, inviting even. Like if there'd been a couple of chairs in the parking lot he would have told James to sit down with him and have a beer. "How was your drive? No bad weather? Accidents? Nothing like that?"

"It was fine," James said.

The guy ran his gaze over the truck. James could almost hear the bent mirror screaming, *He's lying!*

"You sure?"

It wasn't an accusation, but James's gut pinched anyway. "Almost got run off the road by somebody. Hit a ditch. But, you know, other than that, fine."

The guy's finely trimmed eyebrows drew together like a concerned father's and he put his hands in prayer position at his chest. "You're all right, though?"

"Yeah. I'm good." James forced himself not to wipe the sweat off his forehead. "Look, I'm sorry about the mirror—"

"Don't worry about the mirror. I'm not worried about the mirror. I only care about you, for starters—"

"I'm fine."

"And the cargo inside."

"Oh. That's fine too."

"Is it now?"

The guy pulled off the sunglasses to reveal pale brown eyes full of questions. James hoped he didn't look as full-out idiotic as he felt. Yeah, for a guy who'd done six months in prison, he sure didn't know how to cover himself.

"Garo, should I get the girls out now or wait for you?"

It was the first time the other guy from the van had spoken, and Garo gave him a mild reprimand with his face. He was younger than Garo, though he had a couple of years on James. While the older guy definitely had some Latino blood, the other one was pasty white. Though it was pretty clear he had tried to mirror Garo with a sport shirt and a short haircut, he was more or less a smaller, cheaper version. And a lot less bright. He stared back at Garo like he had no idea what he'd done wrong. Couple eggs short of a dozen maybe.

"No business in front of our new friends, C. J.," Garo said smoothly, inclining his head slightly toward James. "We show better manners than that."

He didn't wait for C. J. to give him an answer. James guessed it wasn't the first time they'd had that conversation.

Garo folded the sunglasses and hooked them on his vest, all the while smiling at James. He pulled a key from the pocket of his slacks and approached the back of the truck.

James followed and wondered how long he'd keep smiling when he got there. It was the first time he noticed that this classy dude had a Mohawk going down the back of his head. Even that looked like it had been trimmed with manicure scissors.

Garo stopped and cocked his head. "Where's the lock?" he said.

No malice. Just a question. But James couldn't get his mouth to form an answer.

"Sooo," Garo said. "After your little accident, maybe you just checked on them. Being a good steward and all."

This time it wasn't a question.

Garo lowered his head, the deep eyes still directed at James. "But nothing more, of course."

"No. No, absolutely. Nothing more . . . like that."

As unconvincing as he sounded to himself, James was surprised the guy didn't take him out where he stood. Instead, Garo slid the truck door up and peered inside. James sucked in the dry air until his chest threatened to explode, and he watched Garo's face. One hint that he was going to be anything but full-out decent to the girls and he was going to haul them back to Texas or die trying.

But Garo turned to him, hand extended. "Thank you so much for doing this for us." His other hand squeezed James's shoulder. "You're a good man. Truly. We appreciate it, my friend."

James still didn't breathe as Garo looked back at the girls and spoke to them in Spanish gentle enough to sing them to sleep. James didn't know what he was saying, but Maria smiled immediately. Even Antonia gave him a cautious nod. Whatever it was, it eased some of the tension out of their faces.

Garo softened his eyes at them even as he barked, "C. J.!"

C. J. appeared next to him with two long-stemmed red roses and passed them to Garo, who lifted himself easily into the truck and handed one to each of the girls. Maria took it like she'd just been crowned prom queen.

For a minute James thought Antonia was going to give him a stiff no-thank-you. He'd known her for less than a day and he knew you didn't win her over with flowers from the nearest Safeway. Garo would have been better off handing her a green card.

Yet there was no sign of sleaze. And his voice sounded genuine as he said, in English, "We want you to know we're glad you're here."

Antonia did take the rose, but she looked even more reluctant to take the hand he offered her to get out of the truck. James's own hand twitched at his side. Less than an hour ago he'd been the one touching her soft fingers—and in less than a few minutes she'd be gone. Yesterday he couldn't wait to get this thing over with. Now she looked over her shoulder at him with wistful eyes, hand still trapped in Garo's as he led them both to the van. He wasn't sure he could let them go.

"Here." C. J. smacked a thick envelope into James's chest. "You know who to give this to?"

James pressed it with both hands. "Yeah. So, the girls—where are you—"

"Not your problem anymore." C. J. gave him a smile that was more weasel than human. "Happy trails."

The door closed on the shiny van with a final sound. Maybe they'd be okay. C. J. might be a rodent, but Garo seemed like a guy who insisted on the best. Still, he wanted to stay until they were gone. Just in case Antonia looked back at him, let him know she didn't want to be there.

But even after Garo started up the vehicle, C. J. didn't climb into the passenger seat. James looked around for him and saw him unlocking one of the first-floor motel rooms, about ten feet from where James stood. He didn't open the door all the way, just far enough for James to see a young woman about Antonia's age standing in full view in red bra and panties. C. J. pushed past her, and when she stepped aside, another even younger one appeared, wearing not much more than a plastic smile.

*What the—*

C. J. reappeared, followed by a bevy of girls whose bodies said they were young but whose faces were under too much makeup for James to tell their age. At least they all had clothes on. Barely.

Tottering on strappy stilettos they trailed C. J. to the van where he deposited them inside and took his own place up front with Garo. They drove out of the parking lot, gravel popping under the tires, and disappeared down Fourth Street. Antonia didn't look back. She didn't look anywhere but straight ahead.

James stared at the bulky envelope he was still pressing into his chest. The back of the truck was open and he stared into it too, until the nightmare he'd just witnessed became so real it threatened to cut him in half.

He threw the envelope under the front seat, locked the truck, and stalked across the lot back to the lobby. His breath was coming out in rasps.

The manager was at the counter wiping tobacco spittle from his chin with the side of his hand. James leaned in until his forehead almost touched the Plexiglas.

"You know what's going on out there?" he said.

"Nah. But it looks like you were just involved in some kind of transaction. Wanna talk about it?"

James would rather talk to a plaster wall, although this wasn't much different. The guy's voice was as dry and lifeless as everything else around here. And he was way too interested. James cleared his throat.

"I'm tired. Been driving for a while. Got a room for the night?"

"Only rent by the hour."

James closed his eyes, but Antonia and Maria were still there. Leaving in that slick black van that had something to do with this pit of a—

He looked up to find the man watching him, obviously more aware than he let on with his chew and his blank voice.

"Thanks anyway," James said and started for the door.

"But if you're looking for something fun to do while you're in town . . ." The voice dipped. "And by fun I mean maybe some company to lift your spirits . . ."

James turned to see the guy palm a card from behind the counter and slide it through the opening where cash transactions were likely made. Credit cards probably weren't accepted in this den.

"Take my card," he said. "Go ahead."

James stared at it. Did he want to know, or not? He picked it up and read the front. *Party Time Rentals.*

"Call the cell number on the back," the guy said. "Let 'em know Rodney sent you."

"I'm good, I think," James said.

But that was about as true as the ad on that business card.

# 14

ANTONIA ALLOWED HERSELF to let out a long but quiet breath. When Mr. Garo had helped her down from the truck and she saw the heinous excuse for a hotel, she thought for a horrified moment that they were going to stay *there*. Being ushered into a van with clean floors and a new smell assured her they were headed someplace nicer.

Until that scruffy person who resembled a hamster brought five other girls in. Antonia didn't get a good look at them as they climbed into the seat behind her and Maria and she wasn't going to turn around and stare, but she could smell them now as Hamster Boy climbed into the van and Garo nosed it out into the intersection. The perfume they were marinated in smothered the clean scent and took Antonia's optimism down with it.

Stale alcohol was in the mix. And the faint odor of male sweat. Working as maids in a place like that . . . apparently they came into contact with all manner of nastiness. But did they scrub toilets in *those* outfits?

That didn't fit with the starched uniforms and high tippers she'd been promised.

Neither did the street they were now driving on. Antonia glanced at Maria, but her sister seemed oblivious to the barren yards and shabby apartment complexes that lined it. Nose practically pressed to the window, she wore that fascinated big-eyed expression that appeared anytime she was faced with something new. Life was all wonderful to Maria. As she said when they were at the top of the mountain looking down over the city, everything in America was beautiful.

Up front, Mr. Garo and the hamster—she thought she'd heard him called C. J.—were discussing whether to take them all out to breakfast. Behind her the other girls were strangely silent, except for some deep-in-the-throat breathing, which meant at least one of them was asleep. Antonia hadn't been told anything about working nights. Or a lot of other things, apparently.

The van took a turn onto a street with a little more promise. Sidewalks. Large brightly lit stores. Trees bowing over the entrances to parking lots. It was looking a little more like the town James had shown them from the mountain.

James.

Still clutching the rose, Antonia folded her arms tightly across her chest and angled herself away from Maria, who was sitting up straighter and smiling out at all the possibilities. What was happening right now . . . there was a lot about it that wasn't falling in line.

Met by a slick man with testosterone almost oozing from his pores.

A ride to an unknown destination with other girls their age who obviously weren't high-class waitresses or chambermaids.

Handed roses instead of information.

And the worst: all of it happened in front of a sleazy dump in a part of town she couldn't help associating with drug deals and purse snatchings and stabbings.

That was where James had taken them. He had his "orders,"

he said. Whatever was unfolding right now, he knew about it. He had to.

She tightened her arms until her ribs protested. She couldn't let that happen again: almost being taken in by a nice . . . all right, a handsome face and a sad story. She saw a good man there, but even good men could go wrong. Look at Papa.

They were climbing a hill now and leaving the stores and restaurants below. Houses—lovely houses—spread almost as far as she could see. Wherever they were going, at least it seemed safe and cheerful, as if people were raising children and building lives here. Somehow this didn't fit either.

Maria gave a delighted squeal and pointed with her rose to a house on a corner where two teenage girls sat together on a wooden swing, laughter on their faces. Antonia didn't have to guess what dreams were swirling in her sister's head.

Let them swirl. No need for Antonia to worry Maria with her misgivings, no matter how deep they were digging.

---

James was whipped as he drove down Lake until he found a street he could turn right on, since they didn't seem to believe in left turns in this town. Second Street took him along the edge of downtown where the high-rise casinos created empty canyons between them. Not much happening on Sunday morning except the ringing of church bells to his left, near the almost-dry Truckee River, and two older people moving stiffly across the street, determined to get that exercise if it killed them. The rest of the area seemed to be sleeping something off.

He wasn't sure exactly what he was looking for until he found it: the Silver Miner's Motel, which looked like the Ritz compared to the Lake Inn—but, then, what didn't? It appeared to be clean, cozy, if you were into that. Michelle would've made him turn in.

He did.

The atmosphere on the inside was all the outside promised. Clean as his mother's house. Good lighting. Vertical blinds that let in cheerful stripes of early sun.

Even the guy who greeted him looked like that uncle you liked to visit in the summer as a kid. Sixty-ish, graying, and up for some good-natured sparring in the family room. The cream cowboy hat would've looked cheesy on anybody else.

He put down the magazine he was flipping through. "How can I help ya, friend?"

James felt his shoulder blades let go. "Need a room. Just for the night." He would actually have to get up at noon to start back but "just for the day" didn't sound that good.

"All right." The man slid a card and pen across the counter. "Just fill that out." He scratched at his short salt-and-pepper beard. "Where you coming from?"

"Houston. All your rooms have AC, right?" The air was dry and hot as a blow dryer, and if he didn't get cooled off soon his head might explode.

He looked up from the card to see the guy staring at him with small blue eyes made bluer by the shade of his western shirt. Some of the good ol' uncle had faded from his face. "Business or pleasure?" he said.

"Business. About that AC—"

"That your truck?" He jerked his chin toward the window. "That one there?"

"Ye-ah . . ."

"Whatcha haulin'?"

James felt the hair on the back of his neck bristle. Did every truck driver get this kind of scrutiny or was it just him? "Uh . . . just cargo, man," he said. "Nothin' really."

That seemed just about as satisfying to this guy as it had to that gas station attendant back in New Mexico.

"You look beat," the guy said, without empathy. "Drive straight through?"

"Yep."

The man put both hands on the counter, arms as hard as his face suddenly was. "Now why would you have to go through all that if you're just haulin' nothin'?"

James felt his own face harden and he dropped the pen. "Look, I just need a room."

"What do you think I'd find if I opened up the back of that truck?"

*Nothing* was the correct answer this time, but if he gave that again he was never going to get a bed.

"I don't know what you're getting at," James said instead.

"I think you do. Let's say we go have a look."

"Let's say we don't and you mind your own business." It was too late to keep the rising anger out of his voice. His breathing was rapid.

"Why don't you get that truck off my property?" the guy said. He wasn't disguising his anger either.

James shoved the card back across the counter and took a step back. "What is it with you people?"

No answer.

James pushed his way out the door and into the glare of a town he was starting to hate again.

# 15

THE VAN MADE SO MANY TURNS deep into a labyrinth of desert-colored houses, Antonia couldn't have found her way out if she wanted to. And she wanted to.

It was a middle-class community with cedar fences and tabby cats in windows and well-tended rock gardens surrounding manicured patches of lawn. But the people in this van didn't fit here. That much was clear.

In the front, Garo and C. J. were having a conversation that took place in tight mutters and looks laced with meaning. She was sure they weren't discussing breakfast. She couldn't have eaten anyway. Her stomach was roiling.

In the back, the sleeping girl moaned as if she'd dozed into a serious nightmare and was struggling to get away from it. Another girl told her to stop freaking out. She would probably say the same thing to Antonia if she saw her face right now—she could feel her skin pinching in over her nose. Even Maria startled out of her dreamy survey of the neighborhood and looked back at them, eyes huge.

The girl still chiding the sleeper to "get your act together" folded her arms on the back of the seat between Antonia and Maria and rested her chin. Heavy streaked-blonde hair hung on both sides of her face like curled drapes.

"She doesn't do mornings," she said. "Catch her in a couple of hours and she'll be like a whole other person."

Maria looked at Antonia as if she were asking for permission to smile. Antonia did it for her.

"She is tired," Antonia said, and didn't add that this girl must be too. Thick mascara more than smudged the skin under her eyes, which was already dark blue and slightly bagged.

"She better get over it," the girl said. "Those are the hours. You learn to deal."

The words were matter-of-fact. Everything about this girl, including the just-short-of-obscene cut of her T-shirt, said, *This is just the way it is.*

But what *was* "the way it is"? Antonia glanced at the other girl who was now sitting up, too-black lanky hair half covering her face, eyes staring out of a vacuum. She looked like she'd left her mind somewhere else. The rest of them didn't look much different.

"You don't need to worry," the blonde whispered. Her large green eyes darted to the front seat and back. "Garo treats us real nice. You just have to be cool and do what he says. It's easy enough."

Maria bobbed her head and smiled a watery smile. Antonia couldn't quite get there this time.

"I think this is a terrible mistake," she said to the blonde. "We are here to work."

"Oh, it's work, for sure. And mistake or not, you're here."

"How long will they keep us here?"

"Depends on how much you earn." The girl patted Antonia's shoulder. Her fingers were dry and cool. "You girls are both pretty. Job security, right? You'll do fine."

*At what?* Antonia wanted to shout at her.

But the girl dropped back onto the seat and jabbed the

brunette, who was drifting back into her stupor. The van turned into a driveway and rocked to a stop in front of a proud garage painted in beige tones. It was almost as big as the house.

"This is it," the blonde whispered.

Antonia filled in the rest. *Mistake or not.* She pulled Maria's hand from her lap and squeezed it, though she wasn't sure which one of them she was comforting.

Garo opened Antonia's door and held out his arm. "We have arrived, *bonitas*," he said. "Your new home."

Maria giggled and jumped out. Antonia wished she could be as easily reassured. That was hard with Garo leading the way up the front walk like a feudal lord and C. J. following them so closely she could feel the heat of him on her back. Anyone watching would have thought they were being carefully guarded. Her throat tightened.

It closed together when she stepped across the threshold into a tiled entryway. It opened out into a large bare room scattered with girls—young women—probably twelve of them sitting and sprawling and sleeping on the wheat-colored carpet. With the exception of a few lawn chairs there wasn't a single piece of furniture to be seen.

"Honey, I'm home!" C. J. said.

Most of them didn't even look up. A few rolled their eyes and went back to the focal point, which was a flat-screen TV on a stand before the fireplace. Several of the girls had positioned sleeping bags and blankets and backpacks repurposed as pillows in front of it and were vegging in the same kind of vacuous way as the brunette from the car. Antonia took in a breath, just to make sure there was air to breathe—the room was that lifeless.

"C'mon, let's go—let's go. Walk!"

Antonia got a shove in the back, administered by C. J. Maria received one too and stumbled forward into Garo.

"C. J.—*por favor!*" Garo said. His voice was sharp for the first time. "Gentle with these two." He softened his face and took Antonia's hand. Nodding to Maria to follow, he said, "Come here," and led them through a wide doorway into a spacious kitchen.

Antonia saw no more décor here than in the front room. The counters were bare except for a coffee pot and a blender and a roll of paper towels. No stools sat up to the bar Garo leaned on to face them.

"What's your name?" he said to Antonia, his tone creamy again.

"Antonia," she said. Why didn't he know that?

"Antonia." He pressed his hands together as if he were praying and let them rest in front of his mouth before he said, "That is no surprise, huh? It means 'beautiful' or 'praiseworthy.' 'Priceless,' *sí?*" His eyes, a light shade of brown, shimmered like gold lamé. "That is what you are and that is the way you will be treated."

Did that include being hauled here in the back of a truck like a pair of cows?

He looked steadily, first at Maria, and then at her. "You two have boyfriends? Both of you? One of you?"

Maria let out the expected giggle. Antonia could almost hear her thinking about the three crushes she'd had in the last six months alone.

"Not now, or not ever?" he said. Probed, actually. "Never?"

Trini passed through her mind, but she shook her head and nudged Maria gently.

She'd swallowed the giggle by now and looked uncharacteristically confused. She shook her head too.

"C. J.!" Garo called toward the front room. "See, this is why we are very gentle—not moving them around like they are dogs or animals, because they have something very valuable, okay?"

C. J. muttered an "Okay" as he entered the kitchen.

Garo gave him a hard look.

"I don't know what I was thinking," C. J. said. "I beg your pardon. My bad."

*Just stop*, Antonia wanted to say to him. *You don't mean a word of it.*

"Okay," Garo said.

C. J. turned to the lethargic group scattered around the room. "All right, listen up, evening crew. I want you to get a lot of sleep today. There's football all day today. Preseason." He studied his watch. "And you know nothing complements violence like a little nooky. So wheels up 6:00 p.m., all right? You know the drill."

Garo moved away from the bar and stood between Antonia and her view of the response from the girls.

"You have to be exhausted, *sí*?" he said. "Let's get you to your rooms."

He nodded to the blonde who'd been in the car with them. She put her arm around Maria and started to draw her away.

"Wait." It was out of Antonia's mouth almost before it was in her head. She grabbed for her sister's hand, but the blonde pulled Maria out of her reach.

Garo shook his head, looking almost fatherly. "The other girls will take good care of her . . . mentor her. You have my word. She's okay."

As long as Antonia wasn't entirely sure what they were mentoring her *for*, she wasn't letting her sister out of her sight. But she had to be shrewd.

She closed her eyes. When she opened them to Garo, she hoped they were respectfully imploring. That was what she was going for. "Maria is very young," she said. "Let me facilitate . . . ah, ease her into this new place."

His gaze narrowed. Clearly he wasn't convinced, but she couldn't let this happen. Lowering her voice to a purr, she said, "For you."

Whether he believed that motive or not, his eyes were at least amused, maybe even a little respectful. *I'm smarter than you think, señor,* she wanted to say to him.

"To be helpful, yes," he said finally. "That's very smart."

The other girl let Maria go and Antonia grabbed her sister's hand. They followed Garo out of the kitchen and down a hall.

***

This house was bigger than it looked on the outside. The carpeted hall was lined with closed doors, to bedrooms and bathrooms, Maria assumed. She was still wondering why there were no pictures on the walls or furniture other than camping chairs when Garo opened double doors at the end of the hallway and made a grand gesture into the room. Maria actually gasped out loud.

This room—the master bedroom from the look of it—was fully furnished with a king-size bed and gold-framed mirrors and soft-light lamps on the marble night tables on either side.

Right in the middle of that bed a dark-skinned girl with a tangled mass of curls lounged against the massive carved headboard with a glass of wine in her hand. Two things about her made Maria stare. She had blue eyes that didn't match her African look, and a figure so perfect it couldn't be real. It was hard to miss every line of it in the leopard-skin dress that clung to her like plastic wrap.

She looked up expectantly, but immediately her face drew down to a point. Frost formed in her eyes. Obviously Antonia and Maria were a surprise, and not a happy one. Maria thought they might be freeze-dried on the spot.

Garo seemed unfazed as he ran his hand across Antonia's back. "Daisy, this is Antonia." Maria felt invisible.

Daisy uncurled herself from the bed, never tilting the wine-glass. "Welcome to the family," she said.

Translation: *I hope you die.*

She padded across the thick carpet straight to Garo and put her very-full lips on his cheek. He turned his head just far enough to avert the kiss.

Daisy ran her gaze over Antonia and Maria. "Fresh off the boat and very pretty." She gave Antonia an acid smile. "Congratulations."

"Daisy, if you will, please," Garo said and looked pointedly at the door.

He stepped back to make room for her, but she still brushed against Antonia as she passed.

"Enjoy it while it lasts," she whispered.

*That* couldn't be good.

When the door closed behind Daisy, Garo again devoured Antonia with his eyes as if Maria wasn't even in the room. "I want to know everything about you," he said.

Antonia still hadn't let go of Maria's hand and she squeezed it now

"*We*," Antonia said, "are paying a debt . . . that our father owed—"

"*No más.*" Garo waved his hand like he was dismissing a

mosquito. "I inherited this debt, so now . . . you work for me."

Maria was still trying to figure out what that could possibly mean when Antonia squared her shoulders, like she always did when she was about to set somebody straight. Usually their mother.

"We are here to work, in *restaurante* . . . as maids—"

"No." Garo brushed Antonia's cheek with the backs of his fingers. "You're too beautiful to work in a restaurant . . . as a waitress. No, no, no, no."

Maria wanted to wave her own hand and say, *Hello! What about me? How about my audition?*

"Trust me," Garo said. "This is much better." He beckoned with his hand. "Come. Get comfortable. Sit here."

He was still talking to Antonia like she was the only other person there, but Maria perched on the opposite side of the bed and ran her palm across the bedspread. She'd never felt satin, but this had to be it.

Garo sat next to Antonia, whose back was rigid. "You're not like these other girls," he said. His voice reminded Maria of honey. "You're different. *Special.* I'm going to take care of you . . . and your sister."

At last. Only, as Maria watched him tuck Antonia's hair behind her ear, she wasn't sure she wanted to be noticed. There was something a little creepy about it.

"We'll take care of each other," he said.

Yeah. Definitely creepy.

Garo stood up and looked down at Antonia with his eyes only half open. Like his lids were too heavy. What was *that* about?

"You must be tired from your trip," he said. "I insist you get some rest."

He crossed to another pair of double doors and pushed them open to reveal a bathroom that chased all thoughts of creepiness out of Maria's head. A large tub was tucked into a bay window, and towels even thicker than the carpet hung from brass racks. Double sinks, a set of shelves containing neat rows of bottles and jars and zippered cases, candles burning on the counter and sending up curls of vanilla scent—Maria had never seen anything so rich.

"Please," Garo said. "Run a bath. Relax. The lotions, soaps, makeup—all that girl stuff I know nothing about—anything you find here is yours. And anything in the clothes closet is yours to keep. Everything is of the highest quality." He floated a smile over Antonia. "Just like you."

Antonia hadn't said a word, so Maria waited until Garo was out the door before she tried to lighten up the moment. "I'd like him a lot better if he didn't look like he was going to drool on you. At least this is, like, luxury—"

Antonia's arms went around her, and she cut off Maria's sentence by pushing her face into her neck. When she didn't let go, Maria's heart began to pound, just like her sister's was doing. If proud, confident Antonia was frightened, she should be too.

Even if she had no idea what to be afraid of.

# 16

JAMES WAS NO STRANGER to despondency. Or despair. Or straight-up depression. Most days, three o'clock in the morning crept into every hour, trapping him in a mental middle-of-the-night. Ever since the day he lost Michelle in that terrible accident and had trouble escaping the wreckage to find her body, he'd hardly had a moment when he wasn't either plunging into a dark abyss or trying to claw his way out of one.

As he sat in a dark biker bar several streets over from the Silver Miner's, he couldn't decide which it was right now. The dull maroon counter reflected none of the halfhearted light from the fake Tiffany hanging lamps and the jarring neon beer signs on most of the walls.

It was no better on the outside. The crowd of Harleys and Yamahas squeezed together in the parking area was a jeering reminder of his own refurbed Indian—another casualty of his six-month stint at Kegans. He'd signed it over to his mother to sell to cover some of Emerson's expenses. Not that he cared about riding a motorcycle again. The thing had terrified Michelle. She was convinced he was going to end up smeared across a highway someday.

The irony was a razor to his soul. It should have been him.

Everyone would be better off if it had been him instead of that priceless woman.

He pushed his almost untouched glass of bourbon aside with the back of his hand and picked up his cell phone. The photos he swiped through did nothing to help. Once again, he'd done it to himself and everyone he touched.

He wasn't going to get to Dallas in time to see Emerson, another promise he couldn't keep. Never should have made, actually.

He'd already hung out here in Reno longer than he should have. No way he was getting back to his real job on time tomorrow, and Chad and whoever was waiting for their money weren't going to be happy about his late return either. He wouldn't be getting any more of these gigs.

Not that he'd take one. James tapped his phone screen and stared at the dazzling smile and bright eyes that gazed back at him. Even though Antonia's English was stilted, you'd have to be blind not to see how intelligent she was. And confident, even in the middle of things she didn't understand. Things *he* didn't even understand.

James clicked the pictures away and turned the phone facedown on the bar. He curled his fingers around the bourbon glass but he didn't drink from it. Why get any more muddled than he already was?

Or was he?

He dragged his hand through his hair and closed his eyes, but he couldn't shut out what was right in front of him. What that otherwise dim dude Rodney at the Lake Inn suspected. What the needle-eyed manager of the Silver Miner's had practically accused him of. What every clerk in every gas station and mini-mart between here and Houston seemed to have known by instinct: he had dropped two innocent, unsuspecting women into the slimy hands of men who weren't going to get them jobs as waitresses or maids or rock stars. Dear God, he was an idiot.

James peeled his fingers from the drink so he wouldn't hurl it across the room and riveted his eyes to the wineglasses hanging above the bar. Hopefully that would keep the cigarette-saturated person who had just taken a seat two stools down from trying to strike up a conversation. He had to think what to do.

Head back to Houston and find out if he still had his job? Face the probability that Chad was going to pull all his support? Try to explain to Emmy why he'd just let her down for the thousandth time?

Or try to find out where those two guys with the van had taken Antonia and Maria and—do what? Rescue them and take them back to Houston in a truck that didn't belong to him? James grunted. Wouldn't Social Worker Barbie have a good time with that?

He sure wasn't going to find any answers in this place. He looked up to get the bartender's attention for the tab and found himself locked into the gaze of a guy across the bar.

Mr. "Get Your Truck Off My Property" from the Silver Miner's. He'd have known that hate anywhere.

James stifled a groan and fumbled in his jeans pocket for some cash to cover his drink. They could keep the change. He didn't need another confrontation.

He couldn't even locate the money before the guy was a foot from him, eyes narrowed in on James like the barrels of a shotgun.

"Shouldn't you be heading back?" he said. His voice was like sandpaper. On sunburn.

"I'm just tryin' to have a drink, man," James said.

The guy turned the shotgun gaze on the bourbon. "That always helps."

James waited for the urge to throw the contents in the man's face and then knock that stupid cowboy hat off his head, just for starters. But it didn't come. Something about the level way he looked at James made him feel nothing but defeat. Because after all, the guy was right. He knew exactly what had gone down.

"How did you know?" James said.

The guy pulled in his chin. "How could I *not* know? Box truck on an overnight trip from Houston. Haulin' 'cargo.'" He sniffed. "And the more questions I asked, the more squirrelly you got."

Why James felt the need to defend himself, he had no idea. "I was just a driver. Didn't know anything about it."

He shook his head. "Didn't know about it? What's 'it'?"

James flattened his hand on his cell phone and struggled for words. "I needed the cash and it sounded like an easy gig—"

"Shut up."

James looked up at him sharply. The guy's eyes glinted.

"If you're looking for sympathy . . ." He tugged at the brim of his hat, pulling it farther over his eyes. "You should go. You pretty much make me sick."

Before James could follow that suggestion, the guy started to walk away himself.

And for some reason, James couldn't let him go.

"I need help," he said.

The man turned slowly. "What's that?"

James picked up his phone and thumbed his way to the selfie of Antonia. A sneer curled the guy's lip, until James held the photo up to his face.

"Please," James said.

He watched as the man took in the picture. His upper lip slowly moved away from his nostrils, and a gauzy look came into his eyes. His jaw muscles still twitched. His mouth remained hard. But James knew he was seeing what he saw in Antonia: innocence he couldn't leave to be ravaged.

"Her and her sister," James said. "I want to . . . undo it some-how." They were words he hadn't been able to form in his own head moments before, but they were crystalline as they came out of his mouth. "I don't know how, but . . . look, you obviously know something about this stuff."

The guy said nothing. The tension around him was palpable. The smoky dude on the stool behind him grabbed his beer and moved farther down. Any minute, every eye in the bar was going to be on them, every fist waiting for the fight that would make their night.

"Help me," James whispered.

The man continued to look through him. James had no hope that he would see anything but shame.

"You regret it?" he said.

James nodded. "More than you know."

A hand shot toward him, and for a crazy instant James thought he was about to be punched in the stomach. But the man was offering a handshake.

"I'm Dale," he said.

James tried not to deflate as he put his hand into the steady grip. "James," he said.

Dale glanced over his shoulder. "Better if we don't talk here." With two fingers he pushed back the brim of his hat. "You still need a place to stay?"

# 17

ANTONIA SCRUTINIZED THE DRESS in the full-length mirror on the closet door. She wasn't one for checking herself out—thanks to Mama's monotonous warnings about being conceited or vain . . . or having so much as a sniff of self-esteem. If she and Maria had any positive image of themselves at all it had come from Papa.

She knew he wouldn't be happy with the girl who looked back at her from the mirror. Shoulders slumped. Eyes shooting darts of fear from a lowered face. Hair attempting to hide the gnawing realization of what was happening here.

"Hold that chin up, *mi hija hermosa*," he'd be saying. "You are the daughter of Eduardo Hernandez. She does not cover herself in shame. Stand up straight!"

Antonia followed those instructions as if her handsome father was there behind her, flashing his wise eyes, smiling his knowing smile. She watched herself transform as she tilted her chin and squared her shoulders and tossed back her hair. This was the Antonia Hernandez he had loved into being. No matter what went down in this place, she would be that person.

But she had to shake off the father thoughts and the tears that lined up behind them. There was no room for weakness. She focused on the dress instead.

It was a silk blend, dusty rose, with spaghetti straps and a bodice that fit as if it had been draped on her by the designer. Cinched in at the waist and falling out gracefully to her knees—it bordered on stunning. Yet somehow it didn't feel as real as the frumpy-squaw muumuu James bought for her.

Antonia had to shove that thought away too. He had seemed so . . . true. Carrying a heavy load of baggage, yes. Haunted by his own demons, definitely. But she thought she'd seen something authentic in him.

Until he let these men take her and Maria away. She fingered the cross that hung between the triangles of pink. He couldn't hide the guilty look that strained his face. He knew. And he let them go anyway.

In the mirror she could see Maria behind her, curled up under the covers on that ridiculously enormous bed, sleeping the sleep of the ignorant. It would have been one thing for James to turn Antonia over to Garo and—what was the other one's name? Some initials? She could find a way to handle this. But to allow them to get away with her sister—she couldn't forgive James for that.

"Good choice."

Antonia jerked her head toward the door. The streaked-blonde from the van was just closing it behind her. Antonia was immediately self-conscious. As much as she tried to ignore her mother's messages, she could almost hear her saying, *She caught you looking at yourself. She'll think you are—*

"Don't be shy," the blonde said. Her green eyes were shiny with admiration. "You look good."

Antonia shrugged.

"No, seriously, you do." The girl circled her, nodding like a boutique clerk going in for the sale. She held out her hand to

Antonia and uncurled her fingers, revealing a tiny green pill. "And this will help you *feel* good."

The last pill Antonia had taken was an aspirin for a headache, six months ago. She had no experience with drugs, but she was certain this one wasn't for medicinal purposes.

"No, thank you," she said. She hoped she sounded more polite than put off, which was how she felt.

However Antonia sounded to the girl, she seemed to dismiss it as irrelevant. "They make it way easier," she said. "Sorta like an off switch."

Antonia didn't have time to sort that out before the girl nodded toward the bed. "How's your sister holding up?"

Whether this girl knew which button to push or she'd stumbled on it by chance, Antonia didn't know. And she didn't stand a chance against it. The tears she'd been holding back crowded into the back of her throat.

"I do not know," she said. "This is too much for her. This is too much for—"

"Anyone?" The green eyes lingered on the sleeping Maria. "I remember being new."

The silence that fell was soft. Antonia knew about buttons too. They seemed to find *her*.

Antonia smiled at her. "What is your name?"

The blonde looked as if that were a novel question. "Amber," she said.

"And where are you from?"

Amber sat down on the bed, satin crinkling under her, and pulled her knees up to her chin. "Doesn't matter. I'm from here now." She tilted her head at Antonia so that the blonde curls fell down her arm. "So are you."

Antonia swept that aside. "Did your family owe someone money too?"

A guffaw burst from Amber but she put her palm up as if to erase it. "No . . . I'm just a regular idiot. Got 'boyfriended.' You know what I mean by that?"

*Not a clue,* Antonia thought. She shook her head.

"It's like this: met a cute boy online . . . messaged back and forth . . . sent him pictures . . . blah, blah, blah." Amber opened and closed her hand like a mouth. "One day he sent me a plane ticket to Reno. I'd never been anywhere, so I thought it sounded kinda fancy."

Antonia sank to the bed and nodded her on. Her insides felt heavy.

"Didn't tell my parents. Didn't tell anyone." Amber stared over Antonia's head. "The first day was amazing. A . . . mazing. But that night . . ."

Antonia didn't nod. She wasn't sure she wanted to hear the rest.

"I guess he drugged me. I woke up in the back of the van with a bunch of men."

"I am so sorry," Antonia said. She had a hard time swallowing.

"It is what it is."

Amber extricated herself from the bed and slipped into the bathroom. Antonia heard water running. When she came out she was holding a half-filled glass.

"I don't know why I just told you all that. I usually don't, although . . ." She twisted her mouth. "I guess nobody ever asked me before. What would be the point? Everybody here has pretty much the same story. Except you, probably."

Antonia stayed quiet.

"Anyway, Garo treats me better than my old man ever did, so there's that."

Antonia stood up and touched Amber's arm. Coping or not, she couldn't just hear this girl's story and do nothing. "I will pray for you," she said.

Amber lifted her over-groomed eyebrows. "Honey, you got a rough couple of days coming up. You should pray for *yourself.* And take one of these."

She held out her hand and the glass. Antonia took a step backward and watched the green eyes widen at something behind her.

Antonia turned and felt the stinging slap before she saw the hand that administered it. Daisy's incongruous eyes were inches from her face. Antonia smelled the stale odor of wine on her breath as she bore down.

"You think you can take my man?" she said. "I earned him!"

She left no space for an answer but knocked Antonia to the floor, flung herself on top of her, and drew back a tightened fist. Her teeth were bared, her nostrils flared. But all Antonia was aware of was Maria's terrified voice rising from the bed.

Antonia's thoughts pounded. *Don't let her see this. Don't let her—*

"What the—hey, knock it off. Knock it off!"

It was Initial Boy's voice screeching above it all. B. J.—R. J.— Antonia didn't care what his name was. She was just grateful that he wrenched Daisy off of her, though he had to hold her from behind by the waist to keep her from coming at Antonia again.

Eyes flattened into slits, Daisy fought like a wild thing to get free of him, all the while screaming, "They can't keep you nice and safe in here forever!"

To Antonia's horror C. J.—yes, that was it—thrust Daisy against the wall and held her by the chin.

"You want me to tell Garo you were smacking his new piece?" he spat as much as said to her.

Daisy didn't answer. She only directed her venomous eyes down at Antonia. Eyes shot with as much pain and fear as hatred. She was like a cornered snake.

C. J. pulled his arm across his body, the back of his hand stiff and hard. As it lashed toward Daisy's face, Antonia flung herself between them and flattened against Daisy.

"Stop it!" she said. "Listen to me—please."

C. J.'s hand froze in mid slap. Daisy chugged hot breaths into her back.

"It was not her fault," Antonia said. "It was a confusion, okay? I am very sorry."

Stunned was clearly not a feeling C. J. experienced often. He stared from her eyes to her nose, where she could feel something wet trailing onto her lip. She didn't wipe it off. She hardly dared to move at all, much as she wanted to go to Maria, who was now sobbing. From the corner of her eye she could see that Amber had strung her arm around her.

"Out," C. J. said finally.

He held the door open as Amber pulled away from Maria and left, with a wide-eyed look at Antonia.

"I said out," C. J. said to Daisy.

She drew herself up, the thin veneer of pride restored to her face. But as she made her way past C. J., she glanced back. Antonia thought she caught a brief look of confusion, and maybe just a hint of admiration.

C. J. shoved her into the hall and the door closed behind them. As Antonia grabbed a tissue for her bloody nose and hurried to put her arms around Maria, she herself was no longer confused.

The situation was all too clear.

# 18

THE LOBBY OF THE SILVER MINER'S INN felt different than it had several hours before. James chalked that up to the fact that Dale was no longer sizing him up like the Honorable Wilson Benton peering down from the bench. Been there, done that. Didn't need it.

As Dale tapped on his computer keyboard and rummaged in a drawer, his face was still stern—probably a permanent condition—but not threatening. With every keystroke he seemed to cut James a little more slack. His eyes had lost their squint and James could no longer hear him gritting his teeth. This was clearly not a dude you messed with . . . but he might be one you could trust.

Dale slid an old-fashioned-style key across the counter, one with a diamond-shaped plastic thing announcing the number. "I'd say it's the best room, but if the truth's known they're all the same."

James wrapped his fingers around the key. "I appreciate this."

Dale rounded the counter and motioned to the two tweedy upholstered chairs that were cozied up to a low round table covered with a fan of *Reno Tahoe Tonight* magazines. Dale dropped into one seat, James the other. He wanted to unwind, but he was so coiled up he was afraid a good breath would snap him in half.

"Seriously," he said. "You didn't have to—"

"Look, I got a soft spot for hard-luck cases." Dale allowed a smile. "Being the former president of that club and all."

"Can I give back my membership?" James said.

"We'll see."

Dale crossed one leg over the other knee and folded his hands on his trim midsection. He was pretty fit for a guy—what?—in his late fifties, early sixties. One of those men whose only sign of age was the peppering of gray in his beard and the experience in his eyes. Which were once again probing James.

"What're you hoping to do for these girls?" he said.

"That's just it," James said. "I don't know."

Dale didn't say anything. That was too lame to leave hanging in the air.

"If someone tips off the cops," James said, "those guys who took Antonia and Maria will go to jail, right? That'd be a start."

Dale grunted. "No one goes to jail . . . except the girls."

"What—"

"—and they're so scared they won't turn over on anybody, even for their own good."

He ended with a shrug that got under James's skin.

"So what, then?" James said.

Dale stretched his arms over his head and leaned back in the chair. "That's the nine-billion-dollar question."

That was it? That was all he had?

James shifted in the seat. Dragged his fingers through his hair. Bit down on his cheek. Dale waited.

"What type of guy even gets into that?" James said.

Dale gave him an even look. "I'm looking at one."

"Whoa, man—"

"Normal guys. Businessmen. Bankers. 'Sanitation engineers.'

Employed, unemployed, married, single. You name it."

James scrolled through his mental contact list. Chad? Brent Weisman? Pimples Pardue? Probably any one of them . . .

"Am I right?" Dale said.

"I guess."

Dale leaned forward, eyes even more intense, if that was possible. "Sex is the new drug trade, man, and everyone wants a fix. And in the age of the Internet, available on every device . . . you go online to look at girls. You feel that rush, yeah?"

James didn't, but he motioned with his hand for Dale to go on.

"But eventually just *looking* isn't enough, right? So maybe you go get a massage. Start chatting somebody up." Dale turned both palms up and sank back into the chair. "It's a slippery slope, and it doesn't take much to fall further down every day until you're in a hole." He flicked his thumbs. "Every click is like cosigning that exploitation."

"I don't get it, though," James said. "I thought prostitution was legal in Nevada."

"Common misconception. It's only legal in certain counties, and Washoe isn't one of them. Besides, even in the places where it's legal, that only covers licensed brothels." Dale grimaced. "So, yeah, there are plenty of opportunities for freelancers."

James scratched impatiently at his own beard. "So what's this got to do with helping those girls?"

"Sex is money," Dale said, without hesitation. "And where there's money, there's a lot of bad dudes messing people over to get their hands on it. Like the ones you were dealing with. 'For the love of money is the root of all evil.'" Dale jerked his chin. "You ever heard that one?"

"Shakespeare?"

Dale let another smile out. He seemed to ration them, as if he only had so many left. "Nope. Even bigger."

Whatever. James slanted forward. "So do you know how I can help or not?"

Dale nodded. "First thing you have to do is get a good night's sleep. You can't do anything for anybody walking around like the living dead."

James didn't protest. He'd been feeling more dead than alive for a long time.

---

The sun was trying to make its way through the slats of the blinds into the room Maria had thought was the definition of luxury. Now—ever since that Daisy person attacked Antonia—it felt like the exact opposite.

Maria turned on her side, facing away from Antonia, who had been sleeping in little cat naps ever since they turned out the lights. Maria knew because she herself hadn't even closed her eyes. All night she watched the dreams wrestle on her sister's face, listened to her almost cry out before she muffled herself back to sleep. Antonia might be able to act all confident and in control when she was wide-awake, but she couldn't hide her fear when she was unconscious.

And right now, that was scaring Maria spitless.

She tried to smile into the pillow. *Spitless* was almost the word Josué used when he jumped out at Maria from around a corner or put a rubber spider in her Coke. She would give anything to hear him say it now, even though she always told him he was being immature. It was attention and she loved it.

*That* kind of attention. The kind that made her laugh and smack his arm and glow from the sparkle in his eyes. His or whoever else had a crush on her. Her best friend, Tia, told her there were several.

But she didn't love the kind of attention they were getting here. The looks from that C. J. guy that made her feel like she didn't have any clothes on. And the ones from Garo, taking a survey of her body as if he were giving her points. Ten for that nice tight butt. Only two for the almost-flat chest. *Not everyone can look like Double-D Daisy,* she thought, *but who would want to for this kind of attention!*

Maria rolled back over and watched Antonia. She was breathing deep and even, and she wasn't making anxious sounds. Maria chanced sitting up and leaning against the headboard. If she had to lie here much longer in this bed-prison she might make some pretty anxious sounds herself. Loud ones. Which would bring people running. People she didn't want to see.

She ran sweaty hands up and down the silky sheets, which did nothing to dry her palms. Everything felt slithery here.

Not like home where, at least before all the troubles, there was always sunlight and constant warm smells coming out of Mama's kitchen and somebody laughing. Usually Papa.

That was before he started coming home from work with lines in his face and his eyebrows pulled down over his eyes. Before Mama tightened up on Antonia and her more than ever, like she thought they were about to be snatched from their life and she wanted to hold on to it.

Maria wished she could have. After Papa died, everything changed. Curtains pulled over the windows. No friends and aunts and cousins coming by. Mama cooking like she was trying to kill something. And tightening. Always tightening.

A pain shot through Maria's fingers, and she realized she had them tied up in a tangle that blocked off the blood flow. She wiggled them and tucked her hands under her thighs.

When C. J. and Daisy and Amber had left the room last night, and Antonia put on her it's-all-fine face, it took everything Maria had not to scream, *I wish we never came here! I wish I never left Mexico!*

That would have gotten her an I-told-you-so look.

Maria had been left out of the plan to come to the United States at first—until she did enough listening through doors and pressing herself against walls to overhear Antonia and Mama discussing it. Her first few arguments—and her one major meltdown—did nothing to persuade them that she should come with Antonia. They wouldn't listen when she tried to show them her audition piece, the one thing that would convince them she was more of an asset than her sister.

She'd only managed to get her way by threatening to run on her own if Antonia didn't take her. *I can't stay here with Mama,* she'd said to her that night when Antonia found her packing. *She will smother me.*

Antonia got that. She was getting her share of the suffocating too.

Maria squeezed her thighs together. How was it any better here? They hadn't breathed freely since they climbed into the back of that truck, on the other side of the border. Except for when they stood looking down at this city, with James. Her whole new life was all around her then.

And now? Maria stared down at the carpet. The sun-stripes were brighter now. The day was about to start, and whatever was going to happen in it wasn't going to be good. That much was clear. Nothing they'd been promised was going to come true. And what *was* ahead made her blood turn to ice, right in her veins.

Beside her, Antonia stirred and slowly opened her eyes. They searched right away and found Maria, and they smiled.

"Morning," she said.

Maria slid down beside her and closed her eyes. One thing *was* for sure: as long as she could stay with Antonia, she could do this. Whatever it was, they could do it together.

# 19

James didn't expect to sleep but he was too exhausted not to. Although six hours didn't put a dent in the fatigue, at least he looked less like—what had Dale called him . . . the walking dead?—especially after a shower and a change of T-shirt. He'd only brought one pair of jeans and they were starting to fall off his hips like those kids who walked around with their pants around their butts. They would have to do until he accomplished whatever he could for Antonia and Maria and headed back to Emerson.

The next step was going to have to be food. He hadn't had anything to eat since that diner cheeseburger, and his stomach was threatening to eat itself. No way he was getting back in that truck until he had to, so he set out walking.

The street was Monday-morning dead except for the ubiquitous clang of the slot machines. The air was dry and almost cold. He'd forgotten about the major temperature changes here. It could be ninety degrees at two in the afternoon and drop to forty by 10:00 p.m. In the middle of summer. He rubbed his bare arms and spotted a '50s retro place tucked into the shadow of one of the towering hotel-casinos—he didn't know which. They were all starting to look alike with their luring LED grins.

The diner had red counter stools and booths and a black-

and-white linoleum floor, and Elvis's voice replaced a bell on the door. The jukebox and the vinyl used as wall decor touted it as a tourist draw, but the current clientele appeared to be local. James could feel the ownership of the booths as the waitress in short shorts she shouldn't have been wearing led him to an empty one. One bag-eyed guy all but stuck a No Trespassing sign on his table.

"This okay, honey?" said the waitress—Julie, according to her name tag.

"As long as it doesn't belong to anybody," James said.

She winked a heavily made-up eye at him. "It does, but he's already been here today."

James ordered the Love Me Tender Special and tried not to gulp down too fast the coffee she set in front of him. It was bitter but at least it had caffeine. He might be human after all.

While he waited he pulled out his cell phone and got on the Internet—and then stopped. How did you Google sex-for-sale sites? The keyword couldn't be "prostitutes." Maybe "escort services." He thought of the card the manager of the Lake Inn gave him but it was back in his room. Having it in his pocket was like having something nasty crawling on him.

He positioned his thumbs over the phone screen but he couldn't bring himself to type anything. Thinking about it made him not want the Love Me Tender after all. He literally squirmed in the booth.

Maybe if he went at it like research. He thumbed in "Sex trafficking Reno."

Instantly the screen was filled with a well-oiled woman clad in nothing but a thong who invited him to climb into the phone with her. Behind him a throat cleared.

James slammed the cell facedown on the table but it was clear Julie, who was standing there with his breakfast, had seen it. Her eyes were stone hard, and she didn't call him honey as she put the plates onto the table. The "More coffee?" came out grudgingly.

The urge to set her straight faded as she headed for the coffeepot. He was just glad he hadn't driven the truck here and parked it outside.

The beginning riff to "Jailhouse Rock" signaled the opening of the front door—that and the chorus of greetings for a uniformed police officer. He acknowledged them all with nods that reminded James of a dashboard dachshund and took up what appeared to be his usual residence on a stool at the counter. Julie filled a coffee cup for him before she approached James's table with the pot. She answered his thank-you with a grunt.

If he hadn't been about to pass out from hunger he might have left. But he was almost drooling at the surprisingly appetizing smell of pancakes and bacon. And seeing the cop set him thinking.

Dale said notifying the police only got the girls arrested, and he couldn't even conjure up an image of Antonia and Maria in handcuffs. But if he couched it right . . .

James took a few more mouthfuls and observed the officer. He appeared to be in his early forties, although he could be younger. The dry air and the wind and the twenty-four-hour living seemed to age people here like saddles. He was built largely of sinew on slight bones that made him resemble Barney Fife, right down to the hat two sizes too big. He would have been comical if not for his hardened air and a certain hollowness around his eyes.

Julie put a plate of eggs and toast in front of the officer almost before he had his hat off, and the cook in the back called out to him, "How was Tahoe?" A conversation ensued that included most of the other customers in the place, all of whom seemed to know that his wife's name was Sondra, he drove a '93 Mustang he'd rebuilt himself, and he was trying to quit smoking.

Whether it was the beloved-cop-on-the-beat thing, or the fact that James could no longer sit there and do nothing, he wasn't sure. He drummed his fingers a few more times on the table and then slipped out of the booth and joined him at the counter.

The cop's badge read Melton, and at close range he looked older and more wizened. Smoking was probably the reason for that. Between the lines in his face and the saturation in his clothes, James pegged him for two packs a day. But his eyes weren't unfriendly as he said, "Can I help you?" His voice had a rasp to it.

James glanced around, hoping Officer Melton's friends had gone back to guarding their respective territories, but they were all openly eavesdropping. He leaned in as close as he could without giving the cop a reason to draw his service revolver.

"Yeah," James said, his voice quiet. "I think so."

The officer's eyebrows lifted, but beyond that his face didn't move. James decided to just go for it.

"There's something going on around here that's, you know . . . illegal. There's a motel. The Lake Inn, over on Fourth and Lake. Girls are . . . there's prostitution happening."

Melton took a long drag from his coffee cup, probably much the way he inhaled on a cigarette, and searched James's face with practiced eyes. He couldn't have gone deeper if he'd had a warrant.

"That's serious, son. And how do you know this?"

"I saw it."

"Just saw it?"

James could have sworn he heard a snicker, although he

was talking so low, so tightly, he'd have to be wearing a wire for anybody but Melton to hear him. It was enough to make him consider bagging this whole idea.

Melton reached into the pocket of his knife-pleat-pressed uniform shirt and pulled out pad and pen.

"Lake Inn?" he said as he wrote.

James nodded.

"And your name?"

"James."

"Last name?"

James opened his mouth but closed it again. If he'd actually thought this through he would have known he'd have to identify himself, which meant a background check, which meant . . . a lot of things, none of them good.

"Just James," he said and climbed off the stool.

He pulled out twice the cash the breakfast was worth and dropped it on the counter. He caught Julie's eye just long enough to make sure she saw it and headed for the door. The stares followed him, as did Officer Melton's voice.

"How do I get ahold of you in case I have any questions?"

James stopped, hands on the door bar. He should probably just keep going. But what if this guy really was going to pursue it? Who would get Antonia and Maria back where they belonged?

He stared at his reflection in the glass. "I'm over at the Silver Miner's Inn," he said to it.

"Thank you for the information," Melton said. "Mind if I eat now?"

His audience laughed. James left.

His phone rang all the way to the motel and he heard the voice mail signal, but he didn't listen to it until he was back in his room. As he expected, it was Chad.

"James, buddy," he said in his usual animated voice. "Sounds like everything went as planned. Need you to head back so I can take care of our friends on the other side of this, yeah? Call me."

James didn't. A knock on the door gave him an excuse not to.

"Yeah?" James said.

"It's Dale."

James opened the door to two large Styrofoam cups emitting steam. Dale handed one over and nodded him out.

"Let's take a walk," he said.

James followed the plaid shirt down the outside stairs. The railings were painted silver and the slats resembled mining picks. What the place lacked in amenities it made up for with cheesiness, but at least the coffee was good. Better than the Elvis blend.

Dale led the way to the box truck in the parking lot and motioned to it with his cup. "First things first. You need to get this out of here. There's a Walmart over on Seventh Street. You can leave it out on the edge of their lot until you do whatever you're gonna do with it."

James lowered himself to sit on the back bumper. "Maybe I should just drive it back to Houston," he said.

"To be honest, I'm a little surprised you aren't halfway there already."

"I'm a little surprised myself."

Dale pushed his hat back slightly. "If you need to go somewhere while you're here you can borrow one of the bikes I have out back. You ride?"

"Been awhile, but yeah."

"Good."

Dale put a foot up on the bumper and sipped through the hole in the lid of his cup. He did everything as if he were in complete control. James needed to get himself some of that.

"So what's your plan?" Dale said.

"Maybe go back to the Lake Inn and see what I can see." James had no idea where that came from, but even as it left his mouth it sounded like a logical next step. If anything about this was logical.

His phone buzzed and he considered not looking at it. But then, it could be Emmy.

*Mom*, the screen told him. She probably wanted to chew him out for promising to come see Emerson without checking with her first. It was actually pretty amazing she hadn't done it before now. His thumb lingered over the pick-up button, but he let it go to voice mail and stuffed the phone back in his T-shirt where it sagged against his chest. Or was that his heart he felt?

"So what's stoppin' ya?" Dale said.

James looked up sharply.

"From going over to the Lake Inn?" Dale said.

It was getting to be a thing, opening his mouth and not being able to get anything out. He leaned his head against the truck.

"You all right?"

"Yeah," James said. "I'm fine."

"Y'know . . . I don't like liars."

Again James had to give him a double take. The eyes that looked back at him weren't eyes you told anything except the truth to. But he dropped his own gaze straight to his lap.

"Anything to do with those teddy bears on your bed?" Dale said.

There was no sarcasm in his voice. If anything he heard a trace of empathy.

So James said, "I can't get it right. I have *one* person in the world I actually mean something to, and that's my little girl. But I just keep—"

He closed his eyes and leaned his head back again, letting it bang against the back of the truck this time. That did nothing to stop him from choking up. And yet the words just kept coming.

"She's already lost her mom. And she's sitting there at my mother's waiting for me to show up like I promised." James looked straight at Dale, right into the judgment he knew was going to be written all over him. "And I'm not. I'm not gonna make it. I should just forget about all this and get in this truck and go wrap my arms around my little girl. I mean, right?"

The expected face-tightening didn't happen. "You should do what you need to do," Dale said. "You're a father—most important job in the world. And your daughter needs you."

Dale motioned with his head for James to get up. He unlatched the back truck door and slid it open with a muscular arm. James stared into the dump-like mess of plastic bottles and dirty cast-off clothes. The smell of urine was still strong enough to gag him.

"Every one of those girls you're trying to do right by—not just the two, but all of them—they have a father who loves them too." Dale brought his face close to James's. "So if you're hearing a little voice in your head telling you to stay, that there's something bigger at play here, you might want to listen to that voice."

If Dale had punched James in the chest it couldn't have hit him harder. His instinct was to back away before it came at him again.

"I'm not hearing any magic voice, Dale," he said.

"It's there. You're just not listening. Yet." He crushed his coffee cup. "Now get this truck off my lot. It can't stay here."

*Neither can I,* James thought as he watched Dale stride across the parking lot to the office.

But he couldn't move. The guilt that drilled into him screwed him to the concrete. He should have saved them. He should have known and he should have taken them away from here. No matter what it cost.

# 20

From what Antonia could see of the sun that fought to come in through the still-closed blinds, it had to be noon. Amber had taken Maria off to lunch but nobody had offered Antonia any food. Not that she could eat. Her lip was swollen on the inside—Amber told her that was Daisy's signature—and her stomach was in a painful knot that squeezed all the way up her throat.

Feeling like a caged bird in a pink floral dress—the most innocent-looking garment she could find in the closet—she perched on the edge of the bed she'd barely left since she arrived. If she wasn't trying—unsuccessfully—to sleep she was holding Maria and lying to her. *Everything is going to be okay. We'll get out of here and find jobs. You can trust me—it will be the way we planned.*

Maria seemed to have believed her. Maybe because she wanted to. Antonia wanted to believe it herself, but that was harder to do the longer she sat here watching Garo mix drinks at a bar that miraculously pulled out of the wall. He had his back to her, which gave her time to come up with an excuse not to consume whatever he was concocting.

*I was not raised in a house with drink* probably wasn't going to cut it, even though it was true. Her parents never had alcohol around, even on special occasions. She herself had only had a single drink ever. A tequila with Trini. He'd tried to convince her she'd be completely chill, relaxed like she'd never been before. In retrospect, it had been one more ploy to get her to sleep with him. Which she didn't.

*I do not like the taste of it* wouldn't be likely to work either. She did think it was like drinking the vinegar her mother used to clean the windows, but Garo . . . he wasn't going to buy that. Everything here was the best, he claimed—the clothes, the sheets, the hairspray—so why would the liquor be any different?

Antonia folded her hands under her chin and stared at the carpet. He had been nothing but ingratiating since the moment they'd met, but Daisy's words hissed in her head: *Enjoy it while it lasts.*

She'd seen the way he turned his head when Daisy tried to kiss him—the distasteful look in his eyes. And the way he disregarded the other girls while he slathered his attention on her. His presence maintained a crucial tension between protective and menacing. Just watching him pass through a doorway, his shoulders brushing the frame, his head nearly grazing the top—he could shield whatever he wanted. Or he could crush it.

He turned now, and Antonia stood and leveled her shoulders.

"For you," he said. He lifted her hand and placed a short-stemmed glass in it. The pale amber liquid smelled stronger than Trini's cocktail. Antonia fought back the urge to retch. She couldn't have gotten any of her rehearsed excuses out anyway, so she merely said, "No, thank you."

Garo drew in air slowly through his nose, drawing his height up with it. "I went to the trouble to make you a drink," he said, voice like syrup. "The least you could do is try it for me. *Por favor?*"

Try it. Not chug the whole thing down.

Antonia nodded and put the rim of the glass to her mouth. She let the liquid touch her lips and licked them. Garo pressed the glass against her mouth and tipped it. She managed a gulp and felt her eyes squeeze shut.

"An acquired taste, perhaps," Garo said.

He pushed the glass against her lips again, and more of the bitter stuff spilled into her mouth, and more as he held it there.

When he finally pulled it away, he looked amused enough for Antonia to risk a question. "Where is Maria?"

"Maria . . . Maria is with the other girls. Making friends because it's time."

Antonia nodded, and because he was watching her so closely she forced herself not to show the anxiety that pumped through her anew. The thought of Maria being separated from her any longer set every nerve straight up and bristling.

"You see that she should?" Garo said.

"Of course."

"It's time for you too." He moved closer, until his broad chest was almost touching hers, and tilted her chin up with his drink-free hand. "I can be your friend."

He moved his big hand into her hair, and Antonia felt even her scalp tensing. She prayed for God to help her not throw up.

"But my friendship comes at a cost. Okay?"

He set his drink down and took her face in both hands. With a twist on the gentle side of rough, he turned her head and buried his hot lips into her neck. "Hey," he murmured. "It's okay."

"*No puedo*," she said. "*No puedo.*"

Antonia pulled back, nearly losing her balance until Garo closed his fingers around her arm. There was nothing tender about this touch.

She set her drink on the bar, splashing startled alcohol over the sides. "This is not right." Her voice was clogged with repulsion and tears. "I cannot do this. I am not supposed to be here. I cannot."

Garo's face darkened a shade with every word that left her lips. "You play a game with me? *Juego?*"

"No! No *juego*! I will work—to pay back every penny that I owe. But not like this. You have my word, but not like this, please."

The pleading—the blatant begging—didn't register in his hardening eyes. He pulled Antonia by both arms into his face and spat a string of Spanish into hers. "Every girl in this house wants to be in this bed. But I don't want the other girls in this house. I want you. Why?" Her gave her a jerk. "Because I try to love you."

"This is not love!"

"No?"

"This is not what love looks like."

"Then you choose what love looks like, okay—you decide," he said in searing Spanish as clear as her own. "I will have you . . . or I will have Maria."

A near scream tore from Antonia's throat and she wrenched away from him. "No! No, no, no! She is a child—"

Garo pressed her aside and opened the bedroom door, calling out to C. J. in the hallway. "Bring in Maria!"

Antonia didn't trust her English for this. She screamed in Spanish, "No! Don't touch her! Please! She has done nothing!"

Garo didn't look back at her. C. J. appeared in the doorway as if he'd been waiting nearby, and he was holding Maria by the wrist. Her face was so blanched with terror, her eyes so stricken,

Antonia knew her sister would retreat to some place she'd never come back from if she didn't do something—

Garo stepped toward Maria and brushed the back of his brutish hand against her cheek. Antonia hurled herself at him and wrapped both arms around one of his.

"Stop! Let her go!"

Garo kept his fingers on Maria's face, rubbed his thumb against her cheekbone. Panic shot through her eyes.

"Garo, take me instead." Antonia tried to lower her voice, tried to make her plea sound less desperate. "You said it is my choice. Take me." She pulled his hand from her sister's face and pressed it against her chest. "I want to, I swear. I want to. It is my choice."

The next cry in the air came from Maria. She flung her arms toward Antonia, but C. J. caught them and held her against him. Her sobs shuddered through Antonia. But better she cried for this than for what Garo would do to her.

Garo gave Antonia an ugly smile. "Everyone has a price." He nodded toward the glass on the bar. "Now finish your drink." To Maria he said, "You can go. *Ándele!*"

C. J. didn't give Maria a chance to protest any more. He whisked her from the room and shut the door soundly behind him.

Garo was looking directly at Antonia's drink. Only fear for Maria kept her from throwing it in his face. Fear for herself made her pick it up and choke the entire contents down as he said, "*Bueno. Bueno.*"

Garo took the glass from her and set it back on the bar. His every movement seemed to be in slow motion now, as if there were no need to rush because Antonia wasn't going anywhere. He let his gaze slide down her body and returned it to the middle of her chest. Antonia reached instinctively for her cross but he got to it first.

"This doesn't go with your dress," he said. He snatched it from her neck and tossed it aside as if it were a piece of trash.

Antonia saw her hope go with it. Yet, as Garo said to her, "Now lie please. *Por favor* . . ." she was glad the chain was no longer around her neck. There was no place for God in this.

She swiped at her tears and lowered herself to the bed. Her body felt heavy, as if it were shutting down. What was it Amber said? *It's like an off switch.*

Maybe there *was* room for God. She prayed that whatever was in that drink would take her far away.

"Good girl," she heard Garo say.

Far, far away.

---

In the kitchen, Maria stopped crying and struggling, and as she'd hoped, C. J. let go of her. She hugged her arms around her body and stared at the counter top until he grunted and wandered off to the table. Maria watched him through a panel of her hair, long enough to make sure he was engrossed in dropping green pills into bags and bantering with Amber, who was trying to bargain for some. Only then did she edge her way toward the hall, keeping herself rigid against the hysteria that was rising in her.

She knew as she flattened herself against the wall and inched toward the bedroom—she knew what Garo was going to do to her sister. She had never had it done to her, but she knew about it, and she knew Antonia didn't want it.

She tried to gather the courage to scream, to pound on the door, to do anything to stop Garo from hurting her sister. Even if it meant bringing harm to herself. That was her plan, until she reached the bedroom. Then she froze in fear.

Maria dropped to her knees on the floor in front of the door and started to sob.

"You shouldn't be here," a female voice whispered.

A warm hand closed on Maria's shoulder, but she knocked it away.

"Seriously, come out here with me." It was that blonde girl, Amber, and she sounded almost sympathetic. It wasn't enough to make Maria abandon Antonia.

"Come on—"

Maria wrenched herself into a ball, face smothered in her knees. Amber left her alone to suffer with her sister.

# 21

JAMES PROBABLY COULD HAVE walked from the Silver Miner's to the Lake Inn that afternoon, but he'd already hiked back from the Walmart after he left the truck there in the dry heat that had burned off the morning chill. He was steeping in sweat and had run out of clean shirts. Riding one of Dale's motorcycles four or five blocks in the relentless sun that scorched the east side of the street should be enough to dry him out, if not shrivel him up. He was amazed every person here didn't look like a raisin. On second thought, most of them did.

Once he got to the motel and saw a car parked in every other spot along the front, he decided to leave the bike in the back next to the end unit. The Harley wouldn't attract as much attention as that conspicuous truck but, still, the less obvious he was, the better.

Speaking of obvious . . . as he started down the row of rooms, trying to look like he was casually headed for his own, he spotted a black passenger van and got a sick taste in his mouth. He might never look at a van without wanting to heave.

As he neared the lobby, a door to one of the rooms opened and a man exited—middle management from the look of him— dress shirt tail hanging out of the back of his pants, circles of sweat under the arms. The door stayed open long enough for James to see a half-dressed girl inside, holding a small mirror and crimping her dark hair with her fingers. His breath caught, but as the door swung shut he saw that she was both too young and too hard to be Antonia. He should feel relieved, but he didn't. No, Antonia hadn't just been used—and possibly abused—by the swaggering project manager now climbing into his rental car. But if she was there, he could scoop her up and put her on the back of the bike and make sure it never happened again.

The rest of the doors were closed between there and the front of the motel, and the only person inside the lobby was Rodney, sitting on a stool and slopping Chinese food into his mouth from a soggy box.

James wanted to deck him and possibly cram those chopsticks up his nose.

Instead, he pushed open the door and stepped into the damp air, chilled by a noisy swamp cooler in the far window.

"Can I help you?" Rodney said, mouth full, soy sauce dripping into his chin hair.

"Yeah," James said. "I'm looking for a girl."

Rodney shoved in more noodles and talked through them. "I don't know anything about any girls, but if you're looking for a company that puts on parties, I'll grab you a card and you can—"

He rose slightly off the stool, lunch still in hand, but James waved him down. "I got one already."

Rodney dropped the sticks in the box and smeared his hand over the lower half of his face. Grease now striped both sallow cheeks. "Oh yeah, I remember you. Give 'em a shout and let 'em know Rodney sent you."

He put the box to his lips and tilted his head back. James didn't know what disgusted him most at that moment.

He stepped back out into the heat and leaned against the wall in the one available patch of shade. He'd pretty much expected that response from Rodney—expected it, dreaded it, and hoped for it—so he'd brought the card this time. He fished it from his T-shirt pocket and thumbed the number into his phone. Rehearsed lines ran through his head—the ones he made up on his trek back from Walmart.

They died on his lips, though, as the call went to voice mail. "If you are looking for party rentals, please leave your number and we will get back to you."

Nobody with a voice that insinuating rented tables and tents. When the recording beeped, James launched into words he'd rather choke on than say: "Yeah. I'm looking to party with one of your girls. Slender. Mexican. Brunette." He paused only long enough for a breath. "Her name's Antonia . . . I think." Geez, could he sound like more of a jerk? "So, give me a call back on this number—"

James pressed End harder than he had to. All the air went out of him, and with it every whiff of integrity he'd managed to hold on to since Michelle died. But this was the only way, wasn't it? How else was he going to find out where Antonia and Maria were?

Rodney apparently had no problem with it at all. He waved to James through the window and gave him a thumbs-up and a knowing leer that made James want to hurl. Again.

The phone rang in his hand and he almost dropped it before he could get sweaty fingers to answer it.

"Hey, man, you called this number?" The voice, different from the one on the recording, was vaguely reminiscent of one he'd heard recently. Although all these dry-throated Nevadans sounded the same to him. "You looking for somebody to party with or what?"

"Yeah," James said. "Her name is . . ." He consciously measured the pause. "Antonia? I think? Yeah, that's it."

"Just tell me what you're looking for and I'll hook you up."

He wasn't taking the bait. James tightened his hand on the phone. "Mexican. Real pretty. Dark hair—"

"Dime a dozen. Lake Inn. Knock on the door for room 126. Bring cash."

"How much?" James said.

He was answered with a click that repeated up his spine. Man, this was vile.

James dropped the phone back in his pocket and squinted across the parking lot to room 126. The sun-bleached door opened and a scrawny figure stepped out, already lighting a cigarette as if he were preparing for a wait. James felt his muscles go taut. It was that guy—the smaller sleazy one who had picked up the girls with Garo. He wanted to break the little weasel over his knee.

But this was the only chance he had. Antonia and Maria could disappear like dust if he didn't take it.

He started across the lot and wondered what he was supposed to look like. How did you walk when you were about to exploit a woman just because you could? What expression did you wear on your face?

C. J. had no trouble with the expression on his. Before James could even get out, "Guy on the phone told me to come to room 126," suspicion was scribbled all over him.

"I know you," he said. He dropped the cigarette and ground it out with his heel, never taking his eyes from James. "What are you doin' here? What do you want?"

"Just to . . . spend some time with that girl I dropped off."

He might as well have said, *Just to give you this check for fifty thou*, for as much as C. J. bought that. His eyes were flat as he folded his arms across his narrow chest. James knew he could take him if it came to that, but where would that leave him? He forced what he hoped was a sly smile onto his face.

"Can't stop thinking about her, you know? You said if I was looking for some company—"

"Not with her. She's not on the menu yet, Romeo." His smirk was so condescending James had to shove his hands into his pockets to keep from smashing him through the window. "If you're serious, I got other girls that are just like her and more eager to please."

James shook his head. "I'm willing to pay. I got money."

"I know you do, and plenty of it." C. J. gave a derisive laugh. "It's my man Garo's cash."

"I've got my own money."

C. J. moved closer to James, clearly not caring that James was a head taller and a good fifteen pounds heavier. "Not getting money back to the proper hands is frowned upon."

"Leaving tonight." James swallowed the bile in his throat. "I just wanted to . . . get one in before I left."

"Not gonna happen with her, bro."

"I'll give you a thousand."

C. J. hesitated, cigarette pack in hand. He pushed the cigarettes back into it and switched the pack for his phone. "Stay here," he said.

He turned his back and walked several doors away. James watched him as he whispered, head down, into the cell, glancing over his shoulder once. The hot walkway burned into the bottoms of James's sneakers and he felt like he was melting into the concrete. With every word he said to C. J. he was getting deeper into a dark world he was going to be hard put to find his way out of.

But it was too late to back out now. And with Antonia and Maria trapped in it—too wrong to.

# 22

ANTONIA PULLED THE SILKY SHEET, the velour blanket, and the satin bedspread up to her chin. It still wasn't enough to stop the shaking, probably because the tremors were happening on the inside, where a piece of herself had been ripped out to leave her cold and hollowed out. At least with Garo out of the bed, his back turned to her as he talked on the phone, she could let the tears course down her face.

She'd managed not to cry through all of it, although that was probably because of whatever he'd put in her drink. After the initial pawing and groping, its effects had slowly turned her repulsion into apathy.

It wasn't her fault. She knew that. But as she lay there despising Garo, she hated herself more. How was she going to live with what had just happened?

"How much?" he said into the phone.

Antonia couldn't tell what the person on the other end was saying, but it was obviously C. J. talking. His rooster screech was unmistakable. She hated him too. So much hating for someone who had known only love in her life.

"Really," Garo said. "For the hour?" C. J. squawked something but Garo cut him off. "She'll be there in fifteen."

He kept his eyes on Antonia as he hung up and dropped the

phone on the bed. There was nothing but contempt on his face, but she didn't care. If the "she" in question was her, that meant she was getting out of this room. And since she'd been so cooperative, she could probably get Garo to let Maria go with her, wherever he was taking her.

Garo held out his hand, and Antonia pulled hers out from under the covers. He grabbed it and yanked her from the bed. She wanted to reach back for the sheet to cover herself, or snatch up the pink dress that lay on the floor at her feet, but there was no getting free of his grasp.

"Wow. *Bonita*. One thousand dollars for an hour." He sniffed loudly. "That's a pretty good price for someone who is priceless, *sí?*"

He turned away. "Get dressed quickly, please. We leave in five minutes."

Antonia didn't bother to take up the sheet when the door closed behind him. She stood there, naked, and stared after him until her fists were balled and her teeth clenched. Until all she could feel was anger. It would have to be the anger that saved her. As long as she loathed this, she wouldn't be sucked into accepting it.

Ever.

---

As James leaned against the outside wall of the Lake Inn lobby and waited for C. J. to come back with the verdict from Garo, an impressive sunset was forming over the Sierras. Feathers of coral and purple painted the sky above the casinos and cast even them in a magical light, but James couldn't appreciate the beauty. Everything seemed ugly right now.

Uglier than the inside of a prison cell. Uglier than the hell he'd lived in since Michelle. After all he'd seen, all he'd learned that human beings were capable of, he'd never experienced anything this base. The pull at him to run and the push at him to stay were ripping his gut apart.

Crunching gravel on the parking lot heralded the arrival of a van, a white one with the Party Time logo on the side. It pulled up in front of C. J., who still stood in front of one of the first-floor rooms. He stuck his phone in his wrinkled shirt pocket and fixed a smile on his face that no self-respecting used-car salesman would have worn.

James watched as four men climbed out, each a dead ringer for the middle-management guy he'd seen leaving one of the rooms earlier. They looked dubiously at the Lake Inn, but C. J. wasn't giving anybody an opportunity to back out. He approached them, still grinning stupidly and giving them the deal loud enough to be heard over the wheezing buses across the street.

"Hey, guys! You look ready to party! They told you the terms over the phone, right? Fifty bucks for a key—that gets you started."

He was handing out the keys in question and collecting wads of cash as he continued the spiel.

"Everything else is extra. Have fun." He shifted the smile from inane to lurid. "And don't forget to tip your waitstaff."

Everyone in the line now seemed willing to overlook the accommodations and scattered like ants with their keys in their hands. James's thumbs itched. He wanted to call the cops so bad. After he got Antonia.

C. J. waited until all four doors closed before he strode toward James like he was about to sell him a Camaro. Unlike his open manner with the others, he didn't speak until he was in James's face.

"She'll be here in fifteen."

"Thanks," James said.

"You pay it all up front."

James nodded and produced the ten hundred dollar bills he'd rolled up in his jeans pocket. C. J. flipped through them, lips moving as he counted. He might have been the ugliest part of this yet.

Apparently satisfied that James wasn't trying to rip him off, C. J. plunked a key in his hand and said, "One hour. That's it."

That was all he was going to need.

James checked out the number on the plastic key holder—124—and hurried in that direction, away from the weasel who was boring holes in his back with his colorless eyes. He buried all thoughts of stuffing the bony little jerk in the dumpster and let himself in.

The room was horrible. Not blatantly dirty. In fact, it smelled like Clorox unsuccessfully masked by cheap rose-scented air freshener. But the walls were a dark, depressing green and the carpet was dirt brown and trod thin. The furniture consisted of a nightstand with the veneer peeling off the corners and an under-stuffed chair by the window that might once have been gold but had faded to an indeterminate color that looked a lot like baby poop.

And there was, of course, a bed. Queen-size with a dip in the middle of the mattress, covered by a forest green bedspread bearing a stain shaped like California.

Nothing about it suggested romance. Sensual—forget it. No woman could possibly be turned on by these surroundings. It struck James like cold water in the face that she probably didn't have to be. Her pleasure was the last thing on anybody's mind in this room.

James parted the Febreze-saturated drapes with one finger and looked out into the parking lot. The shadows were growing longer, and so was the wait. He hoped C. J. hadn't started the meter yet. Actually, darkness would be better for getting Antonia out of here. And Maria—

James stopped in his attempt to pace in what little space there was. They wouldn't bring that kid here, to one of those self-serving jerks who had piled out of that van. Right? He grabbed the back of his neck with both hands. Okay, one thing at a time. First Antonia. Then he'd figure out how to get her sister.

A timid knock sounded. The door opened before James could get to it, and in that instant he realized he hadn't turned on a light. He didn't have to. The silhouette in the doorway couldn't have been anyone else's.

"Antonia," he whispered.

The door slammed behind her and she fumbled for the light switch. Shot in the face with a glaring overhead bulb, James had to squint at her. But *her* eyes were wide open.

His planned explanation stuck in his throat. He couldn't say any of it to this young woman who had done almost a complete transformation in less than twenty-four hours. The dark eyes were puffy and rimmed in a raw-looking red, and her lip was slightly swollen and angry. The unmistakable aura of drugs clung to her as closely as the low-necked mini-dress she was wearing. Finger bruises marked her bare arms.

"James," she said.

"What did they do to you?"

James took a step toward her, but she shrank away from him and collapsed against the wall between the door and the window. Her sobs were so savage they seemed to be shredding her soul. When James squatted beside her, she pummeled him with her fists until he moved out of her reach.

He had to find words—any words.

"Antonia . . . I swear I didn't know this was going to happen . . . I'm so sorry. I'm *so* sorry."

"How are you here?" In spite of her almost-uncontrolled crying her voice was surprisingly low and sharp. She was having nothing but the truth.

"I . . . I gave the man some money—"

"You pay to have sex with me?"

"No! I paid to get you here."

James watched something cave in her. "How much am I worth?" she said.

"Come on," James said, hand out. "Let me get you off the floor—"

"Don't. Touch. Me."

"I'm trying to help you."

"Do you not think you help enough?"

The twist of fear and betrayal and rage was so tight, James couldn't even begin to know which one to deal with first. He held up both hands so she could see them and tried to steady his voice.

"I'm gonna get you out of here," he said.

"How could you just leave us? Did you not see what they were? When they bring out those girls—"

"I did, and—"

"You left us!" She flattened her palm in the air between them. "I am so happy my father is not alive to know about this."

A layer of anger fell away, and she wept.

"I'm here to make it right," he said. "But we don't have much time. I have a motorcycle in the back. We don't have a lot of time, so—"

"My sister." Her voice was sharp again.

"We'll get Maria too, I promise, but I gotta get you out while we have a chance—"

"No." She tossed back her hair and jabbed a finger at him. It was no less effective because it was trembling. "You do not understand. If I leave, Garo . . . he will hurt her."

"You have to trust me."

Antonia shook her head, slowly, emphatically. "That word . . . is broken for you. Hear me: I will not leave Maria in the hands of those men."

The room closed around him. Defeat was always claustrophobic. But giving up was worse. James moved to the chair and folded his hands in his lap. They were shaking as hard as hers.

"Here I will stay," she said.

"Okay," he said. "Then I'll stay with you as long as I can. Why don't you try to get some rest?"

She glared at him with those dark piercing eyes and set her chin. Beneath the grief she was trying so hard to hide, she was the one beautiful thing he could still see.

---

Maria decided the only reason she had stopped crying was because she didn't have any tears left. She supposed that could happen. She'd never sobbed as much or as hard as she had since she'd been here.

That must be normal for new girls, seeing how nobody had bothered her since Amber left her outside the bedroom door. Since she'd crept into the "family room," as they called it, not one of them asked her what was wrong, probably because they knew. Although, as indifferent as they seemed to be about everything, she had to wonder if they'd been half as scared as she was when they first came. They watched TV and did each other's nails and stared into the refrigerator like they were at a sleepover. Even the ones who seemed out of it just found a corner and slept.

Right now, though, the room was empty except for her—and Amber and Garo, who were whispering in the doorway to the hall. Maria ignored them and pulled her knees in to rest her forehead on them. She was super tired. As much as it would have been good to get out of here and go where everybody else had gone, she could barely move. Everything ached, including her chest. Could you have a heart attack at sixteen? Probably not. That pain was just anxiety, right? It made her nervous not knowing where Antonia was. She could ask Amber, but she was pretty sure you didn't interrupt Garo when he was talking right into somebody's mouth. Hadn't he ever heard of personal space?

Maria couldn't think about him being that close to Antonia. She curled into a ball against the wall and wished for sleep.

Feet padded across the carpet and a warm body sank down beside her. Maria could smell the honeysuckle lotion she'd sampled in the bathroom. It was Amber. Again.

"Hey, sweetie," she said.

Maria's manners automatically kicked in and she looked up. Amber smiled. It seemed real. Kind of.

"How old are you?" she said.

"Sixteen," Maria said.

"Wow. High school." Amber tugged at one of her own curls. "You like school?"

"No." Actually, she despised it. The boring classes and the pointless homework, anyway. The social life was another thing altogether. The thought of it made her want to cry again. Where could all those tears come from?

"Me neither," Amber said. "I hated it." She gave Maria a chummy nudge. "The good news is, if you stick around, I'll make sure you never have to go again."

Maria smiled in spite of herself. First good news she'd had since James fed them cheeseburgers.

Amber stretched her legs out and crossed her ankles. "Here's the deal: we take care of each other here. Like a family. And you and your sister get to be part of that family now."

The glimmer of good took a dive. This was not her family. Antonia was her family. And Mama—as much of a pain as she could be sometimes. And Papa . . . She squeezed her eyes shut. No more tears. Please.

Amber went on as if she didn't notice Maria was about to start blubbering again. "Oh, and if anyone outside the family were to ask you, like, how old you are, you say eighteen."

"Why?" Maria said.

"Um, to protect you, that's all. Or some seriously bad dudes will take you back to Mexico, put you in jail even. And we don't want that."

Maria had to agree with her there. The anxiety was bearing down on her chest again.

"Hey," Amber said in a voice that sounded a little too suddenly cheery to Maria, "I have an idea. Why don't you go pick out a really pretty dress—we've got, like, a whole closet full of them—and I'll help you with some makeup and your hair. And then"—her green eyes sparkled like she and Maria were prepping for prom—"we'll take some beautiful pictures of you. What do you think?"

Another gleam of good news. "You mean, like a photo shoot?" Maria said.

"Exactly. We could even make a little movie if you want."

Maria let herself nod slowly. This was more like what she'd expected. Photo shoot. Video. If she got to sing in it, maybe they'd see what she was made of, and she and Antonia could—

"Come on—I'll show you the equipment."

Amber stood and thrust her hand down for Maria to take it. Maria stared at it for a moment, until she heard a throat clear across the room. She looked up to see Garo giving her an order without so much as moving his lips. Maria nodded and got to her feet.

"This way," Amber said and led the way to the hall, past the monster Garo, and into a different bedroom.

It was white and bright and the only things in it were a king-size bed covered in a purple comforter, a camera on a tripod, and a laptop on the floor.

As Amber closed the door behind her, Maria had only one thought: *Did Taylor Swift ever pose on a bed?*

# 23

THERE MIGHT NOT BE anything darker than a dismal motel room after the sun went down. James flipped the switch in the bathroom and positioned the door so that just enough light spilled out onto the threadbare carpet for him to see without waking Antonia.

She was curled into a knot at the edge of the bed and folded into the half of the bedspread James had pulled over her after she fell asleep. It hadn't taken long—maybe two minutes—after James convinced her to try to rest. She now breathed the long, deep inhales and exhales of someone who hadn't slept well in days. Even at that, the hand on the rag of a pillow was in a tight ball, as if the angry part of her was still wide-awake.

James sat on the edge of the chair, a spring poking him in the backside, and watched her. In just one day the serenity that seemed to come over her so easily had all but slipped away. She wasn't wearing the cross he'd seen her touch so many times on the trip here. God only knew what had happened to it. Her eyes were wary, even when she was drifting off, and her mouth was tightened, maybe so it wouldn't quiver.

James leaned back. She was strong, though, he had to give her that. Strong like Michelle was.

Michelle, who grew up with a father who would just as soon

slap her as look at her, and without the mother who checked out when Michelle was twelve. But she never wore the victim badge. She was determined to have a better life, and make sure Emerson had one. Through twenty-five hours of writhing labor she kept saying to him, "It's all going to be worth it, baby." On the fifth straight night of rocking that baby while she screamed with colic, until the chair was starting to wear through the rug, she was still saying, "This'll pass. We'll be okay."

That woman could get through anything, like a piece of silk sliding through life. Anything except a semi that crushed her—

James stood up and grabbed his head in his hands. He couldn't let the accusations catch up to him—the ones that tormented him if he gave them half a chance. The charge that he could have protected his wife and he didn't. That he could have saved her and he failed. That it should have been him and it wasn't. They were more brutal than anything Judge Benton handed down, because they meant a life sentence, without the possibility of parole.

He looked down at the mass of shiny black hair that spread across the pillow, the brave shoulders that rose and fell with her exhausted breaths, the ready fist that would protect her sister even if it meant losing herself.

James closed his eyes and shut out the vision that crushed the life from his Michelle. He couldn't keep that from happening. He couldn't rescue her. No matter how many different ways he tried to make it work in his mind, he couldn't, and he never would. But this woman was here and he *could* keep her from getting lost in something worse than death itself.

That was why an hour ago he'd paid C. J. for extra time so Antonia could sleep—so she would be ready for what they were going to do. And why he wasn't leaving this dump without her.

C. J.'s voice and his fist slammed against the door simultaneously. "Time's up, man. You're done. She's got a full dance card tonight."

"One minute!" James said in lieu of splitting the door with his own fist.

"You don't have a minute."

James waited until he heard him bang on another door before he knelt beside the bed and rested a hand on Antonia's shoulder.

"I hate to wake you up," he whispered to her. "But we need to go—"

Antonia convulsed and retreated against the wall before her eyes were even open, slamming her head in the process.

"Easy," James said. "It's just me."

She looked down at herself as if she expected her dress to be torn in half and seemed only slightly reassured that it wasn't.

"Please. Come with me," James said.

"But my sister—"

C. J. pounded again. Antonia shrank farther into the wall.

"I'm getting dressed," James called out to him. He stood up and held out his hand. "Last chance. Please, Antonia."

She wouldn't look at him. In fact, her eyes went out of focus as she stared, as if she were in a trance of grief.

The doorknob jiggled—a key rattled—and C. J. shoved his way into the room. His Daniel Craig–wannabe hair was literally standing on end and his jaw jutted forward like an English bulldog's. To say that he was beyond annoyed was an understatement. The chance to take Antonia out of there right then had passed.

But it wasn't the only chance.

James's mind spun as he pretended to zip his fly and brushed past C. J. "She was worth every penny," he murmured to him as he went through the doorway. Outside, he had to spit on the walkway.

C. J. closed the door, and James looked around for a place he could duck into to watch for his next opportunity. He could convince her on the way out of here that they were going straight for Maria, even if he had to throw her over his shoulder, but he had to do it soon. Every minute in this place eroded her spirit just a little bit more.

The door to the room two doors down was ajar. James hurried to it and slipped inside, a moment before he heard C. J. out on the walkway again. James peered through a slit in the curtains. C. J. was at the top of the steps, where someone was obviously coming up. When the man's head came into view, James stifled a surprised curse.

It was Officer Melton. Out of uniform—dressed in a white dress shirt with jeans and a too-big black cowboy hat. His face came to a point as he honed in on C. J.

James felt his lips twitch. He hadn't thought Melton would do anything with the information he gave him—James had actually almost forgotten about it. But somehow he'd gotten through, and that little jackal was so busted.

He coaxed the curtains a little farther apart and watched C. J. back up as Melton reached the top of the steps. He stuck out his hand, and so did Melton. As they shook, James's momentary hope dropped like a lead weight.

"She's here?" Melton said. "The one you were talking about, right?"

C. J. nodded. James couldn't see his expression, but he didn't have to. The cocky tone of his voice was enough.

"High dollar, but worth it. Rave reviews so far and as clean as they come."

A smile sliced across Melton's face. "You give Garo my best."

"Will do. Thanks, buddy. You know we value your friendship." C. J. put his hand on the officer's shoulder and steered him away from the steps. "You enjoy."

Melton headed for Antonia's room, and C. J. took the steps like a self-important terrier. James snapped the curtains shut and turned to go—just as the bathroom door opened and a wild-haired young blonde stepped out.

"Where you going?" she said "You just got here."

She didn't look much older than Maria, except in the denim blue eyes with their deft persuasion. There she was old beyond her years.

She stepped toward him. "I'm Angel," she said in a practiced purr. "What's it gonna be tonight?"

James grabbed her upper arms to move her out of the way, but he stopped and held on tighter. Concern flickered through her eyes and just as quickly flitted away.

"You want it rough?" she said.

"No." James breathed hard through his nose. "I don't want it at all. Just—you need to get out of here."

He let go of her and went for the door. Just as he opened it she let out a scream loud enough to stop Fourth Street traffic. She kept it up even after James bolted out of the room: "C. J.! C. J., help!"

James didn't even have time to swear under his breath. The door to Antonia's room was already closed, and he could hear C. J. shouting obscenities below. He wasn't going to be able to catch Melton by surprise—not without help.

He looked around for an equalizer and found one hanging on the wall right across from the stairs. He didn't stop running as he yanked open a white plastic box containing a fire extinguisher and pulled it out.

He used his foot to bang on the door, and it gave way. Melton whirled where he stood by the bed like a half-dressed Deputy Dog: shirt and jacket off, holstered gun still hanging around his waist. James looked past his gaping mouth to the figure huddled to her chin in the green bedspread, her face ashen and her eyes once more alive with horror.

"What the hell are you doin' here?" Melton said.

White anger shot through James. He smashed the fire extinguisher straight into Melton's forehead. Melton dropped to his knees and then his chest, but he still grabbed for his gun. James pulled up his foot and stomped, hard. He felt the side of the officer's face give way under his shoe. The body went limp.

Antonia let out only a faint scream before she muffled her mouth and leaped from the bed and into the bathroom. James shut the room door with his foot and picked up the pistol Melton had managed to pull from the holster.

And then everything stopped. The air left the room. Antonia was frozen against the bathroom sink, only her eyes moving as they darted from the crumpled body on the floor to the weapon in James's hand. James stared at the cop, willing his chest to move, and it did. A thin trail of blood trickled from Melton's nose and his cheek was already swelling, but he was alive.

"Antonia, we have to go," James said.

He didn't wait for an answer but inched the door open and stuck his head out. C. J. was tripping from the top step and looked up in time to meet James's eyes.

"Hey!" was all he got out before James slammed the door. He turned to Antonia and forced himself not to get her into a fireman's carry and plow through C. J., through everyone and all of it to get her out of here. She was so rigid with terror he knew she would break.

And yet that stubborn courage was still there, squaring her shoulders and steadying her eyes.

"Please, Antonia," he said. "I am begging you—come with me. Now."

Her chin lifted, above the fear and the shock and the certainty of what was going to happen here if she stayed. He watched her gather whatever it took to say, "No. Not without Maria."

C. J. was now hammering on the door and screaming in a voice shrill enough to bring Melton out of unconsciousness. If James didn't get out himself, he wouldn't be able to live up to the words that came out of his mouth: "Then I'm coming back for both of you. I swear."

He sucked in air and flung open the door. C. J. stumbled into him, wielding a pistol. James grabbed him by the front of his shirt and spun him around. The gun flew from his hand and slid out the door, across the walkway and under the railing. James heard it hit the ground below as he bolted from the room and took the steps three at a time. He bounded past the first-floor rooms and around the corner to the bike.

C. J.'s curses gained on him as he turned the key. Nothing. James tried it again, cranking it and giving it gas.

His "C'mon, c'mon, c'mon!" mingled with the torrent of epithets that got closer and louder as C. J. came around the unit. He'd retrieved his gun.

Panic clutching at his throat, James put his whole body into the key and the engine growled to life. James gave it full throttle and careened toward the exit, spraying a shower of gravel and broken concrete over C. J. James could still hear him swearing as he roared the bike onto Lake Street and left the motel behind. He glanced over his shoulder once—to see C. J. barking into his phone.

If he had any sense he was shutting the operation down for the night.

And giving James a few hours to find a way to shut it down for good.

# 24

MARIA WAITED UNTIL GARO turned away from her to adjust something on the camera before she hiked the neckline of her top back up from where he'd just pulled it down over her shoulder. Posed on her stomach in the middle of the king-size bed, propped on her elbows with her feet kicked up behind her, she wasn't going to be able to keep from showing her entire breasts to the world with the top halfway off of her.

Truth be told, she wasn't sure how much longer she could stay in this position no matter where her blouse was. Her back was beginning to hurt, and Garo's face had started to do that flinchy thing it did the day before when Daisy tried to kiss him.

"Smile like you want it," he kept saying to her.

*Like I want what?* she wanted to say. What she wanted was a microphone and some room to move around and sing.

But she didn't say it. Not with the memory of him and Antonia on the other side of that door still burning in her brain. He hadn't touched her and she didn't think he would. He was old enough to be her—well, he was too old for her. But she still didn't want to make him mad. It was like he dealt with sex and anger exactly the same way.

Maria looked up now to find him glowering at her. Fear

lapped at her insides, and she pulled the top back down over her shoulder. But Garo shook his head.

"Put her in something else," he said—probably to Amber, although he didn't look at her.

Amber uncoiled from the floor where she was doing something on the laptop. "What are you thinking?" she said. "Shorts? Maybe a—"

"A bikini. That yellow one."

Maria looked in the direction where he jerked his head. Three microscopic swimsuits hung from hooks on the wall. The yellow one consisted of three triangles and a bunch of thin strings. Amber pulled it down and tossed it to her. Maria let it land on the bed and stared at it.

She couldn't picture herself in the thing. What she could picture was Papa's face, the day she came out of her room in a hot-pink two-piece that was a suit of armor compared to this. He took her by the hand and led her to the full-length mirror in the entryway of their house, where they always took their last look at themselves before they went out.

"Look, *mi hija*," Papa had said, although he kept his own eyes on her face. "This is a beautiful, pure body, one that men will look at and want. But only one man should have it—the man you will love and marry, and not soon. Why let the others see what they can't have?" She'd tried not to roll her eyes. She and Antonia had both heard it all before and really . . . really?

It was what he said next that sent her to her room to change—and that wouldn't let her even touch the pile of strings in front of her now. He said, "Maria, you are a pearl of great price. Do not cheapen your own treasure."

"What are you doing?" Garo's voice grated across Papa's memory like nails on her skin. "Put it on."

Maria shook her head. The tears were coming again and she couldn't hold them back.

"What is this?" Garo was suddenly there, pulling her from the bed by her chin with one rough hand. The hold of his eyes kept her from jerking away. "You will put it on. In fact, you will do everything I tell you to do because you work for me." His fingers tightened. "Or did you miss that when I explained it to your sister?"

"No," Maria said. She could hardly hear her own voice.

"Then what is the problem?" Garo yanked her head back. "Answer me."

Maria was opening her mouth just as a phone rang. Garo dropped his hand and pulled his cell out of his pocket. She was afraid if she moved she would shake apart, so she stared down at the bikini until it became a yellow blur.

"What?"

Garo wasn't talking to her this time. He strode to the door, phone against his ear, his back hard. Amber didn't move, so Maria stayed still and prayed that some miracle was coming through that call that would take him out of here.

"We're done for now," Garo said to Amber. His hand still swallowed his phone as he pointed at Maria. "But I'm not through with you."

When the door closed Maria sagged to the bed and waited for Amber to make this okay. Amber, however, was shaking her head. "He meant that," she said, picking up the bikini. "He's not going to let this go. So—a little piece of advice?"

She waited until Maria nodded.

"You better start cooperating because I know Garo, and he has cut you all the slack you're going to get. No matter how young you are."

Maria swallowed a lump so large it hurt. When Amber turned away to hang up the bikini, she smothered her face with a pink satin pillow until the tears went away.

---

James barely registered that there was a couple at the counter when he burst into the Silver Miner's lobby. Not until the man— a middle-aged Asian with graying sideburns—pulled his petite partner out of his way and stared at James's midsection. Dale followed the guy's gaze and looked pointedly at James. Which didn't prevent James from blurting, "I saw her! It was crazy—"

"Can you just give us a minute?" Dale inclined his head toward the couple.

It was apparently too late. The man was already hustling the woman toward the door and giving James a wide berth in the process.

"Sorry about that," James said as the door sighed shut behind them.

Dale shrugged and nodded at the gun still stuck in the waistband of James's jeans. "Where'd you get the gun?"

"I borrowed it from a cop."

James was already starting to breathe normally. There was something about Dale that made it possible to get a grip. Dale looked slightly alarmed as he glanced at the door.

"Where's the cop?" he said.

"Probably just coming to," James said. Why did he have the sudden urge to laugh? Hysterically.

Dale put up a hand. "I don't want to know any more until you get that bike in the garage and out of sight. Meet me at the pool."

James was glad to have orders and started to go.

"Wait," Dale said. "Give me the gun."

James gladly pulled it out and held it toward him. Reality slammed into him as he watched Dale take it with a towel, wrap it up, and place it in the far back of a filing cabinet drawer. He was in a lot of trouble.

"Go," Dale said.

James did as he was told—stowed the bike and met Dale at the pool. It was modest as pools went—kidney shaped without a diving board—but no other guests were using it at 9:00 p.m., and Dale had pulled two metal chairs together in the shadows by the time James got there. James started to shake again as he sank into the empty one.

"What happened?" Dale said.

James breathed in. Let that out. Breathed in again. Dale didn't press.

"Stuff got a little out of control," James said finally.

"No kidding. I thought you were just going to see what you could see."

"And I saw an opening to get Antonia out. But she wouldn't go."

Dale seemed unsurprised by that, though his face was pinched as he stared at the water. James knew by now not to push him, even though everything in him was screaming for answers.

After an interminable few minutes, Dale pulled his eyes from the pool and back to James. His face was controlled, as if he were consciously barring emotion from the conversation.

"The pimps treat them nice at first," he said. "And then they break them in. Make them dependent." He flipped his hand. "Drugs and all that."

"They'd already given her something," James said. "It was wearing off, but I could see it."

"It isn't just the drugs that hold them, though. Pretty quickly they get brainwashed into thinking they're being taken care of, so they're afraid to leave."

James bristled. "That's not Antonia."

"Yet."

"No—what's holding her is that she can't leave without her sister."

"Fine. But just don't think she's immune. These men are—they know what they're doing."

"Then I've got to get her and Maria out now," James said.

"First things first. Who was this cop you knocked out?"

"One of the johns. Name is—"

"Never mind." Dale put up the hand again. "A lot of them are on the SET—Street Enforcement Team—but not all of them are team players. Not this one, anyway." He tightened his mouth. "Anyway, you're gonna be laying low for a bit. You've got people on both sides of the law looking for you now."

Dale's voice had taken on an edge. James studied his face as it worked to regain that just-the-facts composure.

"Why do you know so much about this?" James said.

Dale glanced away, glanced back. James could see him deciding something.

"Sometimes the flames of tragedy can refine you . . . ," he said. "Burn off everything else until you finally see what's really important." He tilted his head. "Know what I mean?"

"I think so."

Dale gave him a long look and then sat up straight, hands on his knees. "But that's my story. You got your own to worry about right now." His eyes bore in. "And something's changed, hasn't it?"

In that moment James gave up being stunned by the guy's ability to read him. He just said, "I want to shut this whole thing down."

Dale's face softened—or it could have been James's imagination, he wasn't sure. But his tone was unmistakably warmer when he said, "Sounds like that little voice telling you to do the right thing just got louder. Welcome to the other side."

Call it a voice. Or a surge of energy. Or the faces of Antonia and Maria and the curly-haired blonde with the too-old look in her blue-jean eyes crowding into his mind. Whatever it was, it added up to knowing. And James hadn't known anything for sure for a long time.

"Here's the deal, though." Dale's hands talked with him. "This is an all-in type of thing. Once you start down this road, the things you'll see, the things you'll do . . . there's no going back to normal after this. It'll change you."

James almost laughed.

"What?" Dale said.

"Dude," James said. "I didn't start at normal to begin with."

Dale did laugh. "Me neither, brother. Me neither."

# 25

ANTONIA DIDN'T REMEMBER MUCH about the ride in the van from that horrible hotel back to the house. She kept her eyes closed and prayed two prayers.

One was a long *Thankyouthankyouthankyou*, because she had gotten through the evening without being forced to have sex with anyone else. She had seen one man knocked out and his face stomped on and another thrown around like a long-tailed cat, and even though she couldn't say she was sorry for either of them, it had left her shivering. But at least there had been no groping and pinching and yanking off of clothes. She had James to thank for that. James and God.

Her other prayer as they got closer to the house was more desperate. *Please let Maria be safe. Please keep Garo away from her.* She'd counted the girls in the van on the way to the hotel earlier, and most of the ones she'd seen since they arrived were there, except Amber and Daisy. That meant Maria was virtually alone with him, and the thought of that was too much. And so she prayed.

She opened her eyes when they pulled into the driveway. C. J. turned on the light in the van and swiveled to face them. His eye was almost swollen shut and blood caked at one corner of his ugly mouth, but no one asked him about it, or even seemed to notice, for that matter.

"You go straight inside," he said. "Garo wants to talk to the whole group so don't go wandering off."

The curly blonde next to Antonia said, "Is this about that guy who—"

"Shut up!"

The girl shrugged. When C. J. got out of the car, she muttered, "Busted."

Antonia could only hope.

C. J. marshalled them all into the house, and the other girls flopped down on their respective sleeping bags and cushions like this was all part of the routine. Antonia wove through them, looking for Maria, and found herself nose-to-nose with Daisy. She was close enough for Antonia to smell the wine on her breath and see the bruises on her chin.

Antonia steeled herself for another slap. She wouldn't put it past Daisy to do it right here in front of everyone. When Daisy grabbed her hand, Antonia closed her eyes.

"Here," Daisy said into her ear.

Antonia felt something warm and soft and paper-covered in her palm.

"I saved you one," Daisy said.

Antonia looked down at a Taco Bell burrito.

Daisy's lips brushed Antonia's earlobe. "Thank you. Nobody's stood up for me before."

She pulled away and pointed her eyes toward the corner. Antonia followed with her gaze, and there was Maria.

Her sister was huddled on the floor, knees pulled up into her chest the way she only did when she was either scared or determined to shut everyone out. Antonia knew this time it was both.

She went to her. Maria lifted her face and Antonia swallowed a gasp. Her eyes were so shadowed and lined and mascaraed she looked like a trampy twenty-seven-year-old, to say nothing of the shiny shirt that drooped over one bare shoulder and half exposed her budding breasts. When she saw Antonia, her hands went to the hem of the thigh-high leatherette skirt and tugged—as if she could bring it down to cover another inch of her long legs.

Antonia sank to the floor beside her, dropped the burrito, and gathered Maria into her arms. She clawed at Antonia's clothes and began a frenzied whisper Antonia couldn't understand.

"Hush," she said in Spanish. "It doesn't matter."

"He said he's not done with me—"

"Stop," Antonia hissed to her.

She couldn't hear this. She didn't have to. She could only give her hope.

"But he said—"

"He won't have a chance." Antonia looked warily around the room, but everyone else was turning their attention to the kitchen doorway where Garo was parading in. "James—you remember?"

Maria nodded.

"He's going to rescue us. Have faith."

Maria stared at her, questions in her eyes, but Antonia put a finger to her lips and turned to Garo, who was now towering over the room like the slave master he was. Antonia felt anger rush through her and was grateful for it.

"Attention, ladies," Garo said.

Antonia sniffed. As if he thought of them as ladies.

He donned a solemn expression. "It has been brought to my attention that tonight a stranger, an *outsider*, attempted to abduct one of our own." He looked incredulous. "He thought that lies and money could break the bonds of our family."

Garo cocked his head to one side. "He was mistaken, yes?"

A few girls murmured agreement. Most just remained in their usual stupor. Antonia tried to maintain a mask of indifference.

"And even though she only recently arrived, she stood by us. There is nothing more beautiful . . . than loyalty. Antonia, come here."

Antonia went cold. Maria clung to her, but she peeled her hand away and stood up. There was nothing else to do, not with the entire room suddenly awake and watching. Not with Garo commanding her with every iron muscle in his body.

She went to him but she kept her eyes away. Which was why she saw the faces of the girls sprawled about the room like dropped toys. A few were slit-eyed with envy and resentment. Two others gaped as if they couldn't believe what Garo had just said. But what made Antonia stare back were the approving nods from most of them. This loyalty Garo talked of. This family he lied about. They believed it.

That was almost as frightening as the arm Garo used to pull her into him, and the very soft kiss he placed on her cheek. Only through sheer will did she not recoil.

"There are dangerous men out there," Garo went on, still holding her against his side. "They will make false promises, lie to you, then abandon you." He looked down at Antonia, his eyes glittering like phony gold. "But I . . . I will instruct you and teach you in the way you should go. I will counsel you and watch over you."

*Dear Lord in heaven. Did he truly just twist the words of Scripture?* Antonia wanted to be sick. But she could only stand there and hope no one saw her fighting not to vomit.

Garo let go of her and raised both of his arms over the group at his feet. "So tomorrow—Antonia will receive her beauty mark!"

An odd sort of cheer went up—like the rah-rah of a squad of stoned cheerleaders—and it continued as Garo nodded Antonia away. On the way back to Maria, she gazed about her in confusion. One pair of deep brown eyes caught hers, and Antonia watched as Daisy rotated her shoulder and pulled down the wide strap of her black sundress.

Even from four feet away, Antonia could read the word *Garo* tattooed into Daisy's coffee-colored skin. Garo . . . inside a bar code.

Antonia ran for the bathroom.

---

James and Dale sat by the pool until Dale was nodding off in mid sentence. He all but ordered James to go to his room and try to sleep, and James found himself too fatigued to argue. But the fact that there was nothing more they could do until daylight did nothing to help him drift off. The last time he looked at the time on his phone it was 4:00 a.m.

The slamming of a car door woke him at sunup. Only a weak light leaked into the room as he rolled out of bed, muscles protesting from last night's altercation. Another vehicle door banged shut—unusually loud, as if it were in the room with him.

James stumbled to the window and pulled the curtain aside. Dazzling sunlight hit him in the face and he had to squint to make out the car. A long black van. Parked directly in front of the window. Its side door slid open and a blonde with reckless curls stepped out as if she were being pulled by an invisible string. Another girl followed her, and another.

James yanked the curtains open as the next young woman

emerged—dark haired and slender—and his heart lurched. But it wasn't Antonia. It wasn't Maria. Neither was the next one who stepped out and stared vacantly in front of her.

He turned to go for the door but he couldn't move. Garo stepped into the scene, arm muscles rippling as he reached out to take the hand of yet another girl. A younger one—much younger—with lanky legs and a bouncy ponytail.

James slammed his hands against the window. It was Emerson. It was his baby—being lifted from the van by that animal—

A scream tore from his throat "Emmy! *Emmy! No!*"

He threw himself into the glass and pounded, still shrieking her name. When she didn't turn her head, James picked up the chair and crashed it against the window, but it was unyielding. And Emmy neither blinked nor flinched as Garo led her by the hand, straight past him—toward an open motel-room door.

---

James's final strangled cry brought him straight up in bed. His chest heaved, and he could feel sweat running down the side of his face. He untangled himself from the sheet and hurled his body to the window. The curtains were closed—he thrust them open and stared through the glass.

Nothing but a gray morning stared back at him.

He stood there for a minute until he could shake the nightmare off, though it hung on him like the worst hangover he'd ever had. Then he picked up his cell phone and tapped his mother's name. It was a dream, he knew that, but he had to hear Emmy's voice.

It was, of course, Melody's he heard instead. "James, what are you doing, son? First you arrange to come see your daughter without running it by me first. *Then* you don't show up."

"Mom—"

"She sat here all day at the tea party table, waiting for you."

*"Mom—"*

"I had to drag her away from it at bedtime, and then she cried herself to sleep." Melody's voice caught. "You can't just change your mind—"

"Mom—listen to me."

The phone went silent and for a second James thought she'd hung up, until he heard her trying to catch her breath.

"I didn't just change my mind," James said. "It couldn't be helped and I'll explain everything to you later. Just please let me talk to her."

"Are you in trouble?"

"I'm trying to do something good. Can you just—can you put her on?"

Another phone rang. It took James a moment to realize it was the hotel phone on the bedside table. He ignored it.

"I'll explain everything later," he said into his cell. "I just want to apologize to her."

The sigh reached across hundreds of miles. "Okay," she said. "For her. Hold on."

The hotel phone continued to ring, jangling his last nerve. Who knew he was even here?

Except Dale.

His cell phone still pressed to one ear, James picked up the receiver and held it to the other.

"Yeah?" he said.

"They're here, man." Dale's voice was low and urgent. "You don't have time to get out. Just don't make a sound."

James went instinctively to the floor, pressed the cell to his chest, and put his lips against the hotel phone receiver. "Who's here?"

"I'm guessing it's the pimp and his minions. One of them's banged up pretty bad."

"The cop?"

"How did they know you were staying here?"

James closed his eyes. "Because I told him. I told the cop."

"Brilliant. Just lay low. Don't even breathe. I'll try to run them off."

Even as the phone clicked, James heard banging and angry voices from the floor below. He also heard a tiny voice at his chest.

He stuck his cell phone back to this ear and lay all the way down on the floor.

"Daddy?" the small voice said. "Gramma, he's not there."

Her little-girl disappointment cut into his soul. "I'm here, baby," he whispered. "I promise I'm here."

Emmy's voice brightened like a bird's. "Hi, Daddy."

Footsteps pounded up the steps. If James put his mouth any closer to the phone he would swallow it.

"I'm sorry, Em. I'm sorry I didn't make it to see you yet. One day soon, I'll explain, okay?"

If she answered he couldn't hear. Someone was body slamming a door, probably two rooms down. James felt himself tear in two.

"I love you so much, Emmy," he whispered.

"What are you doing, Daddy?"

He put his hand around the phone, but her words still seemed to echo through the room. The slamming and pounding on the next door rattled the glass on his window.

"I love you, you know that, right? Tell me you know that, sweetheart."

"I can hardly hear you, Daddy. Why are you whispering?"

The slamming of fists jarred James's head. But he couldn't hang up yet. He had to make sure she knew.

Voice barely audible, he said, "I love you. More than anything."

"I know. You already said that." Emmy's voice went from cheery to confused. "You sound funny."

And then they were there, kicking his door from the sound of it. Kicking and beating on it and jerking the doorknob. A voice shouted from down the corridor. James froze and once again pressed the phone to his chest, though not before he heard Emmy's frightened voice say, "What's happening? Daddy, are you still there?"

The pounding stopped. More voices, moving away from his door and down the hall. They faded. He waited until they trailed off completely before he put the phone back to his ear.

"Em?" he said.

But she was gone.

# 26

JAMES STAYED ON THE FLOOR, on his back, staring at the popcorn ceiling until his eyes burned. The phone was dead in his hand, but he swore he could hear Emerson's last words whimpering through it.

*Daddy, are you still there?*

Was he? *Was* he still there for his little girl in any sense of *there*? He'd built up her hopes and then smashed them like tea party cups, and now she thought he'd hung up on her.

Or possibly worse. How much of that whole thing had she heard? Beasts banging on doors, trying to kick them in like they were flushing out a fugitive? Yelling words he'd rip someone's lips off for saying in front of her? Really, was there any end to the misery he was putting that kid through? Michelle would—

He cut himself off and sat up. No. Not no, but—no. He had to focus. He had to get this thing done and get back to his baby girl, or he never was going to be *there*.

Outside, all the violent noise had stopped, but he could hear voices—Dale's over all of them. Weird, since most of the time James had to strain to get what the guy was saying. Seemed like the more intense he was, the lower his tone dropped. But right now—

"I don't know any James," he practically shouted.

James scrambled from the floor and followed the signal to the window. Dale was standing down in the parking lot within a foot and a half of Garo, barking like the dude was across the street.

"You have a photo?"

Garo shook his head.

"You just described half the guys in the Truckee Meadows. And look, you can't be banging on my guests' doors and disturbing folks. I'm trying to run a business here, guys."

James could see that squirrel C. J. skittering toward Dale and Garo, and on his heels was Officer Melton, who was still in last night's plain clothes.

Garo held up one finger to them. They stopped on either side of him, battered bodyguards to the brute who never got his hands dirty. At least not physically.

They all had their backs to James, and although he wanted to leap over the railing and bring all three of them down, he crept from the room and made his way down the stairs, making sure to remain out of sight. Three steps from the bottom he could hear them without being seen.

Dale was still broadcasting his every word. He wasn't going to have a guest left in the place if this kept up. James added yet another layer of guilt to the thickening pile.

"You sure you haven't seen him?" James heard Garo say smoothly. "My man James?"

"He's not here," Dale said. "Must've headed back out of town."

James cringed. Thirty seconds ago he told them he didn't know a James.

That obviously wasn't lost on Garo either. "I don't remember anybody saying anything about him being from out of town," he said.

James twisted to look for the best escape route. The only thing to do now was draw them away from Dale.

"Look . . ." Dale's voice dropped in volume and packed it on in intensity. "You're going to leave or I'll call the police."

"No need for this to get messy," Melton said.

"Right," Garo added. "I'd *hate* for this to get messy. 'Cause if this gets messy, you're not gonna like it. We'll see you soon."

From the stone-cold tone he'd heard too many times in a prison yard, James had no doubt that Garo would see them soon, and that kept him flattened against the wall until van doors slammed and the vehicle roared out of the parking lot. When Dale hurried into the stairwell, James stepped out and Dale almost collided with him. He jerked like he was having a convulsion.

"You scared the—"

"I heard all that," James said. "Look, if you want me to just go—"

"Pack your stuff," Dale said.

James felt himself deflate, but he nodded. He couldn't put this guy, or his business, in any more jeopardy. He'd done nothing *but* that to everybody since the minute he climbed into that stupid truck.

"Any ideas where I can stay?" he said.

"Yeah," Dale said. "My place."

---

"Packing" pretty much overstated what James had to do to vacate the room. The two teddy bears took up more space than his one change of clothes and a toothbrush and his phone charger. As he shoved it all in his bag—and collected the miniature shampoo and bar of soap off the sink—he tried not to think about how long he'd been gone. He'd left Houston in the dark-before-dawn hours of Saturday and it was now Tuesday morning. His job was probably history. And Chad—

Chad could drop off a cliff at this point for all he cared. There was no way he didn't know what this whole "transport" thing was about. Chad had radar when it came to other people's business. He never stepped into a bar without knowing who was trolling and who was packing and who was looking for a fight. And when it came to sniffing out women, he was like a Doberman. James had seen him pluck a willing one right out of a bachelorette party at a downtown club. That wouldn't have been exceptional if she hadn't been the bride-to-be. So yeah, Chad knew. He knew, and he didn't give a rip.

James zipped the bag so hard the pull tag snapped off. He dropped it in the wastebasket on his way out. He'd deal with Chad later. If ever.

He followed Dale's black F-150 on the bike, keeping enough distance so he didn't have to eat the dust flying out from the tires. Even behind the helmet Dale lent him James could taste the desert, especially as they drove farther north of town, past the summer-sleepy university and down into a long, wide valley. It was dotted sparsely with mobile homes and low ranch houses and cars on blocks in various stages of wishful refurbishing. No grass to speak of, except for the occasional square in a front yard, scarred with patches of crispy brown, compliments of the drought. The kind of pines it was almost impossible to kill were the only trees. But somehow horses were surviving, most inside split-rail fences, swishing their tails with bored looks on their faces.

It was hard not to wish the only thing he had to worry about was keeping the flies off himself.

Dale took a left and wound up a rise and around a bend, where they were suddenly shielded from the highway by the hill and a row of mature cottonwoods that apparently drank in better times from a skinny stream that was now bone dry. Dale gestured for James to park the bike between his pickup and the house, a log cabin with a metal shed roof and a front porch made of fresh, yet-to-be-stained redwood. Dale had probably done that himself, and the workmanship wasn't bad.

Dale didn't say anything beyond, "Come on in," as he led the way inside. James noticed that the door wasn't locked, which made him unaccountably nervous. But then, what didn't at this point?

The room they stepped into was semidark and smelled like bacon grease and the remains of a wood fire, like somebody had been camping in there. James scanned the place and took in an all-purpose space just big enough to slow dance in. A plank table leveled by a matchbook under one leg divided it from a travel trailer-size kitchen. A closed door probably led to a bedroom, although from the significant dent in the upholstery of the only living room chair, it appeared that Dale had slept there more than a few nights.

"Just set your stuff over there," Dale said, pointing vaguely toward a sinking navy-blue sofa. "You can sleep on the couch." He snapped on a pole lamp and looked at James. "You get any rest at all last night?"

James shook his head and dropped his bag. "I did nod off for a while but I had this dream . . . Anyway, I'm good."

"You're no good at lyin', that's for sure. All right, you hungry?"

"I don't know—"

"I haven't had breakfast so I'm cooking. You might as well eat." He nodded at the table. "Sit down and let me see what I've got."

James scraped a '70s vintage chair back from the table and sat down to watch the top half of Dale disappear into the refrigerator.

"Okay, we got eggs . . . eggs . . ." Dale emerged with a carton. "With a side of eggs. Might be some bread in one of those cupboards."

James started to turn down that offer but Dale's on-the-nose look sent him to a pair of cabinet doors in the corner. A half-eaten loaf sat forlornly between a set of salt and pepper shakers in the form of miniature Corona bottles and a jar of peanut butter with about one knifeful left in it. Gandhi consumed more than this.

Yet another bag of guilt plunked itself down on James's shoulders. Business must not be that good at the Silver Miner's if the guy lived in a cabin not much bigger than his apartment back in Houston—and here he was about to eat everything he had.

He pulled out the bread and turned to see Dale whipping the eggs in a bowl and observing the sputtering of grease in a skillet. Whatever he didn't have was clearly not what haunted him behind those intense eyes. Still . . .

James dropped the bread on the counter by the stovetop. "Why are you helping me like this?"

"I'll never get in the way of a man trying to do good."

Dale poured the eggs into the pan and went after them with a spatula the same way he seemed to do everything—like there was no question that there would be full cooperation on all sides. It commanded honesty.

"I didn't set out to do something good," James said. He

leaned against the counter and was immediately bitten by a spit of grease.

"Watch yourself." Dale held the bread bag up to let it untwist. "I know you didn't drive that truck up here thinking you were on a mission of mercy."

"Like I said—"

"But you can't help it. That's what makes it good." He dropped two pieces of the bread into a toaster older than James's mother. "You can take this however you want, but a little bit of push from upstairs can help an ordinary man do some extraordinary things."

James usually rolled his eyes when somebody talked about "the Man upstairs." Cheesy church jargon didn't cut it—not when God already seemed like a myth he'd been told before his life got ripped out from under him.

But the way Dale said it—while sliding scrambled eggs onto yard sale plates and ordering James to sit at the table with the mere dart of his eyes—it was as real as his breathing and his bullet eyes and his confidence in every word that came out of his own mouth.

Better yet, it wasn't followed by a sermon. Dale just sat down across from him and handed him a fork and said, "Bon appétit."

Dadgum, those were good eggs.

After James inhaled them and two slices of toast smeared with the last of the peanut butter, Dale told him to forget the dishes.

"I want to show you something," he said.

James followed him out the front door and along the side of the cabin.

"They're gonna be looking for you on that bike now," he said over his shoulder. "So that's burned."

James grunted. He was going through vehicles like bags of Doritos.

Dale led him around back and stopped in front of a garage that was twice the size of the house. Like the front porch, it had been recently shored up with fresh wood. Before Dale even slid open the door, James knew he took more pride in this building and whatever was inside than he even did in the Silver Miner's.

The light revealed a tarp covering a long vehicle. When Dale pulled it off, James let out a slow whistle.

It was a Plymouth Barracuda—probably a '73 or '74—deep blue with a black hood and hard top and black stripes. Impeccable condition right down to the gleaming hubcaps. It looked fast just sitting there.

"What have you got under there?" James said.

"Four twenty-six Hemi. I upgraded her with a bigger air intake. She can go from zero to sixty in five seconds."

James pressed his hands to his thighs to keep himself from touching it. The way Dale caressed the thing with his eyes, you didn't just run your fingers over the paint job.

"Anyway," Dale said, "this old gal has got me through some stuff and I think she's got some party left in her."

"Ya think?" James opened his mouth to ask if he could look under the hood, but he left his lip hanging. "Wait—no," he said.

"What no?"

"You're not saying I should drive this?"

"That's exactly what I'm saying."

"But this is your—it's your baby, right? I can't risk something happening to it."

Dale folded his arms. "Look—about two hours from now

about two thousand cars like this are going to start rolling into Reno for Hot August Nights. You'll blend in like butter and those dudes will be hard put to pick you out—especially since they aren't going to be looking for you in that crowd."

"I don't know, Dale."

"I do. How else are you going to find those girls? On foot?"

He was right, of course. James didn't have any other choice. Not with Antonia's and Maria's lives at stake. And all the other girls'.

In a way, even Emmy's.

"Okay," he said.

Dale tossed him the keys. "You bring her back safe."

James knew he wasn't just talking about the car.

# 27

Antonia stood alone in front of the mirror in the bathroom. The master bathroom. That term took on a new meaning that chilled her to the marrow.

It was hard to look at herself now. This Antonia who stared back at her was different from the one she knew. She'd never seen dark half-moons under her eyes before, or known them to be sunken. She hadn't slept more than a few hours at a time since she left Mexico, but she knew the sag pulling at the corners of her mouth wasn't just from fatigue. Or even from hunger, although she'd eaten practically nothing and her cheeks were sinking into her facial bones. Two bites of the burrito Daisy gave her the night before had been long gone.

But she wasn't standing here to watch herself waste away.

Antonia let the strap of the black tank top fall and looked at the reflection of her bare shoulder. The next time she did this, it would be indelibly marked with Garo's "beauty mark," and the irony of that already burned her skin. She would never feel beautiful again. Not after two nights being handled in his bed like a thing he owned—a thing he didn't value any more than he did the towel he'd left on the floor when he finished washing her off of him in the shower. The tattoo he ordered would be her reminder—he'd told her at dawn as he left the bedroom—so she would never forget that she belonged to him.

Antonia watched herself shudder. He couldn't own her heart. She would harden it into a fist before she would let that happen. Which was exactly what she was afraid of—more than she was the needle that would mark her forever or the backhand he would deliver to her face if she refused him. Cementing her soul would mean she could never love, and then why live?

She closed her eyes to all of it and let her head hang, just for a moment, just to let God come in and soften the clench in her chest. It was too soon to give up. She had to hold on for Maria— at least Garo hadn't touched *her* yet. And there was James. What hope he had of finding them, she had no idea, but she had to hold on to that too.

Someone knocked lightly, and Antonia slid both the strap of her tank top and her impassive mask back into place.

"Yes?" she said.

The door opened partway and Amber's streaked-blonde head appeared. Her green eyes were too shiny, as if she'd had several of the pills that matched them for breakfast.

"Your tat's been rescheduled," she said. "Garo had a conflict."

Antonia turned and leaned against the counter so she wouldn't dissolve to the floor. Relief wasn't something she'd felt lately. It was already unfamiliar.

Amber pushed the door a little farther and held on to it with long fingers. "It doesn't hurt *that* much. Not if you prepare ahead of time. I'll make sure you're fixed up."

"I do not—" Antonia stopped herself and smiled. "I will be fine, thank you."

"Trust me, you won't."

Antonia tilted her head. "Do you have one?"

"What—a tattoo?" Amber's whole forehead went down into a V. "Honey, I have five."

"Beauty marks?" Antonia said.

"Beauty—? Oh. No. Not everybody gets those." Amber came all the way into the bathroom and plopped down on the rug. It had the texture of an angora rabbit, and Amber petted it as she talked. "I was never actually one of Garo's girls, not the way you are."

Antonia felt the wave of nausea that was becoming as normal as breathing.

"I'm not saying he didn't sleep with me. He checks everyone out. But I'm more valuable to him on an administrative level." That seemed to amuse her. She giggled at the bunny rug. "But you are special. He might replace you for a while when we get a new girl, but don't worry, you'll be back in here a lot." She leaned forward like she was about to say something that might change Antonia's life. "And that's time you won't be spending out there with the clientele."

She blinked at Antonia, clearly waiting for her to express some kind of gratitude, but another knock, an uncertain one, turned her head. Maria peered around the door, still looking as tousled and sleepy eyed as she had at three years old.

Antonia held out an arm and Maria padded over and leaned into her. Amber abandoned the rug and stood up, arms folded across her chest.

"How's your head today?" she said, eyes on Maria.

Maria lifted her hand to her forehead. "Fine?"

"No." Amber made a clicking noise with her tongue. "I mean, is it on straight?"

Antonia looked quickly at her sister, who seemed to have no more insight into this line of questioning than she did.

"Really?" Amber said. "You don't remember what Garo said to you?"

Antonia watched the color drain from Maria's lips. "Maria? What did he—"

She was cut off by yet another tap on the door.

"Why doesn't *everybody* just come in the bathroom?" Amber said. "Somebody order a pizza and we'll make it a party."

Daisy ignored her as she stepped in. It was the first time Antonia had seen her in anything but black or a jungle print. She wore a buttery yellow mini-dress that made her skin glow.

"You going out with the football captain?" Amber said.

Daisy rubbed the side of her face with her middle finger as she passed Amber to get to Antonia.

"You're being moved," she said.

Antonia looked for triumph in her eyes but it wasn't there. She seemed almost apologetic. Antonia felt wobbly for the second time in five minutes. Out of Garo's bed meant out of Garo's arms.

"I'll find you a sleeping bag," Daisy said. "You can share my space."

"Seriously?" Amber said. "Enough with the coddling already."

Antonia guessed the whole "family" thing must include sibling rivalry.

"Grab whatever you want from in here to take with you," Daisy said to Antonia.

Antonia nudged Maria. "I will get what you need too."

"You might want to hold off on that." Daisy inspected an already perfect fingernail. "She's not coming with you right now."

Maria dug her fingers into Antonia's arm.

Antonia's heart went wild but she kept her breathing even. "Where will she go?"

"To the studio for now."

"To-o-ld you," Amber said under her breath.

Antonia looked back and forth between them, but Daisy returned to her fingernails and Amber smiled at the ceiling.

"Studio?" Antonia said. "I do not understand."

"She does." Amber pointed her finger at Maria like a pistol and started for the door. She stopped midway to look at Antonia through a veil of hair. "How's that praying working out for you?"

When she was gone, Maria pinched a fold of skin on Antonia's arm. Antonia pried her fingers loose without removing her eyes from Daisy.

"Garo said to tell Maria she has to finish what they started." Daisy put both hands up. A pair of gold bangles slid down her arm. "That's all I know."

"No," Antonia said, "it is not."

By now Maria was pressing her mouth with the back of her hand, which did nothing to suppress the tears. Antonia took a step toward Daisy. "Tell me," she said.

"Seriously, I don't know. I'm assuming it was a photo shoot?"

Maria nodded, eyes to the floor.

"He took pictures of you?" Antonia said.

Another miserable nod.

"We have to go," Daisy said. "C. J. and Garo are both gone so I think they're bringing back a new girl. You need to be out of here when they arrive."

Antonia put both arms around Maria, who was sobbing into her hands. Beyond that, she couldn't move. Daisy closed the bathroom door with her foot and stepped into their space until her breath was in their faces. For the first time, Antonia smelled no wine on it.

"I know you want to get out of here," she whispered. "I have no idea how you're going to do that, but for now, just do what Garo says so he won't suspect." She searched Antonia's eyes. "If he does, it'll be bad. You get that?"

Antonia did. All too clearly.

---

Late afternoon was descending when James eased the Barracuda down the winding road to the highway. Shadows capped the brown mountains to the east, and the sun drenched the Sierras to the west with an orange the color of flames. The place could have its own kind of beauty, if it wasn't harboring dirty cops and sex traffickers.

James had to wonder what city didn't. Every town had its underbelly—he'd seen the brutal side of Houston and Dallas and Fort Worth. Who was to say there weren't entire harems of girls like Antonia and Maria in sleazy motels from Newark to San Francisco—all of them caged up by people like Garo and C. J. As he topped the hill that revealed Reno below, all he could see were their faces contorted with the pain and the fear and the begging, their arms straining toward him until the bones left their sockets, their bodies writhing in one big mass of helplessness.

He rocked the Plymouth to a stop at the intersection beyond the freeway separating the college from the labyrinth of bars and casinos, and realized he was strangling the steering wheel. He couldn't save them all, and that thought was almost more than he could manage. This thing was like a monster with tentacles that spread through the streets of everywhere and squeezed out whatever innocence was left. How was he supposed to fight that?

A horn blasted behind him and James pulled across the intersection. From the corner of his vision he saw a figure step into his path. He stomped on the brake, bringing on a whole arpeggio of horn blows and the squealing of tires. The girl in front of him let her hand slide across the hood as she tried to steady herself. She met his eyes with her startled ones and formed her mouth into a lipsticked O. She couldn't have been more than seventeen.

James stuck his head out the driver's side, still being barraged with the trumpets behind him. At least five others had joined in.

"Are you okay?" he said.

The girl tugged at the bottom of a skirt the size of a Band-Aid and nodded before she wobbled toward the curb on pencil heels. She was met on the corner by a guy two and a half times her age who wrapped his hand around her bicep and pulled her into the Circus Circus casino.

"Are you just gonna sit there or what?" someone shouted.

No. No, he wasn't just going to sit here. He was going to do something—anything. Or the tentacles were going to take over the world.

It struck him as he pulled up to the end of the Lake Inn a few minutes later that from here on he was probably never going to see a teenage girl in stilettos and a micro-skirt without wondering if she'd been sucked into prostitution. That dude could have been the girl's father, taking her into the Circus Circus to win a stuffed pony.

Or not.

And that was the thought that made him slide down in the seat with a ball cap on loan from Dale pulled halfway over his eyes and watch the parking lot for the next half hour.

Dale was right: the town was livelier than James had seen it since Sunday and most of it centered around the parade of cars that cruised the streets. Everything from fifty-year-old luxury sedans to muscle cars with dueling mufflers. It was the kind of thing Michelle would have loved. She always wanted to buy him a '57 Chevrolet like the one her grandfather used to have and help him fix it up—have it painted cherry red and put in tuck and roll upholstery. He missed her so much.

James adjusted the ball cap and refocused on the parking lot, which was filling up. Still no van. Maybe they'd switched venues after what went down last night. That wasn't a welcome thought.

The next vehicle to arrive was a taxi, which pulled straight into a parking space in front of one of the rooms like the driver was staying there himself. James chanced sitting up a little higher. The door to the room opened, and he half expected a naked woman to appear. But it was C. J. who stepped out.

He'd cleaned up some since that morning. No bloodstains on his Garo-look-alike shirt. Hair gelled down over the welt on his forehead, hiding it not at all. James squeezed the wheel again as C. J. opened the back door of the taxi and held out his hand as if he were greeting Beyoncé.

It was like watching a train wreck. A small hand crept into C. J.'s. A pair of feet in pink flip-flops swung from the cab and brought with them a girl no wider than a drinking straw. A long braid of thick auburn hair hung down her back. C. J. folded his fingers over her shoulder with one hand and tossed a wad of cash to the driver with the other. He drove off, leaving the redhead clutching a black-and-pink backpack and nodding at whatever lies C. J. was pouring into her ear.

James had his hand on the door handle when his phone buzzed. A text from Dale: *Anything yet?*

*Still no Antonia,* James texted back. *A new girl just arrived.*

*One thing at a time.*

If James hadn't been so pissed off he would have smiled. He'd met this guy, what, forty-eight hours ago, and he already knew James better than anyone ever had, besides Michelle.

The phone vibrated in his hand, a call this time. Chad.

*That* wasn't happening.

A text buzzed next. *Pick up your phone.*

James tossed it across the seat. He couldn't talk to Chad right now. In the first place he had to pay attention, and in the second place he was ready to chew him up and spit him out.

It rang again. The third time James snatched it up. Maybe that was exactly what he needed to do.

He poked the call to life and said, "Yeah."

"What do you think you're doing, man?"

Chad's voice was a screech he'd probably been working up to all day. James kept his own voice low.

"You set me up," he said.

"No one set you up! You said you didn't care as long as it wasn't drugs—and it wasn't."

"No, it wasn't—"

"I got some *real* angry guys on my case here waiting for their money."

He added more. He'd apparently given up his no-cussing vow.

"Things have changed," James said.

"No. No, they're not allowed to *change*, James. What—are you fallin' for one of these girls? Is that what this is about?"

"So you did know."

Chad blew right through that. "Those girls don't belong to you."

"Chad, those girls don't belong to *anyone*."

"You're a freakin' idiot!" Chad's voice shot up. "There are some bad dudes down in Mexico that will kill you—kill *both* of us—if you don't give them their money. And I don't want to die over a bunch of whores!"

James slammed the phone against his chest and held it there so he wouldn't hurl it through the windshield. When he returned it to his ear Chad was still spitting obscenities in creative combinations.

"They're not whores," James said.

"What?"

"I said they're not whores." He already had his finger over the *end call* icon when he finished with, "They're worth more."

He let the phone drop to the seat again and cursed himself for letting Chad break his concentration. He scraped his fingers across his scalp and scanned the parking lot.

C. J. and the girl were gone.

James slammed his palms on the steering wheel. C. J. probably had that poor kid in a room by now. It could be hours before he took her wherever they were keeping the rest of the girls. Everything in him wanted to go pounding on doors, but what good would that do? He could finish what he started with C. J. last night and be no closer to finding Antonia or any of them.

*Think . . .*

Sweat trickled down the middle of his back, and his jaw ached from clenching it. He drew in a long breath and let it out. The only thing to do was wait, even if it meant camping out here until morning. Rodney wouldn't care, although he was probably still waiting on his cut for turning James on to Party Time—

James came straight up in the seat. The black van was pulling around the other end of the motel with C. J. behind the wheel, his right arm draped across the passenger seat where the little redhead sat. James could see that she was white-faced even from across the parking lot, and her eyes were wide with what James could only assume was a creeping realization. Her hand that held a rose shook as if she had palsy.

He slouched down again and waited for the van to turn out of the lot before he fired up the Barracuda. He winced as the engine roared in his ears, but either the revving of the hundred other motors on the streets swallowed up the sound or C. J. was too engrossed in trapping the girl who trembled beside him to notice.

But James still kept his distance as he trailed the van through the maze. One chance. He couldn't blow it.

# 28

THE CONGESTION OF THE Hot August Nights thing cleared up the minute they crossed the freeway, which meant James had to work harder to stay out of C. J.'s view. Several times on North Virginia Street he slowed down and let other vehicles come between them, and once they were on wide McCarran Boulevard heading west, there were so few cars he had to pull off altogether for an agonizing minute to stretch out the space.

Fortunately, when C. J. rounded the turn at Mae Anne Avenue, the traffic thickened with people heading for the Safeway and the gas stations and the cluster of restaurants. Then keeping him in sight was a challenge, and James cut more than one driver off trying not to lose him.

As they drove up a long hill, James squinted to make sure he was following the right black van. They were entering a residential area—a mass of houses built close enough together for their residents to hear their neighbors' toilets flushing. The homes crowded halfway up the barren mountains to the north and tumbled all the way to the interstate to the south.

They clearly weren't going to the dark brothel James had envisioned.

*This* was where they were keeping these girls? In a neighborhood where people taught their kids how to ride bicycles and had backyard barbecues? Actually, this was a stroke of genius, and that gave him another creeped-out chill. These people had this down to a cruel science.

The traffic petered out again, and James pulled into the driveway of a two-story with a For Sale sign out front and a yard that had been taken captive by weeds and sagebrush. He strained to watch where C. J. turned in—to a place four doors down. It was a variation on the brick and siding and bay window theme, just like every other home on the street, except for the red rock gravel that substituted for a lawn and the shades that covered all the windows.

C. J. got out of the van and helped the redhead to the ground. She was still clutching the rose, and she seemed to have shrunk during the ride. Her face was perpendicular to the ground and her thin shoulders strained toward each other, as if she was trying to make herself smaller while C. J. prodded her toward the front door. James held on to the wheel to keep himself from hauling over there and mowing the jerk down.

The door closed behind them, echoing down the street like a loud, *What now?*

Yeah. What?

James lowered his forehead to his knuckles and breathed again. Okay—the purpose of this whole scene was to find out where they were staying. Now he knew, and that was all he could do for now.

He fished around in the glove box and found a half-dried-up pen and a yellowed gas receipt. He scribbled down the address, gave the house prison one more look, and backed reluctantly out of the driveway. Leaving was like pulling out his own teeth.

Dale was, surprisingly, at the house when he got there. By

then James was in a lather. He'd bottled this whole thing up since he cleaned C. J.'s clock the night before, and it was now seeping out of him through his pores.

Dale clearly didn't miss that fact. Probably because James almost ripped the screen door off getting into the house.

He looked up from the chair that fit his body like an old pair of sneakers. "I take it you didn't—"

"Oh, I did. I know right where they are." James tried to pace but there wasn't enough space to make it work.

"And?"

"And I don't know what to do with that. It's in a housing development—and it's not like there's any place to hide the car. No trees—nothing."

James flung his arms out and the pole lamp teetered. Dale caught it with one hand and righted it.

"You want to stop storming around?" he said. "That's the only one I've got."

"Sorry." James pressed the heels of his hands to his temples. "I guess I could go back and try to get in through a window—"

"Or you could use some sense." Dale got himself out of the chair. "You good to drive?"

James steadied his hands and nodded. "Yeah."

"Let's go. I've got a plan."

James followed him to the car, where Dale slid into the passenger side.

"You sure you want me to drive?" James said. "It's your—"

"If you're anything like me, you're calmer when you're behind the wheel. Get in."

James did feel less like coming out of his skin as he eased the Plymouth back to the highway. Once they drove up out of the valley, he could speak without shrieking like a twelve-year-old girl.

"So what's the plan?" he said.

"It's opening night of Hot August Nights. The pimps will all have their girls out working. We'll get eyes on ours and take it from there."

James jerked the car to a stop at the red light and stared at him. "That's your plan?"

"You got a better one?"

"No, but—"

"It's a start. And I can't see you sitting around waiting. Am I right?"

"Yeah." He was. As usual.

James pulled through the green light and tried once again to breathe.

———

Maria was so confused she could hardly see.

After spending all day alone in the studio, chewing her fingernails down past the quick until they bled, waiting for someone, anyone, to tell her what she was supposed to be doing, Amber finally appeared. She jerked Maria out by the arm, slapped her backpack into her chest, and said, "Hurry up. We're leaving."

"Where is my sister?" Maria said.

"It's not my day to watch her. Come on or C. J. will pull you out by your hair."

Maria put one hand on her scalp and grabbed her backpack with the other before it could slip to the floor. Amber bugged her eyes at her and waited for her to go through the door. Apparently she didn't move fast enough, because Amber gave her a shove that landed her into the back of a red-haired girl Maria hadn't seen before. What happened to her pal from last night who was on the same page with her about high school? It was like Amber had had a personality transplant.

Maria didn't have time to figure that out. She was being herded with the rest of the girls toward the front door, where C. J. was literally counting heads. He looked like somebody had recently tried to beat him up. Maria didn't blame them. She wanted to claw at his face herself. He—or Garo—had done something with Antonia. She wasn't anywhere in the line that shuffled from the house, and once outside, Maria didn't see her in the yard or in the van that waited in the driveway with its doors yawning open.

Fear and the wind chilled her arms and she hugged them against herself. Nobody else seemed the least bit concerned that they were suddenly being pushed into the van like they were escaping from something. Nobody except the girl with red hair who stopped right in front of Maria and doubled over.

"What's the holdup?" C. J. yelled from behind her. "Let's keep it moving!"

Maria put both hands on the redhead's shoulders and pushed her ahead like a shopping cart. Somehow they both managed to get into the van and crowd together in the last seat before C. J. could have a chance to catch up to them. A vein was bulging in his forehead. Maria had an image of his head exploding.

"What's going on?" the girl half whispered, half whimpered.

"I do not know," Maria whispered back. "Do not ask. That is better."

The girl nodded and clutched at her own sleeves. Maria took her hand and squeezed it between hers. She didn't know if it made the newbie feel any better, but it kept *her* from screaming, "Where is my SISTER?"

Another girl—the black-haired one who always looked stoned—crammed into the seat with them. In the other two seats the rest of the girls pulled their shoulders up to their ears as the doors slammed and C. J. hoisted himself into the driver's seat. Amber twisted around in the passenger seat and pointed her finger while she moved her lips.

"They're all here," she said to C. J.

No they weren't. What about Antonia? Maria tried to turn to look out the back window but there wasn't room. She couldn't have seen anything anyway with sleeping bags and backpacks piled up to the ceiling behind them.

What was happening? Everyone else seemed to know. Except for the girl beside her who let out a small cry and pulled her hand away. Maria realized she'd been wringing it like a rag.

"I am sorry," she said.

"Shut up back there! Everybody just keep quiet."

Maria bit down on her lip, but any minute now she'd be sobbing anyway. Maybe she would have, if the mop of dark curls in front of her hadn't swiveled around to reveal Daisy's face. She put her finger to her lips and for some reason Maria couldn't understand, she nodded. As if everything was going to be all right. And it so wasn't.

A dull silence fell inside the van. The red-haired girl stuck almost her whole fist in her mouth to muffle the crying that shook her shoulders. Maria searched out the window in the dusk for Antonia. For anything that made sense.

C. J. stopped at the corner Maria remembered from when

they arrived, the house where the girls were laughing on the swing. A hundred and fifty years ago. A dark blue car was idling on a side street, sounding like a big growling animal.

"I'm impressed, aren't you, girls?" somebody said.

C. J. told her to shut up. Maria barely heard him. She was up on one knee, stretching her neck to watch the car as it turned the way they'd just come from.

James. That was *James* driving that car. She knew his scruffy beard and his soft eyes and his big shoulders—that was him. She slapped her palms against the glass but the car disappeared.

C. J. yelled something in English Maria hadn't heard before. Even Daisy's neck stiffened.

"What the hell are you doing back there?"

Maria did understand that, and she slunk down in the seat before Amber could get turned around to see who was doing what.

"Keep them quiet," C. J. snapped at her. "I need to think."

So did Maria. As they turned onto the bigger street and the Reno lights blurred through her tears, her thoughts tumbled like Lotto balls.

James was out looking for them. And now he would never find them.

No, James was part of this. He'd lied to them all along.

No, James was going back for Antonia, who had to still be in that house.

Going back to rescue her like he promised? Or going back to take her—away from here, away from Maria?

She forced herself not to look back again. When she tried to focus her eyes forward, C. J. was glaring at her in the rearview mirror, his own eyes so close together she could hardly tell one from the other.

Maria didn't know what he was seeing on her face—the hope or the giving up. She couldn't let him see either one. Drawing air full of girl smells in through her nose, she made her eyes glaze, told her mouth to stay in a straight line, until she felt like she had put on a mask.

Exactly like the one almost every other girl in the van was wearing. This was how they did it, how they stood it. They just felt nothing at all.

Fear grabbed at her stomach. Because after only two days with them, Maria knew she could do it too.

# 29

JAMES SQUEALED THE BARRACUDA into the driveway of the empty house he'd pulled up to before and jammed it into reverse.

"What are you doing?" Dale said.

"I think that was the van—"

"Where?"

James backed to the end of the drive and ground his teeth—and the brake—as three cars cruised down the street. Suddenly it was the freakin' Santa Monica freeway.

"Where?" Dale said again.

"It passed us just now when we were coming out of that side road."

He barely let the last of the cars get by before he careened out onto the street. Dale grabbed his arm.

"Dude, stop. Just stop."

James slammed the car into drive, but he did put his foot on the brake.

"Could you see who was in it?" Dale said.

"Some—I think C. J. was driving."

"You see Antonia? Maria?"

"No. Not with those tinted windows."

A horn honked lightly behind them. Dale put his arm out the window and waved a red Jeep around.

"We need to follow them!" James said.

"Was Garo in the front seat?"

"No. It was a girl—blonde."

"Then I don't see much point in going after them. They've probably been swallowed up in traffic by now anyway."

Dale motioned for another vehicle to pass, an SUV with three kids pressing against the windows to stare at them and a soccer mom narrowing her eyes.

"We're starting to attract attention," Dale said. "Let's just go to the house and hopefully we'll get Garo *and* your girls."

James pulled the car back into the driveway and put it in reverse again. "You got a plan for that?"

"Going with my gut."

"I gotta get me one of those," James said.

They drove past the house at a crawl, and Dale let out a short hiss.

"Middle-class suburbia. World's best cover. Only thing missing is a swing set."

That and any vehicles in the driveway.

James pulled to the curb and cut the engine. "If Garo's here he doesn't have wheels, and I don't see that happening."

"Unless he's got a car in the garage. Or three. It's big enough."

"I'm gonna look," James said and went for the door handle.

"Wait. We need to go with Plan B."

"Which is?"

Dale fished around under the seat and came up with a Glock. James felt his eyes bulge.

"Just in case," Dale said.

"This is Plan B?"

A smile twitched at Dale's lips, like his grinning was out of practice. "Like I said, you got a better idea?"

James didn't. And as drastic as this seemed, there was probably no other way.

Although he did flinch when Dale passed the gun to him
across the seat.

"You ever shot one of these before?" he said.

James flashed back to a summer when his uncle Bill took him
out behind his shed on the outskirts of Austin and taught him
how to shoot a .22 at a row of empty Mountain Dew bottles lined
up on the fence. *Just in case you ever come up against somebody bigger than you,* he said.

This definitely counted.

James took the Glock from Dale and held it between his
knees, barrel pointed toward the floor. "It's been awhile. But it's
kind of like riding a bicycle, right?"

"No," Dale said. "It's like shooting a gun."

An unfamiliar sound gurgled from James's throat. Dude, was
he laughing?

"Glad you still have your sense of humor." Dale's rusty smile
broadened across his face. He smeared it off with his hand. "Okay,
let's go around to the back. Keep that out of sight until we get
through the gate. If we can."

James stuck the pistol into his waistband, pulled his T-shirt
over it, and followed Dale to the eight-foot fence everybody in
the neighborhood seemed to have, stopping only briefly to con-
firm that there were no cars in the garage. In fact, it was freakishly
empty. Not even a broom in a corner.

Dale strolled like he was showing up for beer and pizza, and
although James tried to do the same, he was pretty sure he looked

as stiff as he felt. If a soccer mom didn't call the cops it would be a miracle. They needed several.

And got the first. The gate was unlocked and they were able to walk right into the backyard. "Yard" being a stretch. A pea gravel walkway went down the narrow space between the fence and the side of the house and disappeared at the corner. The rest of the property was nothing but naked dirt with the occasional weed that had stuck its head out and decided there was no future here. The only lawn furniture were two plastic chairs drawn up to a sand-filled coffee can that contained the upside-down stubs of about fifty cigarettes, most of them ringed with fading lipstick.

The back windows were shaded, including the ones on the door, just as they were in the front. With dusk gathering, James would expect some lights to be on but none leaked through the cracks. That could be a good thing, or a bad thing.

Dale put his hand behind him for James to stop and tried the knob. The door gave way.

Either they were luckier than James had any hope of being, or this was a trap. Dale moved back and motioned with his head for James to go in ahead of him. Seeing how he had the gun, that made sense. At least something did.

James stepped in, pistol raised, and willed every cop show he'd ever seen to come into his brain. What would Danny Reagan do? But the sinking in his chest made it hard to conjure up anything. The kitchen was bare and the room it opened into was also vacant except for a littering of plastic grocery bags and a stray sock. And a rose.

This was a bad thing.

He tried to match his gaze with the sweep of his arms as he continued to point the gun in front of him. Even in the dim light it was clear the place was empty.

James looked back at Dale, who jerked his chin toward a hallway. He let the gun lead him, only half hearing Dale open and close closet doors behind him. This part of the house was basically the same scene—no pictures on walls, no furniture in the first bedroom, not so much as a towel in the hall bathroom, besides three open shampoo bottles emptying their contents in the tub. Another chill crept down James's neck. They couldn't have been gone that long. Five minutes sooner and this would have been a whole different scene.

James moved down the hall to what he suspected was a second bedroom. He pushed the slightly ajar door open with his foot and switched on the overhead light with his elbow, gun still at arm's length.

What he saw made him lower it. And swear.

The room was almost entirely taken up with a king-size bed, stripped of covers. A beer case lay on its side and a video cable snaked along the floor. There were three indentations in the carpet—probably from a tripod.

That by itself wouldn't have left James with his gun arm dangling at his side. It was the photographs strewn across the floor like debris, as if they'd fallen out of a garbage bag and weren't worth picking up.

Girls' faces lured him, their young ripe lips parted like they'd been coached. Tender breasts peeked from necklines stretched over fragile shoulders. Shiny hair spilled over cheeks that should have been blushing over first boyfriends.

But it was the eyes that seized him and wouldn't let go. No

light shined in them. No teenage impishness sparkled. No adolescent rebellion flared. The life had been sucked out of every pair.

All but one.

With his gun-free hand James snatched up a picture half hidden by another. Maria stared back at him. She was posed like the rest, right down to the tip of her tongue caught between her teeth. But her eyes were two dark pools of fear and confusion. And innocence.

Something crackled behind him. James swung around, gun poised, photo floating to the floor.

Dale raised his hands in faux surrender. "Easy there, Rambo. Just me."

"I almost shot you, man," James said.

"Strangely, I've heard that before." Dale pushed the gun barrel aside with two fingers and surveyed the room. His mouth went grim.

James leaned over and picked up the photo of Maria. "What do you think this means?"

Dale frowned at it. "I don't follow you."

"Does it mean they just took pictures of her, or . . . more?"

"No way to know. And thinking about that isn't going to help you right now." Dale nodded down the hall. "One more room, although I doubt anybody's in there. This place has been cleaned out. From the looks of it, they probably don't stay put for too long. When they're mobile it makes 'em harder to catch."

James shook his head as he trailed Dale to the room at the end. "I can't believe we missed them by minutes. *Minutes.*"

Dale opened the door and hit the light switch. James passed him. This room had some furniture—queen-size bed, night table, lamp. Otherwise it was an empty cave.

Probably where Antonia had been raped by Garo.

James jammed the gun back into his jeans and shoved Maria's picture into his pocket. He had to keep doing something or he was going to punch a hole in every wall.

Dale wandered to the adjacent bathroom and back. "My guess is they're headed to a new city. Maybe even out of state." He took off his hat and wiped his forehead with the heel of his hand. "I'm sorry."

James backed into the wall and slid to the floor. Air, anger, and hope went out of him. He sagged there, head down. "She wouldn't come with me. I tried—"

"Yeah, you did." Dale perched on the edge of the bed with his hands folded between his knees. "What else could you do?"

"Something!" James lifted his face. "This is the second time I haven't been able to protect somebody I cared about . . . It's the second time *I* caused it."

He jabbed his thumb into his chest and looked at the floor again.

"You talking about your wife?"

James nodded. "I was driving when a truck hit us head-on. She was . . . she died."

"Not much you can do in a head-on."

"I could have made her put her seat belt back on right. She took it halfway off so she could sit closer to me."

James shut his eyes but she was still there. Michelle. Snuggling up next to him with the chest strap behind her. And he let her.

He stared at the floor beside him, seeing nothing. "I guess that's what happens to anybody who gets close to me. They're destroyed."

And then he did see something . . . something that sparkled amid the fibers of the carpet.

"What?" Dale said.

James dug his fingers into the rug and pulled it out. A gold cross on a chain dangled from his hand.

Dale squinted. "What is it?"

"It's Antonia's." James pressed the cross into his palm and ran his fingertips over it, back and forth until he could almost feel the warmth of her. "She was always touching it, like it was holding her together. Now she doesn't have it. Those—"

He bit back the curse and spread the chain across his hand. Both parts of the catch were on one end.

"It's broken. That—he must have ripped it off of her." James tightened his fist around the chain and cross and slammed it into his chest. It made the hollow sound of defeat.

James didn't know how long he sat there, slumped against the wall with the cross digging into his palm, envisioning Antonia reaching for it next to her heart and finding nothing. Of all the bruising, punching, assaulting scenarios that flashed in his mind like strobe lights, it was the scenario of *nothing* that nearly blinded him. Maria's eyes deadening like the ones in all the other photos. Antonia's prayers dying on her lips. Garo robbing them of life without killing their bodies.

He was only vaguely aware of Dale, and he jumped slightly when his feet appeared next to him and he said, "Let's get out of here. I want to show you something."

Whatever it was, if it wasn't Maria and Antonia huddled in the doorway waiting for him, James didn't want to see it. But he got to his feet anyway and went with Dale out of the abandoned house and through the evening chill to the car. Dale opened the passenger door for him and got behind the wheel himself. James was fine with that. As drained as he felt, he wasn't sure he could even turn on the ignition.

Dale was quiet as he drove the Plymouth up the north side of the housing development and wove out of it onto a gravel road that continued to climb. Part of James wished Dale would say something to pull his mind away from the images still playing out in explosive flashes. Another part was glad of the silence. What was there to say anyway? This was over. And once again, he'd failed. He was starting to understand these brown, barren mountains with their moody shadows. He felt like one of them.

As they rose above the city, ponderosa pines began to appear, sparsely but enough to break up the sameness. Dale pulled off the narrowing road and stopped beside one of the pines that stood apart from all the others. Its clusters of needles were thick and heavy, its branches higher than the rest and knotted with cones. Hard to see how it could survive in this parched place—and not just make it but thrive.

Dale got out of the car, and once again James followed suit. It struck him that if Dale weren't here he wouldn't know which direction to head in, much less go there. His will was starting to splinter.

They stopped a few feet beyond the tree. Dale gestured to a long rock that jutted unexpectedly from the ground, and James took a seat on it next to him. Below, Reno glittered, like it did from the spot James had taken Antonia and Maria to. Only from this angle, the center of the city didn't look like the center at all. It was a small, almost lopsided cluster of lights dwarfed by the expanse that surrounded it. The hills and valleys that rolled as far as he could see. An endless sky turning on its lights as he watched. Houses made tiny by distance, cars rendered even more minute as they moved like lit-up specks along the threads of streets.

"Funny how peaceful it all looks from up here, right?" Dale said.

"Looks can be deceiving," James said.

He knew he sounded like a jerk before the words left his mouth, but Dale went on as if he hadn't heard.

"Sometimes I come up here to find some clarity. To remind myself of the beauty around all that ugly."

James felt something cutting into his palm. He opened his hand and looked at the cross he'd been unconsciously squeezing until it made an imprint in his skin. He tightened his fist around it again, so it wouldn't go away.

"That cross in your hand?" Dale said. "I call that a God shot."

James glanced up at him. "Never heard of that."

"It's when everything feels like it's over."

He was right there.

"When that last little bit of light and hope is slipping away faster than you can chase it, and then *boom* . . ." Dale spread both hands. "Something appears. A little miracle right in front of you that gives you the strength to carry on." He nodded toward James's fist. "A God shot."

James was mesmerized for a moment, more by the sudden unlining of Dale's face than the words themselves. But that snapped like fingers in a vise.

"Or maybe it's just a necklace," he said.

"Nope. It's that little voice you've been hearing . . . made physical."

James waited for the nasty retort to spring to his lips—for the urge to push Dale off the mountain because he didn't get it—but it didn't happen. It wasn't only the fact that he knew not to mess with the intensity when it took hold in Dale's eyes. It was just that none of his usual reactions were going to change any of this. And he had no idea what would.

He let his head fall back. "I just don't know what to do, man."

Dale picked up a chipped-off fragment of the rock they were sitting on and sent it skittering down the hill. "You know *what* to do. You're just struggling with *how*."

James stared at the stars, half expecting the wind to blow them around the way it—the way everything—was whipping him around.

"You know the direction to walk in," Dale said. "So you point your feet and you start walking. The stuff in your path?" James felt him shrug. "That's not up to you."

James slowly pulled his gaze from the sky. Dale's voice had gone soft, something James hadn't heard in it before. Bald intensity, yes. Deep emotion, no. It landed on him, and he couldn't turn away.

"The two of us," Dale said, "we've done some bad things. Agreed?"

"I know I have," James said.

"We've been villains, outcasts . . . the kind of men I wouldn't want to break bread with now."

James felt his self-loathing rise. "I'm so tired of all that."

"Yeah. But if we were perfect, man, we'd already be in heaven." He rubbed his hands together, hard, and James waited for sparks to fly from them. "We've been put here to learn through this journey. And the pages of our stories are still being written."

ame.*

"You sound like Antonia," James said.

Dale nodded. "Then she's a smart woman."

She was. She was smart and she was beautiful in her soul. And she was slipping away.

He didn't try to keep the anxiety out of his voice. "But what if it's too late to ask?"

The seldom-used smile returned to Dale's face. "It's never too late. Look at us two unlikely characters up here . . ."

He stood up and extended his arms until they could have out-spanned an eagle. He inhaled, deep and strong. "This, my friend, is grace."

James knew the look on his own face was helpless, if not desperate. The hope of grasping even a piece of what Dale was living was so out of reach.

But something was new: the almost blinding realization that he wanted it.

Dale turned to him, hands parked in his pockets. "A man's legacy isn't measured by the stuff he *had*. It's measured by the people he *helped* . . . and then the people *they* helped . . . and the ripples continue. I might not be the wave . . ." He leaned down and picked up another bit of rock. "But maybe I can be the pebble that starts it. You know?"

James did. It snuffed out the flashes and dulled the knife-thrusts and he could at least say, "I like that."

Dale put his foot on the rock. "What do you want them to say when you're gone?"

James rubbed his arm with his opposite hand, as if that would take the chill from the wind. "How do you *know*? I want to . . . I want to get it, but how are you so sure about all this?"

Dale let out a grunt that could have been a laugh. "I'm not. But I believe with all my heart that there is something bigger than me, and that it's profoundly loving . . . and that it gives me purpose."

He looked down at James, who could only look silently back.

"With everything Antonia's been through, do you think she still believes?"

James didn't even have to think about it. "I know she does."

"Well, that's faith. And it's a good place to start." Dale pulled his foot from the rock and pointed a pistol finger at the scene below. "So what do you say we move forward and see what happens?"

James stood up and followed him, once more, to the waiting car.

# 30

EVEN WITH HER LIMITED ENGLISH Antonia knew that almost every word Garo had spit since they peeled away from the house was something profane. He swore about everything.

Having to take this new-smelling black car out of the garage.

The stream of traffic coming down from the neighborhood.

The worse clog of it on these downtown streets.

The people surging all around them from the clanging casinos and the darkened bars and stepping out in front of them.

Not that the car was moving faster than a turtle could crawl. And wherever it was they were going, Garo wanted to be there already. The veins in his neck were as big as ropes, and his head was a burning red all the way to the roots of his hair.

All of it—his anger and his cussing and his reckless way of getting right on the bumper of the car ahead of them, until Antonia could see the stubble on the backs of people's necks—it would have set the very tips of her nerves on end anyway.

But far worse than that was her fear for Maria, a fear that made her palms sweat as she clenched them together in her lap. Garo had practically carried Antonia from the house. Truly, her feet did not touch the ground from the moment he whisked her out the front door until he deposited her into the leather front seat like a sack of the week's earnings.

She begged him, over and over, to bring Maria too—or to at least tell her where her sister was now. He never answered. Never said a word as he lurched and jerked the car through the throng of people and, to her small relief, past the heinous hotel where this nightmare had taken its first horrible turn.

They were now leaving the scene of some kind of celebration and entering a long, straight street where the lights were dimmer and the people on the sidewalks fewer and shabbier. They clearly had nothing to celebrate.

She wanted to cry out to every one of them that she knew how they felt. That she too was running out of hope. But unlike the woman pushing a shopping cart piled with old clothes down the shadowy street, Antonia wasn't familiar with this feeling, wasn't resigned to it the way those sloping shoulders were. It was new and frightening and it grasped at her and tried to pull her under. If it did, she would drown in its bottomless waters. And then what would happen to Maria?

No. *Nonononono.* She had to pray. She had to plead . . . beg God, because He was the only hope she had. She couldn't stop now, or it was over for both her sister and her.

Her hand went automatically to her chest and landed on nothing but her now-clammy skin. She'd tried to search for her cross at the house when she was getting her things together but there was too much confusion, and then Garo had grabbed her and flung her from the bedroom. So now she pressed her hand near her heart and closed her eyes. All she could think to implore God silently was, *Please. Maria. Please.*

And *James.*

Because he was her only human hope. She had to believe he was telling her the truth, that he would come back for them both. She saw it in his eyes, so full of her sorrow and his. How he would find her down this sordid road, she had no idea. She could only pray that God did.

The car stopped. Antonia kept her eyes closed until Garo braced his hand around the back of her neck and turned her head toward him. The small bit of peace she'd just felt was snatched away.

"Your little sister is no longer your responsibility," he said, his eyes shining a rancid yellow. "It is mine, and I'm taking care of it."

"Please just tell me where she is," Antonia said.

Bad mistake. Garo jerked her face up to his and spoke into her mouth. The awful brushing of his lips on hers shuddered through her.

"Ask me again and I will make sure you never see her again. Does *that* sink in, my little imbecile? Or do you need it from the back of my hand?"

Antonia could neither nod nor shake her head. She could only get out, "I understand."

He let her go with everything but his eyes. There was no looking away.

"You are hot, *chiquita*. But I don't know if you're worth all the trouble. We're about to find out." He opened the door on his side. "Wait until I come around and get you out. You do not make a move unless I tell you."

Garo slid out and slammed the door behind him. Antonia watched him through the windshield and saw where they were.

She pressed back a sob of horror with her hand.

---

"This is called the Fourth Street corridor," Dale said. He gave James a sideways look across the front seat. "They've cleaned it up a lot over the past couple of years."

"You're kidding," James said.

"Nope."

James would hate to see what it looked like before. Actually, as they cruised down the block, he hated it enough now. A bar that looked like a black hole. A club with a chasing-lights sign in the shape of a naked female. One or two almost-nude human ones trailing listlessly along the sidewalk. They weren't Antonia, but they gave him an idea.

"Can you pull over?" he said.

"For what?"

"I just need some air. I'll meet you at the house."

Dale eased the Plymouth up to the curb in front of the club. "It's a long walk," he said over the blare of dead music.

"I could use it," James said.

Dale didn't buy it. That was clear from his sad almost-smile. But he got it, because he didn't ask any more questions.

"I gotta swing by my hotel," he said. "If you need anything, holler, okay?"

James nodded and got out of the car. Dale hesitated only a moment before he pulled away. For another moment James wanted to call him back. As long as Dale was there, some positive possibility existed. The point in putting one foot in front of the other was clear. In this instant, standing in front of a strip club with a large hairy bouncer scrutinizing him from the door, his inner fight flagged.

Until a cigarette-alto said, "Hey, cutie. What are you up to tonight?"

James looked into the semi-focused eyes of a woman with worn-out leather skin and a floppy smile half full of meth-blackened teeth. He could blink and she would be Antonia. It was a thought that burned through his muscles and set his head straight. He had a better chance of finding her on foot, and this was the place to start.

He put his hand in his pocket. The woman balked until she saw him draw out his phone. It wasn't a badge, and that was all that seemed to matter to her.

"I already have somebody in mind," James said. He turned Antonia's picture to face her. "You seen her around?"

She was way too practiced to let her disappointment show, but her face got even harder as she shook her head. She ambled on down the sidewalk, trying to swing her bony hips and stumbling until she could get her balance again.

By then the bouncer was looking more interested than James was comfortable with. The guy's hand ran up and down the side of his jacket, but James approached him anyway, holding the phone out in front of him.

"Have you seen this girl?" he said.

"You a cop?" The bouncer's voice was like wet cement.

"No, man. Just looking for somebody."

He shook his head. "No. Haven't seen her. Unfortunately."

James backed away and took the urge to deck the dude with him. If he was going to do this, he was going to have to call up every ounce of self-control he had. He'd better find Antonia soon, though, because that reservoir was pretty low.

He continued down the block, ducked his head into a bar and out again, and passed two apparent hookers who looked through him, apparently done for the night. He could have shown them the picture, but he wasn't sure they would have seen it.

At the corner, a girl so thin she looked anorexic stood under the sputtering fluorescent street light. Her dress was microscopic, her heels way too high. Her hands shook as she struggled to light a cigarette.

"Can I help?" James said.

Her eyes sparked interest, but that flame went out. He was getting the sense that he wasn't the corridor's usual clientele. Still, she nodded and let him take the Bic lighter. It was almost empty, but he managed to get the tip of her Marlboro glowing. She inhaled deeply and let out a grateful stream of smoke through her nose. Heading now toward relief, she gave him another look.

James flipped out the phone before she had a chance to make a proposition. "Have you seen this girl?" he said.

She peered closely, first at the picture, and then at him, through long bangs the color of cheap wine. "How much is it worth to you?" she said.

"Depends whether you've seen her."

She gave an unattractive grunt. "I haven't."

James mumbled a thanks and crossed to the other side of Fourth. Two girls were just emerging from a seedy-looking bar. They stopped when they saw him and whispered feverishly to each other. The taller of the two must have won the debate because she stepped toward him when he reached them, protruding her booty and her bosom simultaneously. Neither was well covered.

"Looking for a—"

"I'm looking for her." James held up the phone high enough for both of them to see.

The tall girl curled a full, plum-colored lip and shook her head.

"She your girlfriend?" the other one said.

Her voice was surprisingly smooth, or at least she didn't sound like she'd been smoking since the womb. She brushed back a bleached-dry panel of hair and beckoned with her fingers for James to bring the phone closer.

When he did, she tapped the screen with a purple talon. "We just saw her, about twenty minutes ago."

The other one curled her lip again. "*I* didn't."

"I did. Down there." She pointed the claw. "You saw her too—big stud taking her into that Chinese massage place. Right down there."

"Okay, maybe—"

"Thank you," James said. "Thank you so much—you have no idea—"

"No, I don't," said Lip Curl.

"It's okay. Here . . ." James fumbled in his pocket and pulled out two twenties that he tossed in their direction as he took off where Talon Girl had pointed.

"Come back if she doesn't work out, honey," she called after him.

Her words were drummed out by the pounding in his ears as he ran down the sidewalk, eyes scanning the signs for a Chinese massage parlor. Dale would have called that a God shot. James hoped his next one was a bouncer who didn't look like a young Arnold Schwa—

He froze in mid jog. A hulking figure strode from a door under a sign that read Chinese Massage and beeped open the door of a black Lincoln Town Car. James backed into the shadow of a torn, flapping awning.

It was Garo. Talking into his cell phone as he passed within three feet of James.

"Dropped the *señorita* off," he said. "Come on over with a couple of the others—"

The rest disappeared on the wind as Garo opened the car door, got in, and took off. James didn't need to hear it anyway. As soon as the Lincoln rounded the next corner, he pulled away from the wall and peered into the large window in the front of the building Garo had just left.

Through sheer curtains he saw a young Asian woman at a red-lacquered counter. The sign next to her kimono sleeve read Massage Menu.

This was no God shot. This was a disaster.

James felt for the gun in his waistband, but it wasn't there. He cursed himself for leaving it in Dale's car, but whatever. He had to go for it. This was as close as he'd gotten to Antonia since the sleazy motel, and this time he wasn't leaving without her.

He pushed open the door, which set off a gong that made him jump in his skin. On second thought, it was probably better that he didn't have the gun.

The place was surprisingly well lit and decorated in Sexy Chinese, if there was such a thing. The walls were red, black, and shiny, and cheaply brocaded curtains hung seductively over doorways.

The girl behind the counter, who was actually Asian and not just playing the part, leaned toward him revealing almost all of her breasts. He was sure kimonos weren't supposed to fit like that, even on Geisha girls. Or were they Japanese?

He was starting to feel giddy and light-headed, maybe the result of the heavy cloud of incense that hovered in the air. He breathed through his mouth and tried to get his wits back.

"Massage?" the girl said, as if this was at least the second time she'd addressed him.

James hurried to the counter and turned Antonia's picture for her to see.

"Is she here?" he said. "What I mean is, is she available?"

A pair of tweezed eyebrows rose on her forehead. "You want her?"

"Yes. Yes, I want her. Only her."

Could he sound any more desperate? Good way to get himself thrown out of here.

But the eyebrows lowered and the girl held up a finger. "One hour. Very expensive."

"Fine," James said. "What room is she in?"

"You must pay first," she said.

He flattened his hand on the counter. She pulled in her chin.

"What *room*?" James said.

She put her own icy hand on top of his. "You tell me what kind of massage—"

James yanked his hand away and dove for an ornate metal gate that separated him from the hallway. He turned sideways and rammed it open. Beyond him stretched two rows of more draped doorways. There must have been twenty.

The girl jumped in front of him and planted her hands on his chest. "You can't be back here!"

James grabbed her wrists and set her aside. Whoever she was going to call for at this point wasn't going to be that easy to remove. He had to move fast.

"Antonia!" His voice echoed down the hall. "Antonia!"

Three doors down a drape was pulled aside. James lunged for

it even before a head appeared. Hair hung over one side of her face, and the one visible eye was glazed and half focused, but it was Antonia, crying, "James!"

He took the hall in two long steps and reached for her, but she was jerked back behind the curtain by an unseen hand. The voice was not unheard.

"We're not done!"

James ripped the drapes apart, saw Antonia with a white lace dress pulled down to expose her shoulder, and lost his mind.

A naked sag-bellied middle-aged man had her out to the side by the hair and dangled her like a shrunken head as he screamed again, "Get out! We're not done!"

"Yeah, you are!"

James drew back his fist and landed it square in the jackal's face. The man let go of Antonia and staggered backward, crashing into a table and dumping over a cluster of bottles. He groaned on the floor in an ooze of oil and blood.

"Come on!" James said to Antonia and grabbed her hand.

She didn't resist as he pulled her down the hall at a dead run, women and men screaming around them. Ahead a door was flung open, and C. J.'s all-too-familiar scrawny figure came toward them, shrieking at a pitch that put the rest of them to shame.

James looked around wildly and spotted an unlit Exit sign to their left. Still towing Antonia with a tight hand, he ducked behind yet another curtain and almost immediately collided with a large metal door.

He tried the handle but it didn't release. He could hear C. J.'s voice heading in the other direction but it wouldn't take him long to figure out where they'd gone—even as stupid as he was.

James rammed himself into the door. It didn't give. Behind him, Antonia was softly moaning.

"Hang on," he said.

Desperation and adrenaline pumping up his arm, he came down on the handle again and the door swung open into the night. Antonia swayed, but James took a firmer hold on her hand and scanned the alley they'd stepped into.

Behind him the door banged open and C. J. was silhouetted in the frame, aiming a pistol straight into the thousand-watt lightbulb behind them. James had to take advantage of his momentary blindness. Pushing Antonia out of the way, he swung around, elbow out, and smashed C. J. square in the face. He felt his nose break, but although C. J. dropped the gun, he still struggled to get to his feet, both hands trying to fend off the fountain of blood that poured through his fingers.

"Really?" James said. "Are you that stupid?"

He brought up a knee and got him in the groin. When C. J. hit the ground squalling, James kicked him soundly in the head.

"Shut up," he said.

C. J. lay still and crumpled, blood still pooling. James picked up the gun and threw it six feet away into a dumpster. It was the first time he was ever grateful for his prison experience.

"James?"

James turned in time to see Antonia's eyes roll up into her head. He scooped her up just as she wilted.

"I gotcha," he said, though the way her head was lolling back he knew she couldn't hear him, or anything.

He was grateful for that as he ran down the alley with her in his arms.

# 31

ANTONIA DIDN'T OPEN HER EYES until James had half run, half dragged himself five blocks from the alley and across a bridge over the trickling Truckee River. He was glad when she stirred because even as featherlight as she was, his arm muscles were starting to shake. Not only that, but more than one car had slowed down as it passed, its driver and passengers swiveling their heads toward him with concerned, if not suspicious, looks on their faces.

So when Antonia brought up her head and studied his face, he moved to a bench and sat her up. She immediately began to slide toward the sidewalk and he had to prop her against his shoulder and hold her there.

It wasn't a bad feeling at all, or it wouldn't have been if he didn't have to scan the crowd for signs of Garo. C. J. wouldn't be looking for him anytime soon, but he'd obviously been in touch with his boss, who wasn't going to let this one go without a full-on manhunt.

Fortunately, a concert was happening in the park on the other side of the river—looked and sounded like a revived '70s rock group, with "revived" being a stretch—so people clotted the streets and walkways and shielded Antonia and him from easy view. But he could only linger long enough to rest his arms and then he had to get her out of sight.

He could see the Silver Miner's Inn from there, but not the back parking lot where Dale parked his truck. Besides, that would be the first place they'd look. His earlier plan to walk back to Dale's place was a bust now.

He pulled out his cell phone, but Antonia groped for his hand and leaned her head back to look up at him.

"Hey," he said. "You okay?"

"You came," she said.

"I did."

A sloppy smile sprawled across the lower half of her face. Whatever they gave her, they'd been pretty heavy-handed with it. That, plus the fact that she probably didn't even drink, much less do drugs. Even as she gazed at him her eyes drifted closed. How the heck was he going to get her—

"We have to find Maria," she said. The words slurred, but they were unmistakable.

"We're going to," James said. "I promise you."

"O-kay . . ." Another slack smile. "We-e-e will . . ."

Under any other circumstances he would have let out a major guffaw. As it was, he couldn't keep from grinning. She was adorable even when she was stoned.

"Come on," he said. "We need to get moving."

She nodded and promptly checked out again. He grabbed her before she could slither off the bench and gathered her back into his arms. With the band rocking on and the partying crowd swirling and the nostalgic cars gunning their engines, he had a chance at staying concealed until he could decide what to do.

So he carried Antonia through the mob, ignoring the judgmental looks and the comments like "Don't you hate it when your chick can't hold her liquor?" He weaved and bobbed until they were headed south on what the sign said was Arlington Avenue.

The crowd thinned and the neighborhood improved, which made James stand out like the proverbial sore thumb. He took several side streets, stopping to set Antonia on her feet when she tried to rally and holding her up as they passed older homes converted to law offices and yoga studios.

When a patrol car approached ahead, James steered Antonia under some kind of ornamental tree and put his arms around her. He nuzzled her neck until it passed and turned the next corner.

She giggled.

Even with the drugs it was a pure sound, like a silver bell that rang lightly and drifted away on the night air. He loosened his hold on her, and her knees buckled.

"Up ya go," he said and hoisted her back into his arms.

She let her head fall into his chest, and then she lifted her face to his. "You are bleeding, James."

"It's okay—"

"But you are still handsome. Did you know that you are very handsome?"

James let himself grin. "I'm going to remind you that you said that later."

"O-kay," she said and zonked out face-first into his collarbone.

He wasn't sure how long he carried her after that, staying on the back streets and pretending to talk to her when the occasional car went by. The sky was beginning to gray above the mountains when he finally decided it might be safe to return to the main road and hail a cab. Dale's place was the only logical choice—actually, the only choice. And he had to take it now, before there was no more darkness to hide in.

Back on Virginia Street he crossed to the other side and set

Antonia on her feet long enough to get a taxi to respond to his arm wave and whistle. He managed to open the door, but he had to lift her inside and dump her on the back seat.

"She's had a little too much to drink," he told the driver.

As James climbed in beside her, he wished a hangover was the only thing she'd have to face today.

The cabbie was a Middle Easterner who either didn't speak English or wasn't interested in a conversation with a guy who had to carry his drunk girlfriend home from a party. James was just glad he could follow the directions he gave him and cooperated when James had him drop them off at the bottom of the hill. It wasn't easy lugging Antonia up the incline, but it was better not to leave a trail. Just in case.

When they rounded the bend, Antonia actually snoring with her pretty mouth hanging open, the Barracuda was there, but not Dale's truck. Anxiety started to stir again.

He took the steps in a couple of strides and pushed open the door. Dale wasn't in the main room. After James rolled Antonia onto the couch and snapped on the pole lamp, he tapped on the bedroom door and got no answer. Even as he cracked it open to peer inside, he had the queasy sense Dale wasn't there either.

Something must have come up at the hotel. But he'd left James hours ago.

Okay. Not the time to start freaking out. James spread a bulky knitted afghan from the back of the couch over Antonia and stepped out onto the porch with his cell phone. He probably should have called him earlier, but he hadn't exactly had a free hand. And the less involved he got Dale, the better he felt. Though he did just bring this wanted girl right into the guy's house.

Stop. Just stop.

He thumbed in Dale's number and caught his breath when he picked up on the first ring.

"¿*Qué pasa*, Romeo?"

It was Garo, sounding smug. Cool. In control.

James squeezed the phone. "Where's Dale?"

"You have my girl."

"She's not your girl." The bile was rising. James fought to keep it down, but it burned his throat.

Garo sniffed. "*Amigo*, I don't agree with you. And regardless, I have the old man. And I have her sister. Now, I won't hurt the sister. Not yet. And the old man . . . I really haven't decided yet, but it's up to you."

James grabbed at the porch railing. "I will—"

"Yes, you will. Follow directions and maybe everyone walks home."

He spoke as if he were getting a card game together. James had to swallow—hard—to keep from kicking through the railing.

"I'll take your silence as a yes," Garo said.

"What do you want?" *That* sounded like a yes, but what else was he going to do?

"You're not good at this." Garo gave a hard, short laugh. "I'll make it easy, then." He shifted into a patronizing tone. "You give me the girl and I'll give you the old man."

"And Maria?"

"Oh, she stays with me, but . . . she remains untouched as long as Antonia is returned to me. They're a pair, you see—they are family and you don't separate family."

James wanted to tear the phone apart, but he said, "Where do you want to meet?"

"First—don't try to be a hero, James, or I will kill them both. And I will make you watch."

Though his voice was still even and low, James had no doubt that he would. "Where?" he said again.

"Rainbow Ridge Park. Northwest Reno. Take Mae Anne Avenue. You know it?"

"Yes."

"Left on Simons, left on Rainbow Ridge Road."

James repeated it and hoped it took hold in his brain in between the thoughts of putting his hands around this guy's throat and the visions of Maria and Dale, tied up in some hellhole.

"Eleven a.m.," Garo said. "Be there—or they die."

The phone went dead. But James stood with it jammed against his ear until a voice behind him whispered, "James?"

Antonia stood in the doorway, wrapped in the afghan, sobered and stricken. "Tell me," she said.

---

Maria pretended to be asleep. There was no way she could be for real. Not wrapped in a blanket that smelled like manure and scratched her skin. Not lying on the concrete floor of a cold metal warehouse that reeked worse than the blanket. Not with stark fear shivering through her.

But she pretended anyway, eyes open only in slits so she could watch The Man. Not Garo. Him she hated the sight of. And not C. J., who was even uglier now, with half his face covered in dried blood and his left eye swollen shut and oozing. That hadn't stopped him from beating The Man she was watching— beating him until he should maybe be in a coma.

But he was even more wide-awake than she was. Even duct-taped to a chair with his bearded face swelling like C. J.'s. Although he could never be as grotesque. His eyes were steady like he wasn't afraid at all. He never took them off of Garo.

"It's a charade—this thing you two are doing," Garo said to him. "You know this?"

Maria didn't know the word *charade*, but it was obvious from the sneer on Garo's face that he thought it was a joke. The Man didn't.

"You're a murderer," he said.

His voice was low and steady like his eyes, but it made Maria startle. She had to remember to keep still.

Garo actually laughed, although it didn't sound like any laugh Maria had ever heard. It was hard. And cold.

"I've not murdered anybody yet," he said.

The Man gave a soft grunt. "There is no difference between a murderer and somebody who steals a girl's innocence and kills her soul."

Maria stifled a yes. She squeezed her eyes shut and listened harder.

"Wow," Garo said. "I never thought of that before. That's very deep."

Even without seeing him Maria knew that was a lie.

"Does this help you?" Garo said. "You go through all this—all this trouble for some girl you don't even know?"

"No," The Man said. "It's for my daughter."

Maria opened her eyes to see Garo pull another folding chair close to The Man and sit his large self at its edge. "I don't know what you're talking about, man."

The Man's eyes never wavered. "You took my daughter. Ten years ago."

"My friend, I hate to disappoint you, but ten years ago I was still in high school—"

"You're all the same man. Different names, different faces, but always the same." The Man moved his taped-down shoulders like he wanted to use his arms to talk. "My daughter ran away for a man like you. Swallowed your drugs. Believed your lies. She thought she was in love and you turned her into property."

Garo gave him a sick smile. "And where is your little girl now?"

It wasn't a question really. Maria could tell he knew the answer. But The Man told him anyway.

"She didn't make it to her eighteenth birthday."

"Look, man, this thing is old. Old, old, old. Old Testament old."

He was talking about the Bible? Antonia would be having a fit.

Garo shrugged. "But I'm sure it was just business, old man. Nothing personal."

Maria had to suffocate another cry. As it was, tears were wetting her cheeks. She hoped people cried in their sleep. Not that anyone was looking at her. She'd heard Garo on the phone. He wanted Antonia. James had her and he wanted her, and she, Maria, was the bait. Just like The Man said. She was property.

"You think you're special?" he was saying to Garo. "Do you know what you are? You are the hollowed-out shell that's left after a snake sheds its skin." Maria could hear him breathe in through his nose. He looked at Garo so hard Maria was sure he would drill a hole into his forehead. And then he said, in the lowest, strongest voice yet, "You know there's hope? That's New Testament."

Garo stood up, knocking the chair over. He kicked it out of the way and stalked over to C. J., who was still wiping his bloody knuckles with a rag like he was proud of them.

Maria looked back at The Man. He had his eyes closed, but his lips, puffed up from being hit, moved like he was saying something. She'd seen Antonia do that, especially since they left home and there was so much more to pray about.

Maybe it was time for her to do that too.

---

James nodded Antonia back into the cabin and made her sit on the couch. He positioned himself on the foot locker that served as a coffee table and faced her.

"Look—"

"I heard his voice. Tell me what he said. Please."

He owed her that. He'd put her and her sister through more than they would have had to experience if he hadn't tried to interfere and turned it into a hot mess. He at least owed her the truth.

So he related Garo's instructions to her. He tried to soften the threat to Maria but she knew. She grabbed his hands with both of hers and set her gaze right into his.

"You must do this. Then my sister, she will be alive. Maria will not die."

"I can't just turn you over to him."

"Yes. You can."

James stood up and held his head as he moved from the foot locker to the bedroom door and back. She was right. He did have to follow Garo's instructions or he'd kill both Maria and

Dale without a second thought. But there had to be a way to go there—go to that park—and come away with all three of them. He glanced at the greasy clock over the stove. He had six hours to think of something.

"Okay," he said and turned to Antonia.

She sat at the edge of the couch, head bent, eyes closed, mouth moving silently. She was praying. Of course she was praying.

And Dale was probably doing the same. If he was conscious. Or even if he wasn't—it seemed to come that naturally to him.

James sat next to her and stayed still for what seemed like hours, until Antonia curled up with her head on his lap and slept. James closed his eyes, but not to sleep. That wasn't happening. Just to listen.

At 9:00 a.m., with only a few hours left, he sensed a whisper. And it didn't come from Antonia.

# 32

ANTONIA HAD NEVER SEEN a more stunning park. From where she and James were stopped just above it, bright grass sloped down and curved around carefully planted pine and fruit trees to a playground that must be pure magic for children. The primary colors on the slide and swings and climbing jungles would have made *her* want to run to them and play.

On any other day.

Any other day like this would have been ideal. A blinding blue sky, just like the one on the morning James took them up to the mountain to look down at what they thought would be their new home. White, cottony clouds just right for imagining shapes. Sunlight sparkling on the sand and gleaming off the toy trucks and bulldozers. It was perfect.

Too perfect.

Because the park was alive with mothers pushing pink babies in strollers and nannies sitting on benches with iPads and children romping and climbing and squealing. *Children.*

James let his fist drop to the steering wheel. "That jackal."

"This he did with the purpose," Antonia said.

"Yes, he did," James said.

Then he was quiet again, the way he'd been ever since they left his friend's cabin. She wanted to ask him about this man who had risked his life for her and Maria. But he was so sharply focused she'd kept silent and busied herself with taking a shower and washing her hair and nibbling at the edges of the jellied toast he made for her. Now, just sitting here with nothing more to do, the fears lapped at her mind like an encroaching fire. She tried not to let them burn away the prayers.

"There they are."

Antonia followed his gaze to the swing set placed slightly apart from the climbing area—and gasped. James put his hand on her arm, but there was no need. She was paralyzed at the sight of Maria, sitting on a swing with her hands tightened around its chains. Antonia couldn't see that her knuckles were drained of all color, but she knew they were. And she knew her sister's eyes were frightened and darting like pinballs, looking for her. And amid all of it, Maria squeezed her knees together in an attempt to make up for the tiny tight skirt—an attempt at modesty that went through Antonia like pain.

"Just stay quiet," James whispered.

"She is alone?"

"No. Garo's over there, behind that bench. You can't see him from where you are because of that pole."

Almost as if Garo had heard him he moved into her view, holding his cell phone to his ear with one hand while the other was parked in his pants pocket, surely where he carried his gun. He wore sunglasses and a buttoned shirt that pulled across his chest and strained at his arms—and he looked about as much like a father taking his kids to the playground as she did. Was no one seeing this? That there was a predator standing arrogantly in the midst of their precious children?

The man on the bench looked only a little less suspicious. She

PRICELESS

could see that his face was battered and bloated, even from here, and he held his torso and thighs in a stiff L, as if moving would be unbearable.

"Your friend?" Antonia whispered.

James nodded, his mouth grim. "That's Dale."

Her heart plummeted and took her hopes down with it. As strong as he might be on a normal day, he was too beaten up to be of any help, if James did have a plan. He wasn't telling her. Probably because he knew she would refuse to go along with it.

As she watched, a dark-haired girl of about five ran in Garo's direction on chubby legs, double ponytails flapping at the sides of her very-round head. She was chasing a multicolored ball as it rolled from the grass into the sandy area, straight toward Garo's legs. Antonia clasped her hand around James's arm.

The ball bounced against the shoe Antonia knew had been polished by one of the girls, who would have licked it if he'd told her to. She held her breath to keep from crying, "No!" as he looked down at it, cell phone still stuck to his ear. The little girl stopped and stared up at him. And up. And up. Until she went as still as a cornered mouse.

Antonia couldn't see the full expression on Garo's face, though she imagined a rehearsed kind smile that never made it to his eyes as he squatted beside the little one and scooped up the ball. She thrust both pudgy arms behind her back, but Garo tilted his head and held the toy out to her like an indulgent father. Slowly she loosened her arms and stretched them out to him. His mouth opened in a cartoon laugh and he placed the ball right into her small hands. When she skipped off, he watched until she ran into the arms of a woman with the same round head. They turned away. The practiced grin was erased. The phone went back to Garo's ear.

"He is smart at this thing," Antonia said.

"He thinks he is." James looked at her, his eyes suddenly soft, drooping at their corners. "It's time," he said. "But I have something for you first."

He slid his hand into the pocket of his jeans and pulled it out, fist closed. He held it over her hand until she turned her palm up. When he released his fingers, something warm and light fell against her skin. Her gold cross winked up at her.

"How . . . ?" was all she could say.

"The chain was broken," James said, "but I think I fixed it. Here . . ."

He took it from her and put it around her neck. She could feel his fingers shake as he fumbled with the clasp.

Her hand went to the cross at once and she pressed it there, eyes closed, prayers filling her head anew. When she looked back at James he was watching her.

"You are a changed man, James," she said. "Thank you for trying to help us."

He nodded. So sadly.

"Look," he said. "I'm not sure how this is going to play out, and if things go south, I want you to know—"

"James." Antonia leaned toward him. "This is how it must be."

She watched his eyes, watched for wavering. There was none.

"There may not be another chance for me to say this," he said. His eyes were wet. "But I think—"

"James," she said again. "I know."

Because she couldn't let him tell her. Not when they would never see each other again.

Antonia left the car first. Only Maria, terrified as no child should be on that swing, kept her walking down the hill, forced her to keep going even after James caught up with her and put a steady hand on her elbow and made her want it to stay there forever.

"Hey," he said, lips close to her ear. "No matter what happens, please trust me. Okay?"

She took her eyes from Maria only long enough to look up at him and see the will etched into his face. "I do," she said.

Because what she'd said to him was true. This was a different James from the one who opened the door of that truck and found them steeping in their own filth. Then he seemed to be everywhere at once. Right now he had a direction. And she would follow it.

A cry jerked her head back toward the swings. Maria had let go of the chains and was straining toward her—held back by Garo's hands on her arms from behind. Antonia only had to run a few steps to hear him say, "It's okay, sweetheart. You stay close to daddy."

Right. She had to make this look normal, or something bad was going to happen. Already from the corner of her eye she could see a mother place a protective hand on her little boy's back before she returned to guiding him up the ladder to the slide.

So Antonia slowed down and stopped a few feet from her sister. She could feel James breathing as he stepped beside her. When she glanced up at him, he was watching Dale, whose eyes went straight to him with that same intense look James had been wearing all morning. Something passed between them. And then it was gone.

James turned to Garo, who waited with Maria pressed against him. She looked only at Antonia, pleading with her eyes.

"A playground? Really?" James said, voice low.

Garo turned on the ridiculous smile. "It's a beautiful day for this, no?"

James shook his head. Almost as if he were disappointed. Something was . . . Antonia began to stiffen.

"I'm embarrassed for us," James said, too loudly.

His hand went under his T-shirt, to his waistband. It came out with a gun.

"Look at us!" he said, screaming now and waving the pistol first above his head and then straight at Garo. And Maria.

Antonia's heart raced up her throat. James continued to scream.

"Here we are, carrying guns, holding hostages! I'm embarrassed for us, Garo!"

Around them children cried and footsteps beat the ground. Antonia whirled in every direction, watching mothers grab their little ones with one hand while thumbing their phones with the other. All of them. Cell phones.

*Please, please, please, God, let them be calling the police.*

"Aren't you embarrassed, Garo!" James's throat was raspy but it carried. "Aren't you?"

Garo looked far from embarrassed. He looked stunned and then jammed his hand into his pocket and pulled out his own gun, bigger than the one James now pointed at him. He shoved it against Maria's temple.

Antonia slapped both hands to her mouth. No. *Nonononono!*

"Maybe we go crazy here?" Garo said. "Maybe we shoot everybody?"

His hand gripped the gun handle until the veins in his arm distended. And with his other arm across her chest he still held Maria, who was beyond crying, beyond screaming. Just like Antonia.

"No," James said. Shouted. "We'll take turns. You kill mine

and I'll kill yours. Round and round we go 'cause this doesn't end here." He waggled the gun between them. "We're both replaceable. The girls, they're replaceable. We're all replaceable."

"*Sí*. So, *amigo*—put down the gun. Or I will start with this one." He moved forward with Maria, gun still at her brain. "Watch this one be replaced. One. Two—"

Antonia screamed.

"Wait, wait, wait," James said.

"Put your gun down, man."

"Okay. Here you go."

James set the gun on the ground and pointed to his own forehead. "Right here. Right here."

"*Sí.*"

Garo let go of Maria and aimed the gun at James's head. "Antonia!" he said, pointing in front of him with his other hand. "*Aquí!*"

But she didn't move. Because with a burst of power Dale came off the bench and hurled himself into Garo's side. Antonia froze in horror as they went to the ground in a tangle of arms and fists and curses, both of them clawing for the gun still clutched in Garo's hand.

An iron arm came around Antonia and pulled her back just as the men rolled as one to her feet. Maria was there, clamped to her and convulsing with hard sobs.

James pushed Antonia farther from the fray, Maria still attached to her. "Go!" he shouted.

But his cry was lost in a shot that cracked the air. And made everything stop again.

# 33

JAMES COULDN'T SEE THE GUN. It was somewhere underneath Dale and Garo, who had both stopped moving. Dale was on top, and James willed him to roll away and expose Garo bleeding out on the grass.

But it was Garo who came to life and shoved Dale off of him. Dale fell over, arms flopping to his sides. A red pool was forming in his open chest, stark against his already ashen face. His eyes stared at the sky. Intense even in death.

James heard himself scream, "No!" though the word disappeared in the urgent wail of approaching sirens. There was no way to know whether it was the frantic phoning of the mothers who had now scattered with their children that brought the police, or the 911 call he'd made before leaving the phone on his dashboard. It didn't matter. They weren't going to get here soon enough.

Because Garo stood facing him, breathing hard and slowly raising the gun that had just killed Dale.

James rushed him, head ducked in a tackle that took them both down. He jammed Garo's outstretched firing arm to the ground and held it there with one hand. He used the other to pound his face. Again. Again. Over and over as rage coursed through his body. For Dale. For Antonia. For Maria. For the curly blonde and the rest of them. And for Emerson. Most of all for Emerson.

Garo was every bit as strong as he looked and too full of evil to flinch. James banged Garo's gun hand on the ground until the pistol came loose. He quickly grabbed it and jammed the barrel against Garo's forehead. He pressed his other forearm to his throat for good measure.

Although he didn't struggle, Garo's eyes stayed alive and gleaming.

"Did Antonia tell you about our special night together?" he said, wheezing. "Did she tell you about how we made love?"

James began a slow squeeze on the trigger.

"Police! Drop the weapon!" a male voice commanded.

But it was another voice that stopped him. Antonia crying, "James, no!"

But it stopped him only for a moment. Dale was beside him, dead. Antonia and Maria were behind him, hysterical and changed forever. If he let go of Garo, this might never end, just as he said. And it had to. Didn't it? It had to.

"Drop the weapon or we *will* shoot!" the cop yelled.

"Go ahead," Garo said. Barely conscious but still in control. "Pull the trigger."

*And then you'll be just like him.*

The thought came as a whisper above the shouting and the sobbing and the throbbing in his own head. Louder and stronger. James tossed the gun to the side and put his hands up.

Other hands were on him, flattening him to his back on the grass. With guns trained on him, James turned his head and looked at Dale's lifeless body, blood running out of his chest. It could have been him, James thought, as he began to sob. It could have been any of them or all of them. But it was the one man who didn't have to be here, fighting this fight.

*But you are here.*

James listened, still crying into the ground. Then he put his wrists together and raised them to receive the handcuffs.

---

A woman in uniform wrapped a blanket around Maria as she sat in the back of the ambulance. People shined flashlights in her eyes and put a squeezing cuff around her arm eight times and felt every limb the way her mother did when she fell off the shed roof that time. Her body felt numb and her mind was almost on empty, and she kept reaching over to touch Antonia—her arm, her hand, her face—just to make sure she was really there, really alive.

Maybe you just automatically felt this way after you were rescued from tragedy. She wanted everything to be over, to forget it ever happened, to run away and never speak another word about this terrible experience. But first they must talk with Detective Jackson, the woman who was before them now, asking questions and taking notes.

It actually felt good to spill the whole thing, even in her halting English, about the truck that brought them here and Garo and C. J. and the house and the other girls . . . also James and the other man who had saved their lives. She made sure the detective understood that Dale and James were the good guys, and that Garo was the villain.

"Where is this man named C. J.?" the detective asked.

"You have not catch him?" Maria replied, obviously shaken.

The woman took hold of Maria's hand to calm her nerves and

spoke calmly but firmly to her. "You tell us where you last saw him and we'll get him."

"In a—storage—what is that called? Warehouse! It smell like—uh—" She turned to Antonia and said *fertilizer* in Spanish. Antonia translated. "It take—took—to three thousand to go there from the bad hotel."

The detective paused her pen over her pad. "Three thousand?"

"I count all the way," Maria said.

Detective Jackson actually looked impressed. She stepped away from the ambulance and was soon talking on her cell phone, jabbing the air with her finger.

Maria turned to find Antonia staring at her.

"What?" she said.

"Nothing," Antonia said. "Well . . . something."

Maria felt a stirring of anxiety in the pit of her stomach. "You're mad at me for telling her all that stuff."

Antonia's eyes opened wide, and she squeezed Maria's knee. "No! You were amazing, actually. You remembered more than I did when they questioned me. No, I was just thinking about all the things that happened to you when I wasn't with you." She looked down at the knot she'd made with her own blanket. "I'm sorry I couldn't protect you from . . . did Garo—"

"No, no, no . . . somehow I was protected from Garo, thank God."

Antonia's arms went around her. "Yes, we must thank God."

Maria got still. "And we have to pray for James. You saw them take him away in that police car, like he was a criminal. Do you think he's going to jail for helping us?"

"I don't know," Antonia said. "I hope not." As tears began glazing in her eyes, she turned her head.

"You love him, don't you?"

"Maria . . . I hardly know him."

"What else do you need to know? You know he's brave and honest and strong . . . and good looking."

Antonia laughed, a sort of garbled sound mixed with those tears. "All right," she said. "We'll pray for James."

She put her arms around Maria again.

They stayed that way, hugging each other and whispering prayers until someone tapped on the open ambulance door. It was Detective Jackson.

"The SWAT tcam arrested C. J. Weiss, right where you said he'd be."

Maria smiled at this good news, and then she quickly burst into tears.

"It's done," Antonia said, pulling Maria closer. "You can cry, because it's done."

# 34

THE STREET WAS DARK with rain and hopelessness. James pulled the hood of his black sweatshirt over his head, leaving just enough of an opening to see out of. The air wasn't that cold. Dank but not chilly. It was the chill on the inside that made him pull on the cords to tighten the cloth around his face. Despair always made him shiver.

He kept walking, but slowly, so he wouldn't cover too much ground before he saw what he was looking for. The street was empty, except for the bottles in the gutters and the raucous laughter from the bar the next block over. But he knew she was there. She was waiting too. He could feel her.

A vehicle turned the corner behind him, tires splashing in the puddle that always formed there the minute five drops of rain fell. It slowed down, and so did James. He stopped and pulled a cigarette and lighter from his sweatshirt pocket and pretended to light up. If the driver saw him, or cared that he was there, it didn't prevent him from slowly passing and inching toward the building on his left with the recessed doorway. As if the driver could feel her too.

James watched over the end of the unlit cigarette. The car, a gray generic rental, paused. And there she was.

Tiny. Practically emaciated, even for a girl just out of her teens. Her hip bones protruded beneath the slick skirt, and her collarbones created wells above the low-slung neckline. Earrings swung to her pointy shoulders, longer than the lifeless curtain of unnaturally dark hair that hung with them.

The driver's side window lowered. The girl leaned on the opening with both arms. James could only see her backside tilted up and the stiletto-heeled foot she kicked behind her. Probably saw that in an old movie and thought it was seductive.

Apparently the driver didn't think so. James couldn't hear what they were saying, except when she stepped back and said, "Twenty bucks ain't gonna get you a handshake!"

It was the usual. She wanted more than he thought she was worth. Which was fine with James. He wanted her more.

The car peeled out, fishtailing slightly before it righted itself and disappeared around the next corner. It also would have been fine if the driver had lost control and rammed that rental into the brick wall.

Although, no. Then there would have been cops. The girl would have run away. And he wouldn't be able to do what he wanted.

She was still standing there, all the sexual energy she'd pumped up for the john draining as James watched. The pointy shoulders moved toward each other. The head dangled as if she'd passed out where she stood. Her knees came together, forcing her toes to touch—the pigeon-toed stance she'd clearly had since she was a kid. Because she still was.

James stuck the cigarette back in his pocket and felt around to make sure the money was there. Just as she lifted her face and looked wearily in the other direction, he struck out across the street.

She turned her head, and her eyes sprang wide. He could see the alarm in them, so he held up his hand and said, "It's okay. It's okay."

She let her lids fall back to half-mast. They were so heavy with makeup James didn't see how she kept them open at all. As he got closer, he saw they were blue. Blue and fading.

"Whatcha lookin' for, handsome?" she said. In a voice that should have been leading a pep rally.

"You," James said.

She lowered her chin and curled her lip, just like every other hooker he'd ever met. "Do I know you?" she said.

"You're about to," he said.

He pulled out a hundred-dollar bill and held it up between two fingers. Her entire demeanor changed. She tossed her limp hair back and shook it and stretched a long, thin arm toward him, roped with bracelets from wrist to elbow. But it was her smile that made him swallow hard. Her teeth were perfectly even, in a way only expensive orthodontia could achieve. She was somebody's daughter. Somebody who cared.

She grabbed for the bill but James smothered it in his hand—and smothered his second thought as well. He had to do this. And he had to do it this way.

"I'll pay when we get there," he said.

"And where are we going?"

"I know a place. This way."

She tried to give him a smoldering look. She tried hard and failed miserably. But James led her anyway, down the narrow side street and into a tinted-glass door with a sign over it that read Houston Arms.

Strangling arms.

As they crossed the empty lobby that smelled like dead mice and mildew, James could see that she was nervous. The narrow hips swung. The hair was tossed several more times. The eyes gave him sultry sideways looks. But it was done with all the panache of a Star Wars droid. If she'd ever done this before it couldn't have been more than once.

He took her down a back hallway and caught her as she almost stumbled once when she caught her heel on a hole in the carpet. James had to admit, silently, that he was nervous too. No matter how many times he'd done this in the past six months, his palms still broke into a sticky sweat and his mouth dried out like he was chewing his sock.

He wiped his hands on his jeans. It was never a good idea to let the girl know that.

He stopped in front of a door and handed her the key. Her hand shook as she fiddled with the lock, though he could probably pin that on drugs. From the condition of her teeth, he'd say she was new at those too.

She snapped on the glaring overhead light and looked around, and James knew her heart was sinking. It was a dreary affair. Dark carpet with bare spots the size of Frisbees. Thick curtains that reeked of tobacco smoke pulled across the windows. A double bed with sheets the color of coffee stains and a spread that should have been given to the animal shelter long ago.

The girl turned on the only lamp, an unsteady pole with a brothel-red shade, and doused the one in the ceiling. It did nothing to improve the ambience, but James pulled off his sweat-shirt and tossed it on the back of the chair that looked like it had been stolen from somebody's grandmother's kitchen set.

The girl went on guard. Suddenly stiff as a yardstick she looked him up and down. They usually did that when he shed the down-and-out disguise and got down to his T-shirt.

"Problem?" James said.

"Maybe," she said. "Are you a cop? You're a cop, right?"

"No way." He pulled his jeans pockets inside out. "No gun. No badge."

"What about your sweatshirt?"

She might not have much experience, but she'd been trained well. James shook the shirt over the bed, dumping out the lone cigarette, the lighter, and the hundred. He picked up the bill and put it on the bedside table, in the center of one of the mug rings on its worn varnish.

She let out a long breath. James couldn't tell whether she was relieved or disappointed. Yeah. She was perfect.

"What's your name?" he said.

"They call me Tennessee."

"What's your real name?"

The pause was long. Finally, she said, "Kelli," and then bit her lip.

"Hi, Kelli. I'm James."

She visibly recovered and put on the aren't-I-sexy expression. "Okay, *James*." He saw her swallow as she stepped closer to him. "What are you into?"

Before he could answer, a light tap sounded on the door. Kelli turned toward it like she'd been shot and almost frantically stripped off her short leather jacket.

She thought it was her pimp was his guess. And she'd better look like she was about to go to work.

---

Antonia waited, knuckles poised in case she had to knock a second time. That didn't usually happen. She smiled to herself. James didn't let things go on any longer than he had to. His palms were probably dripping by now.

She heard footsteps approach inside the room and knew he'd squint into the peephole. She nodded at it, and the door opened. James's eyes were two brown pools of gratitude and relief. And something else. Excitement, maybe.

When Antonia stepped in and saw the girl, she could see why. In fact, her breath caught. She looked so much like Maria when they'd first arrived in Reno—not physically, this girl was far smaller—but in the way she attempted to conceal her fear with bravado.

That was, until she saw Antonia. Then she stepped back and shook her head and held up both hands.

"Hey," she said to James. "A couples thing was never the plan. This is gonna cost you more."

If she could even go through with it at all. No amount of eye shadow and push-up bras could hide the fact that the thought terrified her.

"Fine," James said. He patted the pocket of his T-shirt. "We have more. But we just want to talk to you."

Her brows, what was left of them after an overzealous tweezing, lifted and disappeared under the swoop of dye-blacked hair that half covered her eyes. "Go ahead," she said. "It's your money."

The relief was palpable. Antonia was surprised she didn't melt into a puddle.

As always, James took immediate advantage of that. They'd learned that if they waited too long, the girl freaked out and took the money and ran. Back into the arms of her pimp.

"Antonia, this is Kelli," he said. "Kelli, Antonia."

"It is nice to meet you," Antonia said.

Kelli took another step backward, landing against the closet door. "Let me see the money first. 'Cause I didn't know this was going to be a threesome and—"

James backed up too, away from her, shaking his head. "It's not like that. Sorry—I didn't mean to surprise you. Can we tell you a story?"

Kelli folded her arms and rolled her eyes, but Antonia wasn't fooled. The girl's shoulders were already lowering, her knees no longer straining to stay apart. Now if she would only kick off those shoes she could really relax. She still couldn't figure out how they could walk in those things.

"Fine," she said.

James slowly lowered himself into the chair and held his arm out to Antonia. She went to him and stood behind him, hands on his shoulders. He reached up one of his to grab on. Yes, dripping with sweat.

Kelli was toying with a hunk of hair. "Let me just say this is weird. Whatever. Like I said, it's your money—"

"Please," Antonia said. "Just hear us out."

"I'm listening."

With that she was once again the teenager who had probably driven her parents crazy with her attitude and her refusal to play by their rules. A final screaming match and she was out of there, sure she could make it on her own without them breathing down her neck and telling her who to be. And besides, there was "him." Antonia shut out the rest of it.

"A year ago, just about, I met a woman a lot like you," James said, eyes soft on Kelli. "She'd been lied to and forced into the same . . . situation you're in."

Another eye roll, but James went on. Antonia had watched him become immune to those.

"Against her will. Men decided she was worth a certain price . . ."

His voice trailed off, like it always did at this point. Antonia squeezed his hand.

"I fell in love with that woman. And to me, she is worth more than all the money in the world."

He stopped. Waited. Kelli looked from one of them to the other. Antonia saw the sheen of shame in her eyes.

"You have that same worth inside of you," Antonia said to her.

"You've been taught to talk and dress"—James raised his chin at her outfit—"and act like you're cheap." He scooted to the edge of the chair. "But we think . . . no, Kelli, we *believe* there's a God who knows exactly what you're worth . . ."

His voice broke. Antonia had heard it over and over and knew no more words would come.

"God knows that you're priceless," she said.

James stood up and fished a business card out of his T-shirt pocket. He set it on top of the money. And then he waited again.

Kelli was obviously doing everything she could not to cry. Every muscle in her neck was at work. But in spite of her best efforts, a thin trail of liquefied mascara made its way down one side of her face.

"Look, this is my choice," she said.

"And that means you have the freedom to make another choice."

Kelli's eyes were suddenly everywhere. To the window. To the door where her pimp might be lurking, because sometimes they were. Back to Antonia's face and James's. She couldn't settle them any more than she could the hands she clenched and unclenched at her tiny waist.

"I can't . . . I don't know," she said.

"Hey," James said, almost whispering. "This doesn't have to define you."

The girl could only shake her head and cry.

It was time to go. Running into her boss was a chance they couldn't take. It had only happened once, and they never saw that girl again. She disappeared from the streets.

"Our number is on the card," James said. "Call us—it doesn't matter what time it is, and we'll come for you."

She stared at the card in pale silence until they left. Antonia hoped she was still looking at it as they hurried hand in hand out of the hotel. Now there was nothing to do but pray.

Again.

# 35

THE SUN WAS JUST COMING UP over the Hill Country. James's favorite time of day. That first light hinted at possibility after a long night of shadows and doubts.

And driving.

He took one hand from the steering wheel of the Barracuda and stretched his arm behind his head. The drive from the city out here felt long when they had to make it in the wee hours, which is when they usually made the trip.

James glanced over at Antonia to see if she was awake yet. She was just coming out of a doze, blinking anxiously and then settling into her thoughts. Hard memories, from the look of it. That happened sometimes.

He reached his hand out to her, and she folded her fingers into his. He felt her wedding band and then glanced at his. She met his eyes and smiled, melting away the melancholy feeling.

That happened sometimes too.

"Almost there," he said.

"Home," she said.

Best word ever.

They let the sweet silence fall as they wound up the final hill, lined on both sides by crabapple trees. James reminded himself—again—that it was going to take longer than the year they'd had together for her pain to go away. Or at least take its place in a recess of her soul where it would no longer bring her straight up in bed in the middle of the night crying out against the monster. His own images of Michelle's body lying lifeless in front of the mangled pickup truck came less and less often, so he had hope for his Antonia too. The wounds would heal. They'd seen that.

He pulled the Plymouth around the last turn, and Antonia put her hands on the dashboard, face expectant as a little girl's. It never got old—seeing their long, low ranch house nestled against the hill. Getting their first view of the whitewashed porch that ran across the front, lively with women. Or hearing Maria's voice raised in her self-appointed job as herald.

"They're back!"

Before the engine even shut off, the front screen door banged open and Emmy bolted from the house on her long colt legs. She was in his arms the minute James unfolded himself from the front seat, filling him with her smell of Magic Markers and strawberry shampoo.

"Daddy," she murmured in his ear. Just like she had eleven months ago when the events of Reno had been untangled and he could finally come back and prove to every rung in the system that he was fit to be her father.

"Antonia!" she cried and leaped from his arms into hers.

Antonia rocked her back and forth and giggled Spanish into her neck. Yeah, she took the "step" out of stepmother.

"Do we have a new sister?" Emmy said.

Maria was already pulling the front seat forward and leaning over to coax the figure in the back seat.

"It's okay," she said. "Come on."

Maria stepped back and let her climb out. Kelli stood

blinking at the sun and the stand of sunflowers and the shining faces on the front porch. Actually, only one eye blinked. The other was blackened and puffed shut from her pimp's final blow that precipitated her call to James. Hard to see it as a blessing, but maybe it was.

Kelli looked uncertain as a little girl, but not frightened. She smiled when Antonia reached her and put a graceful arm around her bony shoulders. Gently, as if she might break her if she held on too tight.

James breathed in and waited for the words that always thickened his throat, no matter how many times he heard them.

Antonia dropped her arm and took both of Kelli's hands in hers. Looking straight and deep into the fading blue eyes, she said, "You're safe now."

Kelli fell against her, arms flailing to get around Antonia's neck. Clapping like the sound of rain on a tin roof arose from the porch. Maria hugged Emerson, just as close sisters do.

As Antonia led Kelli to the house, the young women on the porch stopped reading and those in the garden stopped working, and they all came over to talk to Kelli—to talk *into* her. Two ladies emerged from the house, powdered with flour and offering cookies. A bit overwhelmed but obviously overjoyed as well, Kelli smiled the white, straight-teeth smile that would never be marred by meth or the cruel fist of an angry master. Not now.

James leaned against the car and considered, as he always did in these moments, what Dale would think of it. Whether it would in some small way release the pain over his daughter, the one Maria told them about. He was here, in a way. In the money he'd left James in his duffel bag along with the deed to his property, hastily signed over as he saw Garo driving down his road. The moment Garo and his men had left the motel, Dale must have known what the outcome would be. That had helped pay for all of this. James wondered if Dale maybe dreamed of the same thing.

As for the money James was given to take back to Houston the day he delivered Antonia and Mario to Garo—Chad's people never tried to claim it. Not after Garo and C. J. were sentenced to spend the better—or the worst—part of the rest of their lives in prison and a five-state prostitution ring was busted wide open. That was the sisters' money as far as James was concerned. They had chosen to combine it with his to make this a place of healing from a disease that was born of the flesh but ate away at the soul.

That was how Antonia put it.

James wasn't as eloquent. For him, it was like this: the only cure for the epidemic was a heart transplant. For people to see in women the worth that couldn't be measured, that God has given to everyone.

James watched the ones in front of him. Daisy leaned back in the porch rocker, textbook on her lap, and propped her bare feet on the railing, wiggling her toes just because she could. Sydney, their curly-haired blonde, sat back on her heels in the grass and wiped her dirt-creased forehead with the back of her hand and surveyed the now weed-free bed of pink and purple somethings. Red-headed Lexi perched on the steps, writing fast and furious on a pad, probably another letter to the father she'd be rejoining soon.

They *were* safe. But that wasn't enough for James. It wouldn't be enough, until the world knew that every life was what Antonia told every hurting girl they met in a motel room . . .

Yeah. That every life was priceless.

Kelli disappeared into the house, practically cradled by young women who not long ago had been exactly where she was. Antonia hesitated in the doorway and turned, almost as if James had called her name. He lifted his chin, and she floated—there was no other way to describe it—across the porch and down the steps. Straight into his arms.

"Happy?" he said into her hair.

"Beyond," she said.

James tightened his hold on her, and she pressed her cheek against his chest. Tomorrow or the next day or a week from now, they'd go back into the city and find another Kelli or Daisy or Sydney . . . or Antonia. They would do it as long as there was room. As long as Dale's legacy held out and the income from his part-time construction work and her ESL teaching continued to support them. And especially as long as God tells them to keep freeing those who are held captive.

Antonia tilted her head back, and as James looked into her face, her eyes seemed to sparkle. No sign of the anxious memories. Just the tenderness of the moment. And that was enough.

"And you?" she said. "Are you happy, James?"

He tucked her head against him again and nodded. Hearing the laughter that danced from the house and landed lightly on his soul was enough. He was happy. Because he was home too.

# ABOUT THE AUTHORS

SOARING MELODIES, DRIVING rhythms, theatrical instrumentation and personal themes are the heartbeat of **for KING & COUNTRY**'s music. The duo, comprised of Australian brothers **Joel and Luke Smallbone**, has accomplished several notable feats on their records. Perhaps the most remarkable is that the award-winning rock/pop duo has achieved the unexpected.

Not only have they ventured into new musical territories, with some of the highlights being a collaboration with hip-hop artist Andy Mineo, their continued creative partnership with artist/producer Aqualung, and their discovery of new soundscapes with producer Tedd T. (MuteMath), but for KING & COUNTRY also managed to surpass the bar that the brothers had set for themselves with their debut album. They raised expectations tremendously with the release of 2012's Crave and a win for New Artist of the Year at the 2013 GMA Dove Awards, where they received six nominations. Billboard also named them as one of the New Artists to Watch for 2012 and American Songwriter called them "Australia's answer to Coldplay."

In just a few short years, they have already won 2 GRAMMY Awards and 6 K-LOVE Fan Awards to go along with 750,000 albums sold, 100 million streams, and sold-out shows, including as part of Winter Jam, the largest annual tour in the world. The band has also appeared on national televisions such as *The View, Jimmy Kimmel Live!, The Tonight Show, Fox & Friends,* and others.

The philosophies of hope and love behind their music were instilled by their parents, who raised their seven children in Sydney,

Australia, before relocating to Nashville in 1991. Their father worked as a music promoter, so the boys often accompanied him to shows. In their teenage years, they also sang background vocals for their sister, gospel artist Rebecca St. James. When Luke was nineteen and Joel twenty-one, the two formed a band and began the journey of writing and recording music.

To Joel and Luke, remaining focused on what truly matters is crucial to succeeding musically. "The best legacy I can leave is if I am a good dad and good husband. If my family environment was out of whack, I don't know if I'd even be able to write songs anymore," says Luke. "A lot of my passion and zeal for life is because I have a wife who counts on me and two boys who look up to me as their 'Dada.'"

The band's powerful name, for KING & COUNTRY, is a reflection of standing and fighting for something greater than yourself. One popular theme that has been with the band from the beginning—and is the foundation for the movie and novel *Priceless*—focuses on a woman's worth and how men must step up and stand out to proclaim that chivalry is not dead. "Part of the DNA of for KING & COUNTRY is this idea of respect and honor in relationships and women being priceless," Joel says. "What we've both found in our beliefs as men is that people are made equal. No one is a commodity and everyone deserves to be loved and loved well."

# PRICELESS

ALSO A MAJOR MOTION PICTURE

WWW.PRICELESSTHEMOVIE.COM

## IF YOU ENJOYED THIS BOOK, WILL YOU CONSIDER SHARING THE MESSAGE WITH OTHERS?

Mention the book in a blog post or through Facebook, Twitter, Pinterest, or upload a picture through Instagram.

Recommend this book to those in your small group, book club, workplace, and classes.

Head over to facebook.com/forKINGandCOUNTRY, "LIKE" the page, and post a comment as to what you enjoyed the most.

Tweet "I recommend reading #PricelessTheBook by @4KINGandCOUNTRY // @worthypub"

Pick up a copy for someone you know who would be challenged and encouraged by this message.

Write a book review online.

**WORTHY**®
PUBLISHING

**Visit us at worthypublishing.com**

twitter.com/worthypub

worthypub.tumblr.com

facebook.com/worthypublishing

pinterest.com/worthypub

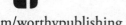
instagram.com/worthypub

youtube.com/worthypublishing